I'm a freak.

"I'm trusting you," I say softly. "I am trusting you with knowledge that people would chain me in a lab for. My girlfriend said I should try to meet you on neutral ground, get to know you, feel out what kind of people you and your husband are before I reveal myself. But honestly, that's not me. Would you feel better if I'd stalked you and struck up a conversation at the coffee house? I don't have time for that. I need help and I need it now."

"What exactly do you need help with?" she asks.

"I'm a freak, Dr. Mullen," I say. "I can produce that protein in my brain. I can regenerate any part of my body."

Systematic

Book 2 of the System Series

Andrea Ring

Originally published in 2014 by Square Gorilla Press. http://www.squaregorilla.com.

ISBN 978-0-9893825-7-1

Cover art and design:

Jay Walsh, http://meanoiche.blogspot.com

Acknowledgements

Jay, you've done it again. Thank you.

Dedication

To Christina. I have the time to write because of you.

Note to My Readers

The Prologue included here is actually the ending of *Nervous System*, Book 1 in *The System Series*. Since it ends on a cliffhanger, I wanted readers new to the series to be able to see how Book 1 ended.

But if *Nervous System* is fresh in your mind, skip right to Chapter One.

Cliffhangers are polarizing things – some readers love them, and others hate them. The purpose of the cliffhanger in Book 1 was to end where the story naturally ended. I hope I've done enough as a writer to get you to care about the characters and be invested in their story, regardless of how Book 1 ended.

Contact me via my website at http://www.andrearing.net with your thoughts, positive or negative. You are the reason I write. Your opinions matter to me.

Sincerely,

Andrea

Prologue

I hang up the phone and replace Dad's pillows. I leave his room and enter Vivian's.

Vivian breathes softly. Her heart monitor beeps quietly with every heartbeat. My own heartbeat pounds like a war drum in my ears.

I sit in the chair next to her bed and look at her. Vivian is the reason I am here, in this room and on this earth. If things had been different for Vivian, I wouldn't even exist.

"I'm sorry," I whisper. "I'm sorry for what you went through."

Vivian doesn't respond.

"I'm Michael's son. Mikey. You knew him a long time ago. He says you loved him. I know what it's like to lose someone you love. It sucks."

I laugh at my own words.

"I think I can help you."

I stand up next to the bed and fumble with the side rail. I finally get it lowered. I drag the chair closer to the bed and kneel on it. Leaning over, I take Vivian's hand in mine. Her hand is warm.

I take a deep breath.

I lay her hand flat on the bed and place my palm over hers. It is not a perfect fit; my hand fits inside hers but doesn't match up. I place my hand so that the tops of our palms line up, and each of my fingers is placed perfectly on top of hers. I press down.

I will my skin to fuse to hers. My hand feels like it's been dipped in fire, but I don't dare mess with my nerves. I ride the pain and force myself to go on.

Finally our skin is perfectly fused. I try lifting my hand, and Vivian's is stuck to it. Her hand lifts enough with mine to bend at the wrist.

I press our hands back down on the bed. Now comes the hard part.

There is a skin barrier between us, and I have to pierce it. Maybe I should have cut both of us before I started this, but it's too late. I'd have to cut us apart and start over. Too messy.

Bone is the only way to go. I force my finger bone to grow out and down. It's painful. I feel the bone tearing through muscle, tearing through skin, until it penetrates Vivian's hand. The heart monitor beeps loudly, continuously. I pause to catch my breath, and the nurse rushes in.

"Thomas, is everything alright?"

I nod, placing my other hand over the one holding Vivian's. There's some blood, not a lot, but enough. I don't want the nurse to see it.

"We're fine," I say. "I'm just talking to her."

The nurse checks the heart monitor and smooths a hand over Vivian's hair. "It's good that you're talking to her. She obviously likes it."

I want the nurse to leave.

"I'll let you know if anything happens other than her heart rate," I say.

The nurse nods. "Okay. I'll leave you alone, then."

She does.

I wipe the sweat from my brow with my free hand. The pain is difficult to think through.

I have the opening to Vivian now, through our ring fingers. I switch from bone to nerves. I extend my nerves along the bone until they are deep in Vivian's hand. I plant the nerve in the palm of her hand and fight the pain to sense what I can of Vivian.

She is in pain, too. Her hand is crying out, ordering her to move away from the source of the pain. But her body is not responding. I connect my nerve to a couple of Vivian's, then I trace those nerves up to her brain. I get as far as the top of her spinal cord. The nerve signal won't go any farther. Vivian's body is lacking the proteins necessary to carry the message on.

I have the right protein. I picture it in my head as I flex my fingers, the protein that allows all the nerves to join up and the signals to travel. I have to get that protein inside Vivian.

I force my body to produce that protein. It floods my brain, and I gasp out loud. All the signals my body is sending out are traveling at super speed, and I'm on sensory overload.

I shake my head to clear it, but I can't get rid of the proteins yet. I have to…do something. I have to send them into Vivian.

It takes me a few minutes to get used to the onslaught of signals. And it leaves me light-headed. Feeling faint but purposeful, I gather all those proteins in my brain and send them on their way along my nerves. Down my neck to my spine. From the spine to my arm. Down my arm to my hand. Down my hand to my finger. Down my finger to Vivian.

The next part is the trickiest. I can sense the nerves I've connected to, but the rest of Vivian's body is a mystery to me. I do not have a direct connection to her brain. So I simply follow the network of nerves. It's like following a rope in the dark. Hand over hand, you let the rope guide you, but you have little idea of where you are unless you reach a hand out to feel. So that's what I do. I follow the nerve in her hand until I come to another one. I sense it. I'm in the meaty part of her palm. I follow that nerve down until I come to another at the top of her wrist. I continue on, following and sensing.

When I hit a nerve connected to the muscle in her forearm, the monitor beeps loudly. I ignore it. I find that outside stimuli are becoming easy to ignore. I process them so fast that they are barely a blip on my radar.

I notice that my breathing has become shallow and labored by the time I reach Vivian's brain. I'm sensing a good portion of her body, the left side, at least, and besides the pain I have caused and the lack of proteins, her body is healthy. As I penetrate the brain, I begin to sense her mood. It is curious. She knows something is happening, but she can't yet feel what that is. I probe deeper into the frontal lobe, and Vivian and I both gasp aloud.

The pain overwhelms her. I had a build up of it, and I knew what was happening and what to expect. Vivian did not. But she's a seasoned Dweller. Before I can say a word, Vivian shuts down the nerves in her hand and arm.

She opens her eyes and slowly rolls them in my direction. "Who?" she says.

I'm in her brain. I know what she wants to say.

"I'm Thomas Van Zandt, Michael's son."

She tries to speak again, but her tongue is too dry.

"I'm not…" I start to say, and then I realize that Vivian doesn't know anything about what she's been through. Her memory stops back at the Attic when Dad was still with her. I can't explain everything to her now, and she shouldn't hear it from me even if I could.

"I'm your son," I say, confirming her belief. "I'm trying to help you. You were lacking the protein necessary to come out of a coma. I'm giving you the protein."

Vivian nods in her head. *You're adorable*, she thinks. *Perfect. I'm so sorry I wasn't here for you.*

Tears fill my eyes. I cannot believe that her first thoughts would be for me. Or her child.

You look like Mikey, she thinks.

"People tell me that," I say, and my vision blurs.

Vivian must be able to sense me, as well. She is suddenly alarmed. *You're sick*, she says. *Where is Michael?*

"Around," I say, trying hard to remember where Dad is.

You need to eat, she thinks. *You need to eat now. Please. Call someone. Where is Dr. Sykes?*

"I don't know," I say, my words slurring at the end.

Cut the connection, she screams in my head. *Cut it now!*

I fight to remember what I'm supposed to be doing. "I'm not there yet," I say. "Almost there. Need to get to the cerbellm."

My mouth isn't working right.

Vivian shuts down more of her nerves, but the process is slow. Her brain is not responding as quickly as she wants it to. But she's making it difficult for me to work. I'm like a salmon fighting to swim upstream.

I can no longer speak. So I think to her.

Let me help you.

No! she thinks. *Not for me. Please! Not for me.* She is sobbing in her head.

I finally reach her cerebellum and repair the deadened parts of her brain. Some kind of chemical had saturated her brain cells and essentially numbed them. I regrow them. I restore them. I give her the power to create the protein on her own.

I bring Vivian back to life.

"No!" she screams out loud.

And my heart sto....

I have perfect awareness, even if I am unconscious.

Vivian is screaming, pleading with someone. "Save him! Save him, please!"

The plea is heartfelt, so I won't dismiss it, but sheesh. There's no need to shout. I mean, I'm right here.

I do a quick internal scan. Whoa – my body's not in great shape. I'm low on, well, everything. Dehydration seems to be the culprit behind my heart stoppage, and the amount of calories I burned in the last fifteen minutes could keep a small army marching for days. And why the hell am I worried about any of that when I'm not getting oxygen to my brain?

A funny "Pfffffftttt," comes out of my mouth as someone pushes on my chest. I giggle in my head. It's like I just farted with my mouth.

I try to draw in a breath, but my muscles don't respond. At least my brain is getting oxygen now as the blood circulates, but if I don't take a breath soon, that oxygen will run out.

Someone puts a damp hand on my forehead and tilts my head back. Dry lips glue to my lips, and someone blows a deep breath into my mouth. Kind of gross if I think too hard about it, but I mentally heave a sigh. I'm getting oxygen.

Lips are replaced with something rubber. I get breaths every few seconds in a pulsing rhythm.

Guys, I appreciate the effort, really I do, but this is not a solution. Where's an IV when you need one? I need electrolytes, a shot of Gatorade. Ice water would be good – my tongue feels like a piece of fruit leather from all these breaths. And YOW!

I curse in my head as some idiot tries to stick the back of my hand with a needle. The needle slips and they miss the vein, I guess because my veins are partially collapsed from the lack of water in my system. I mentally grit my teeth as they try again.

And suddenly I'm intubated and feel like I'm choking. This is supposed to help me breathe? Dear God, I can't even swallow.

I feel it when the magic electrolytes hit my bloodstream and start to circulate. Every cell in my body relaxes in relief. I ride the feeling. And THUMP!

My heart beats.

I still can't open my eyes. I try to speak, but I can't even grunt with the tube in my throat and my facial muscles are frozen in repose. I try to wave, anything to get someone's attention, but my body's having none of it.

So I go to my brain and try to figure out where the disconnect is. There is none. My body is just moving and responding at a snail's pace. It's concentrating on feeding cells and distributing oxygen, and anything else I want it to do just has to wait.

Did I tell you that patience doesn't come naturally for me?

♥

A week later, without any will or warning, my eyes pop open.

Chapter Two

Ten years later…

"Stop squirming," I say, holding firmly to her finger. "You have to hold still."

"It hurts, it hurts, it hurts," Tessa whispers, her eyes scrunched shut.

I almost laugh. Honestly, it's little more than a paper cut. Tessa's acting like she cut off her finger.

"You need something to bite down on?" I joke.

Tessa frowns, her eyes still closed. Then she gropes for my free hand and sticks my finger in her mouth. She bites down lightly and growls.

Wuh. Every thought in my head flies right out. All I can feel is her mouth, and then her tongue as it grazes the tip of my finger.

"Are you done yet?" she asks around my finger.

Oh. Right.

"Uh, no. Hold on. I'm doing it now. It'll sting a bit." Tessa's teeth clamp down, and I tell myself to be gentle and quick or I'll be healing my finger instead of hers.

I lay Tessa's hand down on the kitchen table on a paper towel. I fish the Swiss Army knife I always carry out of my pocket and flick it open. Because I only have one free hand, I put the knife on the table and slide the pad of my index finger along the edge of the blade. I quickly press my wound to Tessa's cut.

I fuse my skin to hers, make a few quick nerve connections. Tessa gasps and her jaw clenches, but she's careful not to bite too hard. Tessa's platelets have already begun to clump together to help the blood clot, but I speed the process along, adding my own clumped platelets and triggering fibroblasts (basically, connective tissue cells) to transform into epithelia, or skin cells. I carefully disconnect my nerves as the skin cells grow and pull the nerves back into my own finger. I unknit our skin, repairing it as I disengage. Ten seconds later, we're both healed.

I grab the paper towel and wipe the blood off our fingers. "Can I have my finger back now?" I ask her.

Tessa slits one eye open and spits my finger out. Darn. "Is it done?"

"Good as new."

She brings her finger up to her face and examines it. "Amazing."

I grin at her. "Been practicing."

"I'll say." She leans in and gives me a lingering kiss. "Thank you."

I pull her against me and sigh into her hair. "You know, I think a proper thank you is in order."

Tessa laughs and bats at my wandering hands. She walks over to the pantry, opens the doors, and pulls out an energy bar. She tosses it to me. "Eat, and maybe I can thank you properly later."

I scowl, rip open the wrapper, and take a bite. "How's it feel?"

She rubs her thumb on her newly healed index finger a few times. "A little numb, but it doesn't hurt."

"Nerve damage," I say, mouth full. I swallow. "It'll be fine in a couple of weeks."

"Wow. I mean, I've seen you do this so many times to yourself, but having it done to me? It's unreal."

I shove the last bit of cardboard bar in my mouth and toss the wrapper in the trash.

"So you have a lot of homework?" I ask her.

"Pre-calculus and Spanish," she says, nodding. "You?"

"Just some reading," I say, "but I can do it before bed. "

"I wish I could do pre-cal in bed, but I need my brain to actually function."

"I'll do your homework, and then we can catch a movie," I say.

Tessa laughs. "One time. I let you do my homework one time three years ago in a crisis, and now you think you can do it all the time."

"I can do it all the time."

"But you can't take my tests for me. I have to be able to do them myself."

"Fine," I say with a mock pout. "We'll do homework."

Tessa smiles. "Thank you again."

Tessa goes home for dinner, and Dad comes home not long after that.

"Good day?" he asks, grabbing a beer from the fridge.

"Excellent," I say, leaning against the kitchen counter. "I healed Tessa's finger."

Dad freezes, his beer can resting against his lips. "You what?"

"She cut her finger slicing an apple and I healed it."

Dad sets the can down on the counter and looks at me. "You weren't supposed to do that."

"It's no big deal," I shrug. "I've been doing it on you almost every night."

"But I can heal myself," he says. "If you screw something up, I can fix it. I can't fix Tessa."

"I know what I'm doing," I say, not meeting his eyes.

Time for the showdown.

I grab a beer of my own out of the fridge and pop the top. Before I can take a sip, Dad swipes it from my hand.

"Hey!" I say.

"What the hell are you doing?" Dad barks.

"Having a beer. I don't have to get drunk. I'll just metabolize the alcohol."

"You're sixteen and you're gonna act like it," Dad says, dumping the beer down the sink. He throws the can in and turns to me. "This has got to stop."

"What?"

"You. Acting like you know everything. Acting like the rules don't apply to you."

I cross my arms in front of my chest. "I don't act like that."

Dad sighs. "Look, it takes one to know one. From one arrogant shit to another, you need to get your head on straight."

I close my eyes and take a deep breath. "I'm bored."

"That's no excuse."

"I'm impatient. I know how to do all these things, and you won't let me."

"For good reason," he says. "Thomas, learn from my mistakes. You still have a lot of growing up to do. You might know the mechanics of healing, but there's more to it – the ethics, the emotions." I stare out the window and Dad puts a hand on my shoulder. "I know you're impatient. You're exactly like me. I've been thinking…maybe it is time for the next step."

I whip my body around to face him, and Dad chuckles. "You mean it? I really get to go?"

"Yep. Get to bed early tonight. We'll drive down to the Attic tomorrow."

Chapter Three

I won't bore you with the details of our arrival. You've seen the movies, I'm sure, the high-security military compounds, where the lead character pulls up to a guard booth outside of an electrified, barbed wire-topped fence, his security clearance is checked, radioed in, the guards usher him inside, and he drives along a tree-lined road to the buildings, only to be greeted by more armed guards, a toady assistant to some senator on some top-secret committee who's holding a clipboard and practically bowing and scraping to see that your needs are met, and all the while it's a cover for whatever secret program really runs behind the scenes.

That's where we are.

Except that we are a part of that super-secret program, so no one tries to distract us from the hidden door with coffee and reception areas that look like parlors.

This is the real deal.

The Attic.

And since Dad's the director, we pretty much have the run of the place. We stride into Building A, our identity is checked again, and we pass through a metal detector. I'm embarrassed at being caught with my knife – Dad just shakes his head – but the guard lets me keep it after examining it for five minutes.

We head left to a bank of mirror-fronted elevators and step on. Dad presses the button for Floor 10, and I am shocked as the elevator shudders and proceeds to drop.

"I thought we were going to the Attic," I say. "You know, attic. Up."

Dad smiles. "It's ten stories below ground."

"Why not call it the basement?" I ask.

"There are twenty-two stories below ground, for one. And second, all of us like to think we're close to God."

"You don't even like God," I remind him.

He shrugs. "Most of us do."

"Us who?"

Dad hesitates. "This…some of the things in the Attic will be hard for you to see."

"I can handle it," I say.

And the elevator doors slide open to reveal a sterile white hallway, stretching to forever.

I step out, and the odor assaults me: nose-wrinkling alcohol, musty algae like in the tunnels of the Pirates of the Caribbean ride at Disneyland, and, under those, a rot, like human flesh left to molder in a dark corner. I take a breath to steady myself and the odor clings to my nostrils and the back of my throat. I retch, fighting it.

Dad puts a hand on my back. "You'll get used to it."

"Not bloody likely," I say.

Dad laughs and pushes me forward with his hand. "Fifth door on the left."

I count the doors as we pass them. They're all the same, white acrylic over stainless steel, no labels or plaques, no hint of what's beyond. I strain to hear some sound as we pass, some indication of life in this sterile hole, but all I can hear is the rushing air from the vents overhead. I try to breathe through my mouth, but that only brings the taste of the stench to my tongue.

Door number five. We pause. Dad swipes his security card, leans in for a retinal scan. The scanner beeps.

"Your turn," he says, handing me a card. I swipe the card quickly and lean into the scanner, fighting to keep my eyes open against the bright light. The scanner beeps.

And the door slides open.

"Deep breaths," Dad whispers, patting my back.

I have the sudden urge to hold his hand, but Jesus, I'm not six anymore.

It's a roomy space, sterile white like the hallway, occupied by only a full-sized bed and a stainless steel bistro table and four matching chairs. A two-headed man sits facing us at the table playing chess by himself. Both heads look up at us as we enter.

"Maybe we should have knocked," I whisper to Dad, though if this guy (these guys?) is like us, he can hear me regardless.

One of the heads looks normal – he's a white guy, forty-ish, with a mop of unbrushed brown hair, nondescript brown eyes, a hawkish nose. The other head looks…wrong. It's too large, for one. Faint gray hairs grow in wispy tufts about a skull mottled with pulsing blue veins. Its eyes are off-center, one half an inch higher than the other, but both are the same brown of its companion. The nose is a blob, squished and malformed.

The smiles of both – thin lips and perfectly straight white teeth – are identical. I shiver.

Dad pushes on my back, signaling that I should move forward, but I don't. He smiles down at me reassuringly and leads me over to the table.

"I want you to meet my son, Thomas," Dad says to them. "Thomas, this is Dacey."

The normal head smiles and nods at me, holding out his hand for me to shake.

"Pleasure to meet you, Dacey," I say, struggling to keep my eyes on his. It's like some sick compulsion, the need to gape at the other head.

"Likewise," he says. "And this is my companion, Tyrion."

I bark a laugh automatically, my nerves fraying my control and decorum. "Tyrion," I say. "Great name. Like the dwarf in George Martin's books?"

The misshapen head laughs heartily, a booming sound.

Dad frowns. "You repaired the vocal chords?"

"Too well," Dacey says. "This is the quietest he's been in three days."

"I'm only startled to see the smart young man," the grotesque head says in a smooth, cultured baritone, winkling his eyes at me. "You are the first to get my Tyrion reference."

I incline my head to him. "An apt name. He's a clever character."

Tyrion laughs again. "Ah, and not only smart, but tactful as well. Perhaps you could give a few lessons to some of our companions in the Attic."

Dad pulls out a chair for me and I sit. After hearing Tyrion's voice, he doesn't seem so scary. Dad takes a seat as well.

"We discussed the implications," Dad begins, but Dacey cuts him off.

"Mike, I had to do it. He needed to speak. All day long he was scrawling out entire conversations until my hand cramped into a claw. I had to."

"You did not have to," Tyrion booms, "and I did not need you to. You Dwellers have too much power, unchecked and untried. He says I've been blathering non-stop for three days, and this is true. We've been in isolation for what? A month now? It's too much for you, my friend. Too much. I am not worth it."

"Shut your hole, Tyrion, before I shut it for you," Dacey says. "This is it. You're here. End of story."

"I could strangle myself," Tyrion says.

Dacey grits his teeth. "Only if you gain control over my arms long enough to do the deed. Shut up. Now."

"What do you mean, Tyrion?" I ask him. "Why do you want to die?"

Before Tyrion can reply, Dacey slaps his hand over Tyrion's mouth. "I created him, just to see if I could do it. An entire brain from scratch. A skull to encase it. A second juncture from my spinal cord, the nerves, the...everything. Just to see if I could do it. And I did." Dacey stands, and he and Tyrion pace the room. "The idea was to see if it could be done, and then to cut off its blood supply, repair the juncture and do away with it. But two weeks into the experiment, he began to communicate. Just small things at first. He had an itch that needed to be scratched, and it required me to relinquish control of my hand. His eyes were tearing and he needed me to blot them. He just…blossomed. And now I can't imagine him withering away."

Tyrion turns his head to Dacey and smiles ruefully. "I always knew the day would come, my friend. Without you, I would never have tasted life. But your life is your own. You deserve it back."

Dacey stares at the wall, away from his friend, and Tyrion takes the opportunity to look at me. "What do you think, Thomas? Can Dacey have a life like this, with me by his side? He hasn't been home in over a year. It's probably rotting to the ground. What solution is there but to get rid of me and move on?"

Dad waves a hand in the air. "Dace, man, why didn't you say you didn't make any arrangements for your home? I'll take care of that stuff."

"A stop-gap measure at best," Tyrion says, "though appreciated. The time has come."

Dad weighs Tyrion with his eyes. "I agree with you, Tyrion. Dacey has let this get too far. This was never meant to be the outcome."

"What does it matter now?" Dacey says, still staring at the wall. "Intended or no, this *is* the outcome. Tyrion is alive and he's my friend. I cannot be responsible for his death. He's a man, Mike!" Dacey flings themselves backwards in the chair. "We're going back, into General Population. No more isolation. I thought I was protecting everyone else from getting attached to you, but maybe that's what I need to get you to see reason. We'll put it to a vote."

"I have an idea," I say, startling everyone. Three pairs of eyes fix on me. "You created an entire brain, a head, the most complex structure of the entire body. Why not create the rest, then surgically separate the two bodies?"

"No," Tyrion says.

"Yes," Dacey says, and his eyes shine with a strange fervor.

"No! You almost killed yourself creating me. You've lost thirty pounds—"

"A high-protein diet, carefully planned, it's but a minor obstacle…"

Dad stands quickly, the legs of his chair scraping across the floor like a microphone whining feedback in our ears. We all wince.

"Think on it," he says. "Nothing's decided. I'll send in Dr. Trent and we'll see what he thinks."

Dad heads to the door, expecting me to follow, I suppose. I hold out my hand to Dacey/Tyrion. "It was amazing to meet you both," I say sincerely. "Maybe we can play a game of chess the next time around."

The two heads exchange a look, and Dacey speaks. "We'd both like that."

Out in the hall, I lean back on the wall and take a shallow breath. The stench is strong out here.

"Wow," I say. We start down the hallway. "I thought you said I was the only one." Dad stops and looks at me, guilt plastered across his face. He knows what I'm talking about. "Well? Why did you lie to me?"

"I didn't lie," he says. "You are the only one we know of who's ever been born with the ability to grow nerves in the central nervous system. You are the only one born able to manufacture Protein TVZ."

"That's what you're calling it? Protein TVZ?'

Dad smiles. "Protein T for short. After you."

I like getting the nod, but it's irrelevant to my point. "Then how do you explain Tyrion?"

Dad blows out a breath. "Dacey was one of five people who volunteered to take the proteins we harvested from you."

I narrow my eyes at him. "That was ten years ago! Why didn't you tell me it worked?"

"It didn't," he says. "Not at first. Dacey had to figure out how to manufacture the protein on his own. He only figured it out a few years ago. Then he had to create Tyrion. It's been an arduous process, and Dacey considers it his life's work."

I stalk off ahead of him. "You could have told me that."

Dad catches up to me and spins me around to face him. "Like it or not, I was not gonna drag you in further until I thought you were ready. Even now, I'm not certain this was a good idea."

I bristle at that. "Why not?"

Dad grips my shoulders tight and shakes me gently. "You have to get it! You have to get that you are not infallible! This is a military facility, for one. Everyone follows orders. And no one, no one, does an experiment unless it's authorized and documented. Do you understand?"

I blink back tears and nod.

"Do you?" Dad bellows in my face.

"Yes. Yeah, Dad, I get it. Loud and clear."

"Good." Then he pulls me into a hard hug. "I know...Thomas, you have the potential to do so much good here. Tell me you're ready. Tell me you'll do the right things, and I'll never bring this up again."

I meet his eyes. "I promise, Dad. But, why didn't you prepare me better? Like, for Dacey?"

Dad looks at me with sympathy. "Would that have helped? I know the imagination you have. You wouldn't have slept these past months, thinking about all the possibilities."

I think about that. He's probably right.

Dad ruffles my hair, something he hasn't done in years. "Stop thinking. Don't imagine. Just go into the next room with an open mind."

He dismisses my concerns by telling me I have an over-active imagination. Typical Dad, avoiding the real issues. But this isn't the time to argue with him.

We continue on until we arrive at door number twelve.

Before I do my scan, Dad says, "This is General Population, where most of us stay most of the time. All our experiments are out in the open, where we can learn from each other."

"Dacey said he hasn't been home. That means that most people don't live here?"

"Most of us have lives outside of the Attic. We may stay for the duration of an experiment, if it proves...if it changes our appearance."

"How do they all explain where they are, to their families and stuff?"

"Everyone here travels for their jobs," Dad says, meaning they all lie.

I don't like this explanation. But I can't think of a better one, so I don't comment.

"Let's do it," I say.

General Population is like a big dorm room, or a military barracks. Cots line both walls, with two table-and-chair sets occupying the space at the far end of the room. There's a kitchen to my immediate left, a door to my right (the bathroom?). Nobody pays us any attention as we enter.

Only about half of the twenty cots are occupied. Dad passes the first one on our left, occupied by someone asleep, and stops at the next, where a doctor is talking to a woman lying on her side away from us.

"This is Cappy. She's working on eyesight enhancements, but they often leave her dizzy, so she works while she's lying down."

It seems awkward for Dad to speak about her as though she can't hear us. I guess that's what he meant when he said they were open here – they must talk about each other all the time.

"You mean, like vision correction?" I ask.

"More like turning our eyes into camera lenses. Automatic zoom in and zoom out. The problem seems to be that the eye is not designed to hold the type of lens needed for zoom capability. She continues to burst blood vessels and even rupture the optic nerve. She's working to get to the point where a new lens will fit and look normal within the existing structure of her eye."

"Whoa," I say.

Dad winks at me.

We move to the other side of the room, where a wiry man barely five feet tall is doing curls with a plastic bottle of water. With his tail.

The tail's about four feet long, hairless and tender-pink, and fully prehensile, like that of a Howler monkey.

"Wicked," I whisper under my breath.

"Hey, Raj. This is my son, Thomas."

"Hello," I say.

Raj nods at us and continues his weightlifting. "Mike, Thomas." He grunts out the words with effort.

"You graduated from the tennis ball, eh?" Dad says.

Raj cracks a smile. "It's working. Slowly," and he grunts, "but surely."

Dad smiles. "Find us when you're done."

"You bet."

"Nice to meet you," I say. Raj nods at me.

"He grew a tail?" I ask.

"This is his sixth one, actually," Day says. "A prehensile tail that can grasp things is actually quite complex. It has to be streamlined for flexibility, yet strong enough to bear the owner's weight and still bend but not break. Raj is trying to build the muscles up naturally to see if this one will hold."

I wince. "You mean, he broke the other five?"

"Four. The fifth looked more like an alligator's tail, since he was trying to make it stronger. Not flexible enough, though."

"So he could barely pick up a tennis ball?" I say.

"He started with nothing. Couldn't even lift the tail. Gravity and the weight of his own body were his first trials."

"How long has been doing this?"

"About four months. Took him two just to be able to keep the tail from dragging on the ground."

We move past Raj. Lying on the cot next to him is a young woman with long golden hair and freckles. We watch her take a deep breath, close her eyes, and hold the air in.

"Watch," Dad says. He points to a clock on the wall above her head. It says 9:14 and thirty-three seconds.

We watch her. The girl appears dead. At 9:24, I start to get nervous.

"Is she okay?"

"Watch."

I shift from foot to foot, trying to keep my circulation going. Dad stands perfectly still. I had no idea additional patience would be required when I finally arrived here.

I wiggle. I fidget. At 9:57, the girl begins to tremble. I can see the pulse in her neck jumping.

"Jesus, Dad, help her."

"Watch."

At 10:02, she expels the last gasp of air from her lungs and bolts upright.

"God damn it!" she yells.

Dad sits on her cot beside her and rubs her arm. My eyes freeze on his flesh touching hers. "Over forty-eight minutes, Viv," he says.

She growls at him. "Not good enough."

"Forty-eight minutes—"

"My red blood cells have stopped adapting, Mike. I've been under fifty minutes for what, three months now? I've hit my limit."

"You know that there's no record of a human being able to hold their breath that long."

"There is now."

Dad sighs. "Are you hungry?"

The fight goes out of her at the mention of her stomach. "A bit."

"Eat. Rest," he urges her.

"I've been at this for years," she says. "I guess another hour won't hurt." Then her head snaps up and her eyes widen. "Thomas," she says.

"Hey, Viv."

Vivian's eyes search my face. "God, it's been what? A decade? You look like your dad, except for the eyes."

"Yes, they're my mother's," I say. "Have you been sleeping with my father this entire time?"

Viv's eyes grow even wider, and Dad jumps up and grabs my arm.

"Jesus, Thomas! Apologize to Vivian right now!"

"I'm sorry I know nothing about your relationship because my father prefers to lie to me."

Dad slaps me hard across the cheek.

"How dare you! You don't have a clue what you're talking about! Out. Now. We need to talk."

But I don't move.

"Mike."

Dad stares at me, fuming.

"Michael!"

He turns to Viv as though suddenly realizing she's here, a witness. "What?"

"It was just a question. He saw something, he reacted. You can't punish him for being observant."

"So I was right," I say.

Dad actually bares his teeth at me.

"Don't help me," Viv says to me. Then she stands and pulls on Dad's arm until there is some distance between us. "We're close, but we are not sleeping together, Thomas."

I want to believe her, but I don't. I notice that all conversation in the room has stopped, and everyone is looking at Dad, waiting for him to react.

"This is not the time or place for this conversation," Dad says, anger still threading his voice.

"I'm a Dweller now, isn't that right? You said that Dwellers are open. That they discuss everything right in this room."

"Not this." And Dad grips my arm, though not as roughly as I thought he would, and takes me to room number seven.

♥

We're in another isolation room, identical to Dacey's but without a chess set. Dad makes me sit while he paces the room.

"We're going to start with your behavior. These people are my friends and my colleagues, and you have no right to speak to them, any of them, the way you spoke to Vivian."

"I apologize."

"When we return to GP, you will say that to her, and mean it."

"Yes, sir."

"No one questions me in public. No one! Not even my son. Ask your questions."

I sigh. I wish that Dad would just spill it, his entire story. Why does he always make me work for it?

"Are you sleeping with Vivian?"

"No."

"No, as in not as this moment, or no, as in you are not in a relationship with Vivian, or no, as in you have not slept with Vivian since I brought her out of that coma ten years ago?"

"All of it."

"How come she came back here? I mean, after all they did to her...you told me she moved to LA and just wanted a normal life."

Dad's mouth tightens. "She tried having a normal life, but it wasn't that easy. Ultimately, she felt that she needed to be around others who understood her."

"But they put her in a coma and basically lost track of her!"

"That was before, Thomas. I'm in charge now, and I'd never let anything happen to her. I only assign experiments that the Dwellers have agreed to – hell, most of them design the experiments themselves. Vivian wants to contribute, and the Attic is the best place to do that."

"So why aren't you sleeping with Vivian?"

Dad sighs and sits in the chair opposite mine. "I thought, at first, that maybe it would happen. Us, as a couple. But it took her a while to get adjusted. She'd missed out on so many things…imagine waking up fifteen or twenty years from now. Technology has changed. Countries have changed. I changed. I'd lived an entire lifetime while she slept. It was too much of a hurdle for us."

"But you're close. You said you're close."

"We are," Dad agrees. "But I feel like an older brother now. I'd do anything for her."

"Then why haven't you ever brought her around? I mean, if you're just friends, you could have brought her over for dinner, at least."

"Thomas, I decided to keep you out of this world until you were old enough to handle it. You don't have to like that decision, but I stand by it."

I sigh in frustration, knowing that I'm not going to get anywhere with this discussion.

"You know," he says, "if you give Viv a chance, you might find you have a lot in common with her."

"I don't have a problem with Vivian. And I want you to be happy, whether that's with Vivian or not. I just…you didn't even tell me you were still in touch with her, and this is the second time, the second time you've lied to me about something major. I don't feel like I can trust you."

Dad's body wilts. "I know. I know you feel that way. Thomas, I've spent my whole life keeping secrets. It's not something I've done on purpose, or without a purpose, I mean. I've been trying to protect you."

"Then why did you finally bring me here?"

Dad sighs. "Because you're needed. The things you can do...they are desperately needed."

So this isn't about me. This isn't about giving me an outlet for my boredom and frustration, or a way of exercising my brain and abilities. This is about some greater good.

And that realization brings to mind all the problems I have with Dad, and why I need to be on my guard. These freaking people at the Attic are the same ones who forced Dad and Vivian to try to have a child when they were eighteen. Vivian actually did have their child, a daughter, and Dad still hasn't worked up the courage to reach out to her, despite finding out about her ten years ago.

Of course, Dad says he's in charge now and things are different. Maybe. But he takes orders from someone, too. Until I know who's really running the show, I can't let my guard down. Dad's not known for his honesty with me.

Which begs the question, how do I know he's telling the truth now? How do I know he doesn't have some hidden agenda?

And now I'm scared, terrified, actually. What if they don't let me leave?

I wipe the frown off my face and stand, projecting confidence I don't feel. "Let's go so I can apologize. I'm sorry for what I said to Vivian, and for questioning you in front of the others. I'll make it right."

"Thank you," Dad says.

"So has anyone else taken my protein?"

Dad shakes his head. "That reminds me. I need to send Dr. Trent in to see Dacey. You gave him quite a bit to think about."

"You mean, no one else had thought of that?"

Dad rises and we exit to the hallway. "Well, regeneration is the goal of a lot of our experiments, but the Dwellers have their limits. Dacey is the first to really try anything so outrageous. Most of us have grown new limbs, but it's a long process and difficult to heal. And remember, you grow a third eye and you'll be stuck in here, so don't get any ideas."

He smiles as we go through the scans and re-enter GP. "Why don't you have your talk with Vivian while I talk to Dr. Trent?"

Raj is still lifting his bottle. I nod at him and reach Vivian's side. She's as still as a corpse. I decide to sit on the floor and wait for her.

Dad approaches a couple of minutes later with a thin man in a lab coat at his heels. I jump to my feet, and we're introduced, again, since I met him ten years ago. He was the one taking care of Vivian when she was still in a coma.

"Dr. Trent and I are going to check in with Dacey. Will you be okay here?"

My heart pounds and I swallow hard. "No problem."

Dad thumps me on the back and they leave. I turn around to check on Vivian and find her sitting up looking at me.

"Uh, hello, ma'am," I say.

"Ma'am? Do I look like I'm old enough to be a ma'am?"

"Uh…miss?"

Vivian laughs. "I'm definitely not young enough to be a miss."

She pats the cot beside her, but before I can sit, I have to apologize.

"I'm very sorry for the way I acted. I was rude. Unforgivably so. I hope you can forgive me."

"That is the best damn apology anyone's ever given me," she says with a laugh. "Now sit."

I sit.

"I was in your position once, you know," she says. "Except I was eighteen, not sixteen, and I was completely alone. Coming here was the scariest thing I'd ever done."

"How did you get here?" I ask, even though I've heard the story from Dad.

"My father died of a heart attack, and my mother couldn't live without him. She waited a few months, until I turned eighteen, then she told me to go to the nearest recruiting office and ask to go to the Attic. She burst her own heart. Literally. Fitting, I guess, since hers was already broken."

"I'm sorry."

Vivian smiles sadly. "Thanks. It just sucks, doesn't it? I mean, so much of life is loss. Pain. It just—"

"Sucks," I say, and we both smile. "I guess you do get it."

"At least you have your dad. Thank God things have changed since I was eighteen, but it's still a lab. We're still a part of the military. It's a tough place to be sometimes."

"I...I've never been thankful for my dad before," I say, and I see Vivian's smile turn into a grimace of horror. "I mean, I love him, I revered him once, but I've never been able to rely on him. I just...I don't think I know him very well."

Vivian starts to cry, but she pays no attention to the tears. "That's gonna change, honey, now that he's brought you to the Attic. You'll see. Your dad is a great guy. Strong. He always does what's right, his duty. Michael Van Zandt does what needs to be done."

She sounds like a disciple called to the pulpit to bear witness. How can I crush such faith? How can I tell her that that's exactly what I'm afraid of?

Chapter Four

Dad and I do finally leave, and I cannot tell you the relief I feel when I'm out in the open air.

"So what do you think?" Dad asks me as we make the drive back to Orange County. "Was it what you expected?"

"In some ways," I say, choosing my words carefully. "All the experiments, the people...you were right. They're doing amazing things."

"We are," Dad says, nodding. "I can't wait for you to be a part of it."

"About that. What's the plan?"

Dad's knuckles whiten as he clenches the steering wheel. "We're finally able to produce your Protein T, as you saw with Dacey. But there are issues. He's had trouble controlling how much he produces, for one. And he's slow at directing it. The protein can basically move throughout his bloodstream, and he can direct it to a cell, but once there he loses control of it if he doesn't activate it right away. From what you've told me, you can move it through cells, blood, whatever, and it only activates on command."

"Hmm," I say, nodding and thinking that over. "Let's take it from the beginning. So he's replicated the structure of the protein."

"Yes, but he couldn't do that until we'd determined the amino acid sequence for him. Your genes dictate the sequence; you're basically pre-coded. No one else is, that we've found."

"So you've got the protein molecule built, you know it's amino acid sequence and, I'm assuming, the fold, or he wouldn't have been able to make the protein work."

"Yep. That's what took so long. The third structure, the unique fold that each protein contorts itself into, was unknown. Dacey had to figure it out on his own."

"So...you have the structure of the protein molecule. You have the fold, so it can perform its proper function. Can Dacey move other proteins throughout his body?"

Dad nods. "Yes. Not as fast as you, but he has the same control you do."

"And he can keep those proteins inactive at will?"

"Yep."

I ponder the mystery for a few seconds. "After Mom died, I tried a few experiments. One time I swallowed a marble to see if I could feel it as part of my body."

Dad's mouth quirks up in a smile. "Yeah? Did it work?"

"Nope. I could tell it was there in my stomach, you know, as a foreign object, but I couldn't sense it like I can the rest of my body. I think that's what's going on with Dacey. He's created a foreign object. His body has no point of reference to recognize it. He's lucky he's been able to use it at all."

"I know where you're going with this," Dad says. "And I'm vetoing it right now."

"You're gifted, but you're not a mind reader," I say. "How do you know what I'm thinking?"

"Because I'm thinking the same thing: genetic engineering."

I sigh to myself – how does he do that?

"It's the only answer, isn't it?" I ask. "If we want someone to be able to use my protein."

Dad stops at a streetlight and looks me in the eye. "Repeat after me: I will not willingly donate my DNA."

"But Dad," I say, "that's ridiculous. My DNA is already out there. My doctor, Dr. Morley, took blood and ran tests years ago. When you took the protein from me for Dacey, surely some of my DNA was transferred. My hair falls out every day—"

He cuts me off with a sharp, "Thomas!"

I close my mouth.

"All taken care of. Repeat after me: I will not donate DNA. And I will not tell anyone that I can heal someone else."

"Vivian and Dr. Trent know," I say sullenly. "Dr. Rumson and Tessa, too."

"And they will take that knowledge to their graves, if necessary. I trust them implicitly."

"But Grandma—"

"Will be fine."

"Why?" I whisper.

Dad sighs. "They knew about you. I had to bring you eventually. And with Tyrion, I couldn't put it off. But if we don't keep a lid on this...look, I'm all for science and progress. But this has to be done systematically and in secret. We do it our way, and in our time, period. I will never, ever see my son put through the things I went through. Got it?"

I stare out the window.

I feel guilt, guilt that I assumed my father cared more about the Attic and its experiments than he did about me.

And then I feel a certain elation, that I will be able to participate, but with someone watching my back.

And THEN I feel, I don't know, uneasy, I guess. I'm going to have to lie. And I've never been good at that.

"Got it," I whisper.

Chapter Five

I sit quietly through Sunday's service, not really paying attention to anything Dr. Rumson says. I've got too many things on my mind.

When it's over, I hover off to the side, waiting for Dr. Rumson to finish with his post-service greetings. I catch his eye while he's speaking to Mrs. Thurman, and he smiles – I think my presence gives him a great excuse to get away from her.

"Will you excuse me?" he says politely, extricating himself from her firm handshake and giving me one instead.

"You look all pent up," he says, pumping my hand and pulling me into a hug.

"I feel all pent up," I say into his shoulder.

"My office," he says, and I follow him into the familiar and comforting space.

I've spent a lot of time here, at least an hour a week for almost ten years. I feel myself relax just being in Dr. Rumson's presence.

We sit, and he raises an eyebrow at me.

"So my dad," I begin. "No. Let me start somewhere else. We've had many discussions about the soul."

Dr. Rumson nods.

"Well yesterday, I...Jesus, this is complicated."

"I am not Jesus," he says, chastising me.

"Sorry," I say. "So sorry. Uh, yesterday, I learned of an experiment, highly classified, I don't have to tell you, I mean..." I pause, fixated on his amused smile.

He nods. "Yes, the Attic, top secret, you don't have to tell me." He chuckles. "So your dad finally caved, huh?"

"He did, but that's another issue for another time. See, this experiment...well, somebody grew a second head."

"Excuse me?"

"Yeah, I know it's out there, but I saw it with my own eyes. A second head, a brain, the central nervous system connections...the freaking thing could breathe. And talk. And think, probably better than most of the people I know. And I'm calling it a thing, but he's not. He's a man. A thinking, feeling man."

Dr. Rumson steeples his hands and presses his finger to his lips. "Go on."

"So what about the soul?" I shriek. "The soul! I mean, did this guy create a soul? Did God infuse a soul as soon as the brain was created? Does he have no soul, but appear to have one? I don't know what to think."

"Tell me more," he says, placing his hands flat on the desk. "He had a personality? Humor? Genuine feelings, separate from the original man."

"Yes," I say.

"Do they...but they are still attached? One body?"

"Yes."

"Then I believe that is the answer – they are sharing the soul."

"So the separate brain creates a separate personality, but the life force they share is the same?"

"Indeed," Dr. Rumson says. "I think it's the only explanation."

My mind reels as I try to process this. "But...they're going to try to separate him. They're going to try to create the rest of the body, then surgically separate."

"It won't work," Dr. Rumson says firmly.

"Can...I mean, is it possible, that the soul could be divided?"

"I don't see how. It's not a physical thing, like this man is trying to create. There's no way to divide it."

"And if it works? What then?"

Dr. Rumson stands and turns his back on me to look out the window behind him. He has a stellar view of the parking lot.

"I don't know," he finally says. "Cloning has worked. And I don't believe it's incompatible with our religious beliefs. At the quickening of life, the soul is infused. Period. I believe that, whether a living thing is quickened in its mother's womb or in a petri dish. But this? I just don't know." He finally turns back and resumes his seat.

"From a scientific perspective, Thomas, do you believe the two men can be separated and live?"

"Scientifically speaking, yeah. Yeah, I do."

"God works in mysterious ways," Dr. Rumson says with a laugh. "I can't wait to hear about the outcome."

I nod, but I don't feel like laughing.

"There's more?" he asks.

I frown, thinking about the more. "Dad wants me to lie about what I can do," I say.

"He has good reason?"

"He doesn't want the military or anyone else to conduct experiments on me."

"That seems like a good reason. But you're not comfortable with it."

"No," I say. "Plus, it will limit the things I can do. Plus...I know what to look out for. Dad didn't have that luxury when he went in. He had no clue they'd do anything nefarious. I know what to expect."

Dr. Rumson narrows his eyes at me. "Thomas, I love you. I want nothing but the best for you. God wants the same. But your arrogance will get you killed!"

I lean back in my seat, stunned by the vehemence in his voice.

"You know nothing! Your father is the one with the experience and the inside knowledge, and if your childhood has taught you anything, it's that your dad withholds information. Now, I believe your father is looking out for you. He withholds only with a purpose. But do not for one minute think you know better. Your life depends on it."

My eyes sting, and I blink hard to keep the tears from falling.

I cannot speak. So I nod.

Tessa comes over Sunday afternoon, and she goes in for a big kiss, but all I have in me is a peck.

She steps back, frowning. "Rough weekend?"

I flop into a chair at the kitchen table and sigh. "You could say that."

Tessa doesn't speak. She takes the chair opposite me and sits quietly.

God, I love her.

"Am I…do you think I'm arrogant?"

Tessa cracks a smile. "I prefer the term *confident.*"

I scowl. "So you do think I'm arrogant."

She reaches out and grabs my hand across the table. "No more than you have a right to be. You can do extraordinary things, and you know it. So what?"

"So…does my arrogance blind me? Does it cause me to try things I wouldn't normally try, or shouldn't try?"

"Thomas, you are the least impulsive person I know. When you act, you think it through. I don't think your arrogance drives you."

"Maybe not *drives me,* but what if I have an overdeveloped sense of my own capabilities? What if I overestimate what I can do, and someone gets hurt?"

Tessa squeezes my hand. "A little self-doubt is not a bad thing. I mean, you don't want to be paralyzed with fear when you have to make a decision, but I think it's good you're questioning yourself. Means you want to do the right thing."

"But that's the problem!" I say, voice rising. "I'm not questioning myself, not really. I believe in myself one hundred percent. I'm just irritated that two people this weekend called me arrogant, and I don't see it."

"That's a little arrogant," she says.

I give her a small smile. "I know."

Tessa takes her hand back and props her chin on it. "So now you know. It's highly possible that you're blind to your own faults, so I think you need my help."

"With what?"

"Remembering that you're not perfect." Tessa stands and leans back on the kitchen counter. She holds up the finger I healed on Friday. "One, you remember every conversation we've ever had, so when we have a fight, you can tick off the things I've said in the past and how they contradict what I'm saying today. That's highly irritating. Two, you drink so much orange juice that sometimes you smell like oranges. Three, you have octopus arms whenever we watch a movie, and I can't pay attention while I'm fighting you off. Four—"

"I get it."

"I'm not finished," she says. "Four, you're often caught up in your own moods, and you forget that I have moods of my own. Five—"

"I do that?" I say, taken aback.

"Case in point – right now. I went to kiss you because I missed you this weekend and wanted to connect. You blew me off."

"It wasn't on purpose," I say.

Tessa smiles. "I know that. I love that I'm the one you dump on. But sometimes I need to dump, too."

"Fair enough," I say. "What's five? I'm almost afraid to ask."

"Well, this may be hard for you to hear, but you're weird."

I laugh. "I already knew that."

"And sometimes it's tough to be in a relationship with you, because we're at two completely different places. I mean, we're at the same school and take a lot of the same classes, but you can take a nap and ace the tests while I struggle through every assignment."

"You don't struggle," I say, but she ignores me.

"It would be so much easier if I were dating a normal guy, who understood what I have to go through every day."

"My day is the same as your day," I say.

Tessa frowns. "And you're proving my point right now. You could teach the classes, Thomas."

I study my fingernails. "Are you saying you don't want to be with me?"

Tessa sits back down. "Of course not. You couldn't pry me off with a crow bar. Thomas, do you know what number six is?"

I shake my head.

"I don't have a number six, and that's number six: you are too freaking perfect. I can sit here and list fifty flaws of my own, but for you, I can barely come up with five."

I have to smile at that. "My turn. So one. One, you are so beautiful that I worry all the time about all the guys at school drooling over you." Tessa ducks her head, and I continue. "Two, you hug me so easily and so often that I'm addicted to it. If there's a time when I don't get a hug, I feel lost. Three, you're such a good listener that I take you for granted. I just assume you'll listen politely and thoughtfully whenever I need you to, because you always do. Four, you have such a great family, especially your mom, that it makes me jealous. It makes me miss my own mom. Five, you're such a good person, deep down, that sometimes you shame me. I'm ashamed that I'm not as good as you."

Tessa stands and pulls me out of my chair. We hug tight, and she strokes my hair, holding my head to her shoulder. "You're right. I do love to hold you," she whispers.

I sigh. "I'm a lucky guy."

Chapter Six

That night, I kick back on my bed with my cell phone. I call Grandma's apartment, and she picks up on the third ring.

"Hello?"

"Hey, Grandma, how are you?"

"Who's this?"

"It's Thomas, your grandson."

"Oh yes, Thomas. Is there something you need?"

"No, Grandma," I say. "I call you almost every night. Just checking in, seeing how things are."

"Oh, you…is this Michael?"

"This is Thomas, Michael's son."

There is a pause, and I can hear Grandma moving around. "Thomas? Thomas Van Zandt?"

"That's me."

"Oh, Thomas, how are you?"

"Good, I'm good. Tell me about you. What did you do today?"

"Oh, we went on a bus. Everyone here went on a bus to the Farmer's Market. Except that old crankpot Donald Mills. He wouldn't get on. Thought he might have to tinkle and have no place to go."

I laugh. "So did you buy anything at the market?"

"What market?"

"The Farmer's Market."

"Oh, yes, we went there today. On a bus. It stunk of old people. Do you know every single person on that bus was old?"

"Really?" I say, just to keep the conversation going.

"Who is this?"

I sigh. "Thomas."

"I have a grandson named Thomas."

I close my eyes. "Tell me about him."

"He's about six years old now, growing right up. And he's so bright. Just the brightest little thing. I miss him."

"I'm right here," I whisper.

"He doesn't come to see me. His father's in the Navy, and they don't have much time for me."

"Well, how about if I come visit you tomorrow? I'll bring some Klondike bars."

Grandma laughs. "Klondike bars! I love those! Tell me who I should thank for them."

"Thomas," I say. "You should thank Thomas."

"Well, I'll do that." And Grandma hangs up.

I put my phone on my nightstand and put my arms behind my head.

"Hold on, Grandma," I say. "Hold on. I'm coming."

Chapter Seven

After school, I walk to the grocery store, buy a package of Klondike bars, and hustle two more blocks to Grandma's place, an assisted care facility.

It's not a bad place, actually. She has her own apartment, and it's pretty tricked out. Above the toilet, a chain hangs that she can pull on to call for a nurse. On the wall next to her bed and in the kitchen are two buttons: one for 911, and one for a staff nurse. She has a TV that Dad and I hung on her wall, and a digital picture frame that I loaded with hundreds of photos. She even has a little patio of her own, where she likes to grow tomatoes and herbs. The only thing she lacks, really, is a stove. We had it removed two years ago when she set the kitchen on fire.

Grandma's decline has been slow but steady. It started a few months after my mom died – little things at first. She forgot to turn off the stove after making tea. She couldn't remember directions to places she'd been fifty times. She confused the remote control with the phone.

Dad and I tried to work around her forgetfulness. At one point, I printed out labels and stuck them to various things around the house – her keys, the phone, the can opener – but she ignored the labels, didn't even realize they were there. One day she called us from the bank in tears, because she couldn't find her car. Except she was sitting in it.

Six years ago, we placed her in this home. I hated to do it, felt like we were betraying her somehow, but our options were limited. We could have hired live-in help, but Dad said he wouldn't be comfortable living with a stranger. In one of my snarkier moments, I asked him, "Why not? I'm living with you, aren't I?"

We feared she had Alzheimer's. Tests, though, showed nothing of the kind. Alzheimer's patients develop holes in their brains, and Grandma's brain is fine, at least when they look at her scans. Her brain is healthy. Her body's healthy. Modern medicine has proved a dead end.

Which leaves me, and my unconventional brand of medicine, if Dad will ever let me use it.

My mom passed away in a car accident when I was six. I was just beginning to explore my abilities at the time, and I wanted to bring her back to life. As soon as I learned about the Attic, I knew I wanted to be a part of it. I was sure that I could find a way to bring my inner abilities outside to help someone else.

It took me a while, but I did figure it out. I can attach myself to another person, hook up my nerves to theirs, and take control of their body. It works, like when I healed Tessa's finger.

And when I saved Vivian.

Vivian had been in a coma for years. I went against my dad's explicit instructions and hooked up to her when he wasn't around. I healed a part of her brain that had been numbed, negating her own healing abilities. Vivian woke up.

And my heart stopped. Literally. My abilities don't come for free, and I'd used up all my energy, strained my poor heart to the point that it couldn't continue to beat. I was lucky. A nurse heard Vivian scream, she gave me CPR, and they kept me alive long enough that I could heal the damage I'd done. It was a delicate balance of giving me the proper nutrients and helping me with my breathing and other functions, to get me to that healed point. Even though I'm happy that Vivian is healed, almost dying is not something I want to experience ever again.

But how can avoid it if no one will let me experiment?

So I've been reading journal articles, keeping up on experiments conducted all over the world. And I've been planning my own experiments. But there's only so much thinking a guy can do in his own head. Dad says I still won't be involved directly in experiments at the Attic until I turn eighteen – I'll just be donating Protein T and theorizing. My only other option to conduct research, short of drugging someone and strapping them to my bed, has been Dad (and Tessa the one time, but I've promised not to repeat that). He lets me heal injuries to his extremities, and I've gotten pretty good at it.

When Dad says I'm arrogant, that I don't understand the ramifications of my experiments, I know he's full of crap. I do get it. I understand that my body has limits.

But I don't really care. And that's not arrogance, it's…I don't know what that is. I want to help people. I want to heal Grandma, damn the costs. If I end up dying, well, we're all gonna die someday. I'd rather die trying to help someone than die of boredom on my ass in front of the TV.

Is that so wrong?

Grandma's door doesn't have a lock, but I knock anyway. She opens it so fast that she must have been standing there waiting for someone to show up.

"Thomas!" she says.

I give her a big hug, relieved that she recognizes me, and wondering how long it will last.

We sit on the couch and I hand her the box of Klondikes.

"Oh, I love these," she says, ripping off the cellophane and taking out two bars. "Plenty for each of us."

We nibble on our ice cream, and Grandma chatters.

"They want to paint my apartment, but I told them the fumes make me sick. I just can't stand that smell."

"Maybe you can stay with us for a few days while they paint," I say, licking some chocolate off my wrist.

"With us? You live with someone?"

"I live with Dad, Grandma. Your son, Michael."

"Michael's here?"

"Not *here* here," I say, "but here in town. You just saw him yesterday. He brought you those flowers." I point to the vase of lilies on her kitchen table.

She furrows her brow, trying to remember.

"Grandma, do you remember the time I tried my Frankenstein experiment?" She looks at me, but I can tell no one's home. "I was trying to hide it from you, and I asked you to make me some beef stew so you'd leave me alone."

Grandma has stopped eating her ice cream. A single stream of vanilla runs down her fingers and drips onto her thigh.

"You caught me, though," I say, chuckling. I get up and grab a paper towel from the kitchen. "You knew exactly what I was up to the whole time." I take the ice cream from her hand, and she doesn't fight me. I clean her fingers and her thigh gently.

"I told you it wouldn't work," she whispers. I whip my eyes to her face, but she's staring at her lap. "You can't create life without God, without the soul."

"You remember that?" I whisper back.

Grandma doesn't reply.

I throw my trash away and put the rest of the softened ice cream bars in her freezer. I sit back down next to her and hug her.

"I love you, Grandma. I'll call you tomorrow."

She suddenly shies away from me.

"Who are you? What are you doing?"

"I'm Thomas," I say, trying to remain calm. "Your grandson. I'm just giving you a hug goodbye."

"Don't touch me!" she says, leaping to her feet. "Stay back!"

"It's okay, Grandma. It's me, Thomas. I'll go now. I'll leave you alone." I back away to the door slowly.

"Don't you move," she says. "You're not getting away with this."

And before I can respond, Grandma lunges for the wall and presses the button for 911.

Chapter Eight

"You okay?" Dad asks as he drives me home.

"Yeah, fine," I say, staring out the window, away from him.

He sighs. "It's such a screwed-up situation. Maybe we should only visit her together."

"Maybe."

"It's hard for me to see her like this, too."

"Then why don't you want to do anything about it?" I mumble.

"I do, of course I do. One step at a time."

"One step?" I say, voice rising. "We're crawling. No, not even crawling. We're standing still. I can do it, you know I can do it—"

"But that doesn't mean you should!" he says, exploding. "I want…what you and I want doesn't matter. What you can do doesn't matter. Grandma wouldn't want you to risk your life for her!"

"You don't even know if I'd be risking my life," I say. "I can just explore her body, find the problem, and who knows? Maybe it's something conventional medicine can fix."

"And if it's not? Once you're hooked up to her, my hands are tied. I won't be able to separate you without your help. You will be in control."

"And that's a bad thing?" I say, hurt.

"No," he says, "it's an unknown thing. You have no sense of self-preservation. You will continue to try to heal her no matter what."

"What if I promise? What if I promise to explore only?"

Dad glances at me, but doesn't reply.

"What, you're gonna question my word now? My integrity? It's all I have."

"I'd never question that," he says, softening. "I believe you'd go in doing the right thing. But you don't think when you're hooked up. You kind of, I don't know, go to a different place in your head. You're so focused on healing that nothing else registers."

"I have to be in the moment," I say. "You want me thinking about Tessa while I'm supposed to be healing you?"

"You're deliberately missing my point. You're focused on the other person's body, not your own. And I need you to focus on both."

We pull into the driveway, and I get out and slam my door. Dad catches up to me just inside the house.

"Listen to me," he says, spinning me around to face him. "Listen. I believe in you. I know you can heal so much more than we've tried. I know there's so much that you can teach us. Believe that I believe that. But you're my son, and your welfare comes before that of humankind. That might sound silly to you, but that's just the way it is. Grandma will hang in there. Healing her is not an emergency. It will happen, but there are things you need to learn to protect yourself before I let you do it. Do you understand?"

I take a deep breath and nod.

"Now, I've brought you to the Attic, and while I'm confident there's no direct threat from the military, just showing up is going to put you on some radars.

You're going to be approached, corporations will make offers...you'll be wanted even if they have no clue what you can do. But you're a minor, and until you turn eighteen, they need my consent. But there are ways they can get around that."

"So you're saying sick people will want me to heal them. Medical research firms will want to hire me. How can they get around you?" I ask.

Dad won't meet my eyes. "Well, if something happens to me—"

"Why would you think something's gonna happen to you?"

Dad sighs and goes into the kitchen. He pours me a glass of orange juice and grabs a can of beer for himself. We sit at the kitchen table.

"I've appointed Erica as your guardian if something happens to me."

"Erica? Tessa's mom? Why?"

"She's one of the few people who know about your abilities, and quite frankly, the only one I trust to raise you properly."

I rub my temples. "But I ask again – why do you think something is going to happen to you?"

"Thomas, to get to you, they have to eliminate me. It wouldn't be hard. They could get a politician to pull strings and send me to a combat zone. Or assign me to a new experiment that leaves me unable to make decisions. Hell, they could just shoot me."

I knock over my chair as I explode to my feet. "What?"

Dad just nods.

"But they…can't get away with that. That's criminal. People who want me to heal wouldn't condone killing."

"You'd think," Dad says, throwing back his beer. "As long as everyone thinks you're just a run-of-the-mill Dweller, they probably won't go to that much trouble to get to you. And as far as the Attic goes, I run interference as best I can while still getting things done, but I take my orders from people much higher up who couldn't give a shit less about the Dwellers. I'm hoping I'm wrong, that I'm just being paranoid. But I'd rather be paranoid than have you end up on the wrong side of someone's experiments."

I pace the kitchen and take all this in. It's a lot to process.

"So we're in danger," I say, leaning back against the counter. "Should I scan the surrounding buildings for snipers?"

"Already done," Dad says, taking me seriously even though I was joking. "I've got some of my ex-teammates on it. They're watching out for any overt attempts."

"What about covert attempts?" I ask.

Dad sighs again and drains his beer. "I've been meaning to have this discussion…look, the bottom line is, secrecy is vital. But if they want us to cooperate badly enough, they'll find a way. Probably by using the people we love. Do you understand that?"

Besides Dad, Dr. Rumson, and Grandma, there's only one person I love. "You mean Tessa?"

Dad nods.

I sink back into my chair. This can't be my real life – it's like a bad movie. Sure, my life's never been normal, but I never worried about my physical safety or that of those closest to me before. And now, just because I was born a little different, Tessa's in danger?

"She's the priority, Dad," I say. "I don't give a shit about me, you, or even Grandma, if it comes down to it. Tessa's more important."

"I know," he says.

"So your teammates, they need to be watching out for her, too."

"Done."

My head throbs. I feel better knowing Dad's got Tessa covered, but she's only in danger because of me. I rub my temples. "So how do you propose we work on research without letting anyone know if I can't work on the secret stuff at the Attic?"

"I think our best bet is a privately funded lab."

"You just said that no one should know. You have the resources and connections. Why don't we build our own lab?"

"All my connections are military," he says. "I'd be in hot water if I took my knowledge to civilians. But you don't have that restriction, as long as you don't divulge Attic secrets. That's another reason I've kept you out of the Attic – you have limited knowledge to reveal."

"But who says civilians won't reveal what I can do?"

"Researchers are notoriously secretive," he says. "Their funding and income depend on it. I'll let you do the legwork and find the ones you want to work with."

Wow. Those are words I never thought I'd hear come out of Dad's mouth. I don't even know what to say.

But Dad seems to understand. He stands and puts a hand on my shoulder. "There's some danger and there's some risk. But I know how much this means to you. I know you're life's not worth living unless you're fulfilling your purpose. I'm doing my best to make that happen."

My eyes sting, and I blink. I wrap my arms around Dad and squeeze, maybe the first time I've initiated a hug since Mom was alive. "Thanks, Dad," I whisper.

He thumps my back and steps away. My head pulses with pain again, probably from my almost-tears, and I shut down the screaming nerves.

"You think I could go talk to Dr. Rumson?"

Dad throws his beer can in the trash. "I get it. It's a lot to take in. Go. But take your car."

I scowl. Dad bought me a Ford Explorer when I got my license, but I don't drive it much. I like to walk to clear my head. "Why?"

"You're easier to kidnap off the street." My eyes grow wide, and Dad laughs. "I'm just kidding. But people can approach you easier if you're walking, and I'd rather not put you in that position just yet."

I shake my head and grab my car keys.

Chapter Nine

I exit my car and lock it. I scan the parking lot and the surrounding bushes, looking for any shady characters who might be lurking.

I see no one.

I barrel through the office door and wave at Dr. Rumson's secretary.

"Hey, Mary Kate. I have something important I need to discuss with the good doctor."

Mary Kate chuckles. "It's always important," she says. "He's actually taking a nap, hasn't been feeling well today. Let me buzz him."

"Oh, no," I say waving her off. "If he's asleep, I can come back."

"No, it's fine," she says, reaching for her phone. "I was supposed to wake him twenty minutes ago. Have a seat."

Mary Kate calls Dr. Rumson, and we can hear his phone ringing through the door. It's a good ten rings before he answers.

"How are you feeling?...Good, I'm glad...It's almost five o'clock, yes. Thomas is here, he wanted to have a word...yes, I'll send him in, and then I'm off for the day. See you tomorrow." She hangs up and smiles at me. "He's all yours." She gathers her purse and stands. "I'll see you Sunday, if not before."

I laugh. "Have a good night." And I enter the sanctuary of Dr. Rumson's office.

"Hey, sir, how are you feeling?"

"Tired," he says honestly. He's sitting on his couch, stockinged feet poking out from beneath his black trousers.

"I can come back," I say.

"Nonsense. Talk to me while I clear my fuzzy head."

I turn the guest chair away from the desk to face the couch and sit. "I might need you clear-headed for this."

Dr. Rumson frowns and rubs his chest. "Oh?"

I stare at the wall. "There's a development, I mean, a wrinkle. Well, it's more than a wrinkle, see, the thing is…there are people who already want to experiment on me. Which we kind of knew. I mean, I always thought it'd be the Attic, but Dad says corporations and sick people are watching me, too, and want me. But they can't get me to do anything while I'm a minor without Dad's consent. But Dad thinks they could get around that by taking him out of the equation, like by killing him. He's already hired security to watch his back, and he's setting up the legal end of things by appointing a guardian for me in case something does happen to him."

Dr. Rumson gasps.

"I know. Heavy, right? Like, completely surreal. I mean, he thinks they'll just do away with him to get to me!"

"Thomas."

My headache starts back up, but I ignore it. "You can't believe it either, right? I didn't believe it. I mean, I still kind of don't. This is the United States. We have laws."

"Thomas."

I finally look at Dr. Rumson. The color has drained from his normally ruddy cheeks, and his eyelids are fluttering.

"Are you okay?"

He shakes his head slowly and flexes his left hand a couple of times. I slide out of my chair and kneel at his feet.

"Where does it hurt?" I say. I can feel my body flood with adrenaline, and my heart flutters like a trapped insect.

"My...arm," he gasps out. "My chest. Can't...breathe." He starts to list to his right, and I reach out and catch him.

"You're having a heart attack," I say, voice trembling. "I need to call 911."

As I lower his head to the couch, Dr. Rumson takes a final rattling breath and goes slack.

"Shit!" I mumble, extricating my arms from underneath his body. I tilt his head back and hover my cheek over his nose and mouth. He's not breathing.

I rip his shirt open, sending buttons flying in every direction. I breathe five times into his mouth, then start chest compressions. I check for breathing again. I check for a pulse. Nothing.

I have to make a decision. Do I call 911 and hope it's not too late, or do I try to heal him myself?

But I'm not allowed to do that! What if I mess up? What if I make it worse? What if someone catches me in the middle of healing him?

What if the five seconds I've taken to think about this have already sealed his fate?

I can't let him die because of some stupid rule.

I leap to my feet and rummage in my pocket. I take out my knife and flick it open. I make a shallow cut above his heart and slice open the meaty part of my palm. I press my hand to his chest.

First the easy part. I extend my nerves, grow them, attach them to nerves in Dr. Rumson's chest. I follow the neural network all the way to his brain, where I take control of his entire body. Now he's mine.

I follow back to his heart. I find a blocked artery, which I easily clear. I order his cardiomyocytes, the heart muscle cells, to start beating again. They do, but there's significant scar tissue in his heart. This is obviously not his first heart attack.

Now the tricky part. I gather the stem cells from under my fingernails and direct them to Dr. Rumson's heart. I flood them with the right protein (Protein T), and will them to regenerate into cardiomyocytes. I break down the scar tissue and replace it with the new cells.

I do a quick search for any bacteria that I've introduced and destroy them. I remove my nerves from Dr. Rumson and repair the cell damage I've done. I heal his chest wound and my own cut. I lean back over him and breathe into his mouth.

I feel the moment when he breathes on his own. I pull back slightly, hesitant to move too far away.

His body shakes, and he starts to cough. I grab the ever-present water bottle off his desk, and hold it to his lips. He takes a small sip, his eyes still closed.

"Can you speak?"

Dr. Rumson tries but ends up coughing again. I give him more water, and some spills out of his mouth and pools in the hollow of his throat.

"Dr. Rumson?"

"What...Thomas?"

"I'm here," I say. "It's Thomas. Just rest. You had a bad spell."

He slowly opens his eyes, wheeling them around until he finds my face.

"When was your last heart attack?" I ask.

His eyes widen. "You...did I..."

I nod.

He closes his eyes for a moment, then opens them. "Help me up," he says softly.

"I think you should stay down for a while," I say.

"Help me up!" he screams, though his voice is barely over a whisper.

I slide my arm behind his back and manage to get him upright.

"Tell me," he says, leaning his head back.

"What do you remember?" I ask.

He scratches absently at the fresh pink skin on his blood-smeared chest. Then he freezes, looking down at the crusting blood and his ruined shirt. "What happened?"

"Tell me what you remember," I insist.

"I...I was feeling tired, so I took a nap. Mary Kate woke me up, you came in...I felt...my chest felt heavy, like an elephant decided to take a shit on it."

I laugh at this, the first time I've ever heard him curse. "That sounds about right." And then I sober. "You had a heart attack."

Dr. Rumson looks me in the eye. "And you healed me."

I shrug.

He pats the space next to him on the couch. "Sit. If I remember everything you've told me, you're about ready to pass out yourself."

"I can make it home—"

"No! Sit." He digs his cell phone out of his pocket. "Pepperoni and mushroom okay with you?"

A wave of sleepiness goes over me, but I shake it off. "Great. Can we order buffalo wings too?"

He chuckles as he dials. "I haven't eaten either of those things in a decade. That's when I had my last heart attack."

Dr. Rumson orders and tells the guy he'll pay an extra $100 if we can get our food in twenty minutes. They show up in fifteen.

As we eat, my sleepiness fades, but the adrenaline also starts to wear off. I'm not in danger of passing out, but I'm exhausted. The repercussions of what I've done also start to penetrate.

But I don't want to think about any of that now, I don't have the energy to think about it, so I latch onto something to distract myself.

"So ten years ago you had a heart attack. That's around the time we met."

"Indeed," he says without offering more.

"So how did it happen? I mean, you weren't giving a sermon, were you?"

"Nothing so dramatic," he says. "I was on the phone."

"Did the person you were talking to call 911?"

"No," he says quietly. "He'd already hung up."

"Did Mary Kate find you?"

"She did. Almost had a heart attack herself, poor thing. She refuses to retire. Says she won't leave until I do."

"Wow," I say, taking my fifth slice of pizza. "So you were at work. Seems pretty peaceful here, I mean, nothing stressful that would bring on a heart attack. I'm particularly interested in stress-induced maladies. It just amazes me how stress can affect our health. But you seem to have a pretty calm life."

Dr. Rumson waves a hand, dismissing me. I shove the last bite of crust into my mouth and grab another chicken wing, staring hard at his averted eyes.

"Wait. You mean it was stress-induced?"

He still won't look at me. "No, no. I said nothing of the kind."

I narrow my eyes at him. "I thought there was only honesty between us."

He stares at the napkin draped on his thigh. "Fine. Stress may have played a role, but I was out of shape. My own fault."

"Family trouble?" I ask around my half-clean chicken bone. I know Dr. Rumson has been a widower for twenty years, and has one married daughter who lives nearby. He's never mentioned any issues with her, though.

"In a sense."

I growl. "This is like pulling teeth. Tell me already."

"Thomas, I don't think—"

"Just from a medical perspective," I say. "You don't have to give away any secrets. Just give me the situation."

Dr. Rumson sighs. "Someone very close to me was in danger."

The gnawed bone drops from my fingers to the floor and rolls under the couch. I stare at him. "Me."

"Thomas."

"Me. I gave you a heart attack."

"Don't be ridiculous."

I stand up and walk out of the office, my fingers still sticky orange, without even saying goodbye.

♥

I want to punch something, mainly myself. How could I have been so stupid?

Granted, I was only six when I called Dr. Rumson that day, just before I decided to heal Vivian. I wasn't sure if I was healing her for the right reasons, and I knew something might happen to me, and I needed him to let Tessa know that Dad had taken me away to try to bring Vivian out of her coma. Of course, Dad thought we'd be doing research without any actual surgery involving me, but my point is, I unloaded on Dr. Rumson. I worried him. I gave him a freaking heart attack.

But the worst part of this entire situation is the fact that a part of me, a teeny tiny part, feels content. And doesn't that make me psycho of the year? Finally, I get actual confirmation that someone I love and trust loves me back so much that me in danger stops his heart, and what's my reaction? I feel loved! Shit! What does that say about my life and my relationships? What does that say about me?

Dr. Rumson is the only person, besides Grandma and Tessa, whom I'd want to live with if something happened to Dad. He's been my rock. And now, I'm not even sure if I ever want to speak to him again. How can I? I might kill him.

Hell, he might not want to speak to me. I certainly wouldn't if I were him.

My feet eat up the pavement as I walk, and then I remember my car. I trudge back to the church, start her up, and squeal out of the lot. I wish someone would start following me, 'cause I could really use a target for my anger right now.

Somehow I end up at Tessa's. I lean heavily on her front door, thinking about our conversation over the weekend. Here I am to dump on her again.

I knock, and Erica answers.

"Thomas. Hey."

"Hi, Erica. Is Tessa home yet?"

She glances at her watch. "Probably another hour. You want to come in?"

I nod, and she opens the door wide and ushers me inside.

"You want a Coke?" I shake my head with a small smile, and she laughs. "Right. Soda rots our body from the inside out. How about ice water?"

"Great."

I slump on a stool at the kitchen island while she fills my glass. I thank her and sip.

"You need to talk about something?" she asks.

I appreciate her approach. She's rinsing some dishes in the sink, not looking at me at all, giving me an out if I need it.

"You're a good mom," I say, but I have no idea where the words come from. "Tessa's lucky to have you."

"Thank you," she says, her hands still busy. "Thinking about your mom today?"

"Not really," I confess. "Just wondering if I'm missing something. I mean, I know I'm missing something, lots of things, but I'm wondering if that's my fault."

"It's not your fault your mom's gone, Thomas," she says.

"I know, but relationships in general. I have a couple guy friends, but it's superficial 'cause I can't share anything about my life. I don't have a mother. I don't have grandparents who can fulfill their role. I have Tessa, thank God, and I have Dr. Rumson, but that's it."

"You have me," she says quietly. "I feel like you're one of my own."

My eyes burn, and I blink hard. "But knowing me might put your family in danger. I can't...I couldn't live with myself if something happened to one of you."

Erica turns off the faucet and faces me. "Life is full of risks. You didn't ask to be born this way, Thomas. You're dealing with it. And we're happy to help any way we can. Please believe that."

"I do," I say, staring hard at my water glass. "But the danger is real, Erica. I have to get away. I have to let Tessa go." I stand, preparing to leave.

"Sit down," she says.

I stay standing.

"Sit down now!"

Okay, so I sit.

"If you think you can walk out this door without even saying goodbye to her, you're crazy."

"But—"

"No buts. I never pegged you for a coward, Thomas."

"I'm not a coward!" I yell. "I'm just trying to do the right thing!"

"Oh, so the right thing is breaking Tessa's heart and running away?"

A tear rolls down my cheek. I angrily brush it away before she can spot it.

Erica sits next to me and places her hand on my arm. "Mike…your dad told me everything. He asked me to be your guardian, and I accepted. I've weighed the risks, and I decided you're worth it."

"What about Ron?" Tessa's dad works a lot, and she doesn't see him much, but Erica's talking as if she made this monumental decision on her own.

Erica sighs. "It's not an issue."

"You mean he agreed, just like that?"

She sighs again and stands. "Look, our marriage…Thomas, it's complicated."

I nod. I have a ton of questions I want to ask, but the answers aren't any of my business. I stand up next to her.

"I'll just go hang out in Tessa's room. I…thanks, Erica. It means a lot to me."

She pats my arm and kisses my cheek. I walk to Tessa's room slowly, my lips split in a grin even though I feel like shit.

♥

I fling myself on Tessa's unmade bed and roll to my back.

I love Tessa's room – it's totally her. Not too girly but still feminine, the room has bright orange walls, covered in her paintings. I can spend hours in here examining them, even though I know them all by heart.

I gaze from one to the next, remembering the times she painted them. The one of a gnarled oak, its leaves just beginning to turn yellow, she painted while I worked on the sculpture for the local library. The one under the window, of me in the Thinker's pose, she painted our first day of high school. I remember how nervous she was the night before, how she'd talked my ear off until two in the morning and I fell asleep in the middle of our one-sided conversation, and when I woke up at seven, I saw the phone was still connected and she was still talking. She claims she fell asleep, too, and called me back the next morning and I mysteriously answered, but I don't believe her.

On her desk, I notice something new, a pencil drawing I haven't seen before. I get up, walk to the desk, and pick it up.

Whoa. It's me holding Tessa, her bent back at the waist and me bending over her. Her hair is flung back, her eyes fluttering shut, her mouth a slack "O" as though she's taking a breath. My mouth is buried in her neck. Her hands clutch my shoulders.

I sit back on the bed with the drawing. If this isn't a hint about sex, I don't know what is.

I hear the front door open and close, and Tessa's cry of "Mom!"

I quickly replace the drawing on her desk and jump back on her bed. I put my hands underneath my head and force my breathing to slow.

Tessa comes in a few minutes later and throws her backpack to the floor.

"Hey, you," she says, a smile on her lips.

I prop myself on one elbow and smile back. "Hey."

She sits on the bed and leans in for a kiss, but I dodge her and stand. "Wait."

I hold out a hand to her and pull her up. She looks at me quizzically. I press my body to hers and wrap my arms around her. Slowly, I dip her backwards. She places her hands on my shoulders and squeezes. I bend forward and bury my lips in her neck.

"Oh," she says on a long sigh.

I kiss, I nibble, I suck. I lick my way up her neck until I find her sweet mouth. And I give her a kiss she deserves.

We straighten slowly, and Tessa smiles. "You saw my drawing."

"How'd I do?"

"Magic," she whispers, kissing me again.

I laugh against her lips. "I love you, Tessa."

"I love you, too."

We touch foreheads, and she hugs me tight. "Something up?"

I shrug. "Tell me about swim practice first. I want to hear about you."

"Regular day, nothing to report. Tell me."

I sigh and sit back on the bed. "Do you think…one day…will you marry me?"

Tessa laughs and sits next to me. "Only if you promise to ask me properly again when we're ready."

I fall backwards. "Marrying me would be weird, though. Our kids would be like me. Or maybe not, now that I think about it. I could probably manipulate my DNA. I know I could. Never mind. Our kids will be normal."

"I'd want our kids to be like you," she says.

"No way. Not if we had a choice. I mean, I could give you exactly what you want. Girl or boy?"

Tessa flops back next me. "I'd want God to decide."

"God doesn't decide, Tessa. It's all about my sperm."

"I know, but I mean, I wouldn't want to decide. I'd want nature to take its course."

"Okay, but I know you want a girl. What if we have three boys first? Wouldn't you want me to make sure number four is a girl?"

"Nope. If we have four boys, then I'm not meant to have a girl."

"But there's not some cosmic force deciding every outcome. There's not some great plan. It's all chance."

"Thomas, you can do so many things...this is something I never even thought about, manipulating our future children. I know you can do good things, but this just seems wrong."

"Why?" I insist.

She shrugs. "I don't know. Don't you think there could be consequences?"

"Sure, if it were done on a large enough scale, like the ratio of females to males could become unbalanced. But we're talking about a few kids, not the entire planet."

Tessa stares at me. "Arrogance alert, Thomas. You are not God."

"I know. I know how it sounds. But God gave me these abilities. Surely I'm supposed to exercise them."

"To a point. There's a time and a place for everything. You shouldn't do something just because you can."

I study my hands and pick at a hangnail on my thumb. "I healed Dr. Rumson today."

Tessa raises her eyebrows at me. "He cut himself?"

"No. He had a heart attack right in front of me."

She gasps and opens her mouth, but no words come out.

"He stopped breathing. His heart stopped beating. The whole deal."

Tessa leaps to her feet. "Food. You need food."

"I ate," I say while she stares at me.

"You...you're probably gonna crash. Maybe I should call your dad to pick you up."

"Don't you want to hear if Dr. Rumson's alright?"

"If you healed him, I know he's okay. It's you I'm worried about."

"I'm fine."

"Let me call—"

"No. Just...will you lie with me, Tessa? Just for a few minutes?"

Tessa's eyes soften. She slips her shoes off and snuggles up next to me.

"You want to talk about it?" she asks.

"Later," I whisper, my two-ton eyelids slamming shut. "Wake me in an hour."

If Tessa replies, I'm too sleepy to hear it.

Chapter Ten

I wake up and all is dark. I'm alone in Tessa's bed, my Converse still on my feet.

I sit up and stretch. Physically, I feel refreshed, but there's too much on my mind to feel energized.

I take my phone out of my pocket and check the time: 9:00 at night. Longer than the hour I was hoping for, but still, not too bad considering the work I did today.

I walk towards the kitchen, and I can hear Erica talking before I get there.

"You're welcome to ask her, but she won't tell you anything," she says.

"Loyal 'til the last," I hear my dad say. "I admit it's noble, but she has to realize what's at stake."

"I'm not going to insist, Mike, unless Thomas is in danger. He'll tell you himself when he wakes."

My heart stutters, hearing them talk about Tessa. She kept my secret. God, what did I do to deserve such unswerving devotion?

I round the corner and enter the kitchen.

"I'm back in the land of the living," I announce. "Haven't slept well for a week. Guess it caught up with me." My insides squirm as I utter the lie that isn't really a lie, but more of a half-truth.

"Really?" Dad says. "You needed thirty hours of sleep just to catch up?"

I gulp. "Thirty hours?"

Erica smiles at me. "You came over yesterday afternoon. I called your dad after you fell asleep."

I blow out a breath and stuff my hands in my front pockets. "Shit. Thanks."

"Yeah, shit," Dad says. "What the hell happened?"

"I…it's a long story, quite boring actually, I'm sure you're eager to get to bed—"

"If you lapse into that bullshit geek speak, I'll throttle you. Tell me what happened."

I roll my neck a few times, working up my courage. "Fine. Dr. Rumson had a heart attack," I say. "He died. I had to."

Dad curses under his breath and stands. He hugs me hard. "Do a scan," he says.

"When we get home," I say.

He shakes me. "Now. Do it now."

"Fine."

I close my eyes and take a deep breath. I feel inside my body, starting from the top down.

"Brain's fine…heart's good…blood's good, low on iron…major organs fine…extremities fine…a little dehydrated…vitamin C will help…hormones are, uh, fine…" I open my eyes and look at my hand. I cannot tell that I'd slashed it open yesterday.

"That's it?" Dad asks. "You're sure?"

"Fat cells depleted, but not as much as you'd think."

"How much?"

"Oh…two, two and a quarter pounds."

Dad nods, obviously thinking. "And you ate yesterday?"

"Five slices of pizza, maybe thirty wings, three sixteen-ounce bottles of water."

Erica sets a glass of water in front of me and I take it gratefully.

Dad gathers his keys from the counter. "We'll talk at home. Thanks, Erica. Thank you so much for helping."

"Of course."

They exchange a brief hug, and Dad heads to the door.

"Is Tessa here?" I ask.

Erica shakes her head. "She's running an errand."

I smile. "She didn't want Dad to pound on her." I throw back the entire glass of water in one long gulp. "Tell her I'll call her later."

Dad insists on leaving my car here and him driving. I don't even think about arguing with him.

"Dr. Rumson is fine, thanks for asking," I say when we get in the car. And then I mentally slap myself – why I am provoking the beast?

Dad's jaw tightens. "I called him after Erica called me. Took him a while to get back to me, but he told me what happened."

"Oh," I say. "So…is he feeling okay?"

Dad cracks a wisp of a smile. "You just told me he's fine."

"Fine," I say. "I know he's fine. But is he…fine?"

"Yes, Thomas. Dr. Rumson is fine."

"What did he say?"

Dad glances at me. "He managed to stay awake long enough to leave Mary Kate a note and to go home. He slept about twenty-four hours. Woke up ten pounds lighter and feeling like he could run a marathon."

My lips automatically curve into a smile. "Really?"

Dad's hands tighten on the steering wheel. "Thomas, you did a good thing."

I don't reply.

"A damn good thing!" he yells, thumping a fist. "It's just...I wish there were an easier way to get around it."

"Around what?"

"You could walk into the Attic right now and solve every research dilemma we have." Dad pulls into our driveway and shuts off the ignition. "But you're too vulnerable. You're a billion-dollar prize. You have to learn to protect yourself, and you have to do it now."

I stare at Dad's profile. "So you want me to take karate lessons?"

Dad blows out a breath and laughs. "This isn't a movie. We'll take normal precautions to ensure you're safe, but I'm thinking about the side effects of your abilities. Right now, your own body is your worst enemy."

I sigh. "You mean the way I fell asleep for thirty hours. It makes me vulnerable."

"Yep."

"That would be useful to combat."

"And the way you burn up calories. You're basically cannibalizing yourself."

"All of us have that problem, though, right?"

Dad smiles. "On a much smaller scale. You're the only one healing other people, and because you're so fast, the consequences are greater. You need to get a handle on it before your heart stops again."

I hang my head. "Okay. I concede. I need to work on this stuff."

"I know," Dad says. "Find that lab. The sooner, the better."

Chapter Eleven

I tell myself to leave Dr. Rumson alone and let him heal. But his text messages have been increasingly difficult to ignore.

Thomas, call me immediately.

You did nothing wrong.

I feel great. Please. I need to talk to you.

Don't do this. Don't throw away our friendship.

You're giving me a heart attack right now, you idiot.

How can you ignore it when someone calls you an idiot?

So on Saturday morning I get in my Explorer and drive the few blocks over to St. Paul's Church.

"Thank God you're here," Mary Kate says when I enter. "Something's wrong."

"Wrong?" I say, adrenaline already kicking in.

"Look for yourself," she says.

I knock twice and step into his office without waiting for an invitation. Dr. Rumson is standing on his rolling chair, precariously balanced on his toes, dusting the top of one of his bookshelves.

"Hey," I say.

"Thomas," he says on a sigh, and he hops down off the chair with the agility of someone half his age and throws his arms around me. "Don't ever do that again, do you hear me?" He grips tighter. "Ever!"

I hug him back a bit reluctantly, but it's impossible to resist a sincere hug. "I'm sorry," I say, squeezing tight.

He releases me and nods. "Me, too."

I sit on the couch while he bustles around. He has several open boxes on the floor, piles of books, and a host of rags and cleaning supplies.

"Spring cleaning?" I ask.

He chuckles. "I haven't done a proper cleaning in here in years. Couldn't work up the energy. But I've got the energy now, thanks to you."

I'm secretly pleased, but I don't want to talk about it. So I say, "You know the other day, when I told you we have a dilemma?"

"Refresh my memory," he says, spraying a shelf with Pledge. I love that smell – it reminds me of Mom. "I'm still a little sketchy."

I tell him about Dad wanting me to find a private lab so I can work on my abilities and my personal safety. "I guess…I've just wanted this for so long, and now that it's happening, it's frightening."

"Well, let's look at your options," he says. "You could do nothing. Don't go to the Attic, don't go to any lab, don't participate."

"But that doesn't get me closer to my goal, which is to actually heal people."

"Then it seems to me you need a facility, one way or the other," he says. He sits down next to me, still carrying his dust rag. The lemony scent tickles my nose. "You could go public."

"What?"

"You heard me. Call Oprah. Call CNN or Fox News. Tell them what you can do. Show them. Find the researcher you most want to work with and plead your case. If you're known, it will be harder for someone to get to you."

"But…"

"But what?" he asks.

"But…going public has consequences for the others. Is it fair of me to out them, too?"

"Who says you have to out anyone? This is about you. You don't have to mention anyone else."

"But they'll ask me. Of course they'll ask me if there are others like me. You know I have a hard time lying."

"Thomas, there is no one like you. That's an honest answer."

Strictly speaking, maybe, but I wouldn't call that answer honest.

"Okay, so what happens then?" I ask Dr. Rumson. "Paparazzi hound me, people camp out on my front lawn so I can heal them?"

"Probably," he says. "And you'll get your share of nuts, claiming you're a fraud. Maybe some death threats."

"Gee," I say. "This option gets more appealing by the minute."

Dr. Rumson chuckles. "Okay, maybe the news route isn't the way to go. Go to a university. Talk to some of the leaders in your field. Find someone you trust."

"I have three people in the whole world I trust, outside of family. You, Tessa, and Erica. I'm not exactly a pro at making friends. I guess that's the scary part."

He pats my knee. "It's time for you to evolve, my boy."

Chapter Twelve

"Okay. Go."

I stride across the room and stand next to a pretty blonde. She's eyeing the paintings on the wall, her arms crossed over her chest.

"Subtle, isn't it?" I say. "The way the light plays across her face. As though the sun's reaching for her."

The girl looks at me and cocks her head, but stays silent.

"Do you like it?" I ask.

"I find it a bit boring, to be honest," she says. "There's not much expression in her face."

"Because it's not about her, it's about the light," I say. I hold out my hand. "I'm Thomas."

She shakes my hand lightly. "Hello, Thomas."

"And you are?"

"Late, actually," she says, turning away from me.

I sigh. "What did I do wrong?"

Tessa faces me and smiles. "You need to play off what I said. Ask me why I think the painting's boring. I don't even know you. I don't care what you think."

I kick my toe into the carpet, frustrated.

"Try it again."

I go back over to the other side of the room and start again. I stride across the room to Tessa.

"This is one of my favorites," I say.

Tessa stays silent. I look at her profile.

"You look like her, actually."

"I do?"

"Yes. You're much more expressive, though. This girl in the painting doesn't have much expression."

Tessa fights a smile. "I think it's a pretty boring painting, to be honest."

I consider the painting. "Why's that?"

"She's not expressing any strong emotion, like you said. It's just a picture of a girl."

"So you like art to express emotion?"

She turns to me. "Don't you? I mean, what's the point of art? To evoke a response."

"I've never thought of it like that. I tend to judge art by the competence of the artist."

"But in what sense? The artist should be competent enough to provoke you in some way."

"So this artist doesn't provoke you?" I ask.

She smiles. "Not with this painting, but there are a few...that one, there, of the guy with his heart on his sleeve, that one provokes me."

I look at the oil painting of me slumped in a chair, a life-like heart in mid-beat throbbing on my arm.

"What does that one make you feel?" I ask her.

"Curious," she says, "about the guy, about why he's so emotional, why there's sadness in his eyes. And it makes me feel sad, like I can feel his pain."

I swallow. "You think he's in pain?"

She holds out a hand to me. "I'm Tessa, by the way. Sometimes, yes, I think he's in pain. But we all feel that. That's why I like the painting. I understand it."

I squeeze her hand. "I'm Thomas. Would you like to have a cup of coffee, talk about it some more?"

"I'd love to."

I throw my arms around her and she squeaks. We fall to the bed, laughing.

"So I did better that time?"

"Perfect," she says, giving me a kiss. "Did you see the difference in your approach that time?"

I roll off of her and prop my head up with one arm. "Sort of. I played off what you said."

"And you didn't lecture me," she says. "People don't like a know-it-all."

I smile. "You know, you just taught me how to pick up a girl."

Tessa smiles back. "I taught you how to make a friend. And I'm counting on you using your powers for good instead of evil."

Chapter Thirteen

Dad and I head down to the Attic for my second visit on a bright Sunday morning. It's more of a beach day than a lab day, but since I'm the one who's been begging to go to the Attic for years, I guess I have to be content.

Content is perhaps the wrong word. I am resigned. And almost paralyzingly nervous.

I regulate on the drive, just a bit. I slow my breathing, keep my heart beating at a calm pace, suppress my sweat glands and the release of adrenaline. If I go in showing fear, they'll probably smell it on me.

"So Dacey and Tyrion are our first stop?" I ask as we cruise up the tree-lined drive.

"Yep. They're still in isolation. Dr. Trent is running tests, trying to come up with a workable plan for Tyrion."

"What's he got so far?"

"Not much," Dad admits. "They're thinking of doing the limbs first, then resting a few months before growing the rest."

"Why the limbs?" I ask. "They're the most useless parts."

"They're the known," Dad says. "We've grown limbs hundreds of times. We know exactly how much energy they take to create."

I don't say anything else. They're going about this backwards, but I just want to talk to Dacey about it. Since he's the only other Dweller who's grown cells in the central nervous system, I figure he's the one to bounce ideas off of.

We're checked in and heading down in the elevator when Dad says, "Vivian is out today."

I look at him, but he's staring straight ahead. "Oh?"

"She's spending the weekend with Jack."

Jack. Jacqueline. My sister. Dad's other child.

"So…have you…"

"No."

Guess that answers that. Dad hasn't seen her, hasn't talked to her. I don't get it, but we've had enough arguments about it, and I don't want to get into it again here.

We exit the elevator, and I fight to keep my breakfast down. I stop at door five.

"You coming in?" I ask Dad, since he makes no move toward the scanner.

"I want to check in with Dr. Trent. You go. I'll be there in a bit."

I nod, slide my card, and scan my eyes. The door opens.

♥

"Hello?" I say, trying to be polite.

Dacey and Tyrion rise from their chair and walk to greet me.

"Thomas," Dacey says, shaking my hand. "Welcome back."

"Thanks," I say. "How are you guys?"

They exchange a look. "Hanging in there," they say at the same time.

They wave me to a chair and we sit.

"So my dad said you guys are planning on the big split."

Dacey grins, and Tyrion sighs.

"The big split," Dacey says. "I like that."

"You would," Tyrion says.

"You're still not on board?" I ask Tyrion.

"We're looking at a year, probably more," he says. "And it's already been a year. Another year without sunlight. Another year without being home. Another year without sex."

"Ouch," I say with a smile.

Dacey just shakes his head.

"I feel your urges," Tyrion says. "This has not been easy."

"It's worth it," Dacey says.

"So you're thinking about limbs first," I say.

Dacey nods. "Those will be the easiest. We know what to expect, and I can grow them in my sleep. I once had twenty toes."

I laugh. "How'd you get rid of them?"

"I cut off the blood supply to them, and we surgically removed the dead flesh."

I cringe thinking about it. "Well, I don't think that's the way to go."

"You don't?" Tyrion says.

"No. The key to the whole thing is managing the strain on Dacey's body, mainly his heart and his calorie output. Why waste time and resources on the limbs?

Tyrion, you can grow limbs yourself after you're separated."

"He can't," Dacey says. "His DNA's not coded for it."

"But you took the cells from your own body to create him," I say. "You passed on your DNA."

"I started with my own sperm cells, actually," Dacey says, "because they were my best source of stem cells. But as you probably know, with the exception of your dad, male Dwellers do not pass on our abilities."

"Hmmm. Okay. I still think you should do the major organs first. A second heart would help take the load off of you, Dacey."

"I see your point," he says, "but I've never done it. Never built a heart. It took me years of planning to get the brain right. You can see my on-the-fly attempts at growing other body parts." He points at Tyrion, who smiles.

"You did just fine," I say. "I can probably talk you through the heart. We can practice. I've grown cardiomyocytes. Took me about twenty seconds to repair about one-sixth of the heart."

Dacey sits up straighter in his chair. "You've healed your own heart?"

So much for my promise of secrecy. Damn me and my mouth.

I take a few deep breaths and consider the situation. Dad wants me to consult with Dacey. I want to help save Tyrion. They are both Dwellers, trustworthy and, ultimately, isolated. Who can they tell?

"No," I say. "A friend had a heart attack in front of me. I healed him."

"You what?"

"Didn't you ever wonder about Vivian?"

"Vivian had a heart attack?" he asks, rising.

"No, no. Vivian's fine. Ten years ago...you never wondered what happened to her?"

Dacey sits back down and shakes his head. "There was nothing to wonder about. They told us she'd been in a self-induced coma and brought herself out of it."

I've entered dangerous territory here, and I know it. This is something Dad would want me to keep quiet about.

"Can I trust you to keep a secret?" I ask.

Dacey and Tyrion are silent, and it's obvious they're communicating.

"Turn your chair," Dacey says, pointing and lowering his voice. "Face me. Yes. Bend forward, just a bit. And whisper. The room's wired."

I stiffen. It never occurred to me that Dacey was under surveillance. My lack of street smarts pains me.

I do as Dacey asks.

"This secret might put you in danger?" Tyrion asks.

I nod.

"Then yes. Absolutely. You have my word." He looks at Dacey.

Dacey is weighing me with his eyes. "If you can heal, Thomas...you have to do it."

"If I can heal," I whisper, "there's nothing I want more. But it has to be on my terms. I won't be stuck down here strapped to a bed."

Dacey nods. "Of course. Your dad knows?"

I nod.

"And he doesn't want the Attic to know."

I nod again.

"We're in," Dacey says. "You have our word. Tell us what you can do."

♥

"You want me to demonstrate?" I ask them.

Dacey nods, and Tyrion says, "What does that involve?"

"Well, if you have a problem in the extremities, like a cut on your finger, it's pretty simple. I can cut my own finger, then attach my finger to yours. I use my own platelets and cells to heal you. Want to try it?"

They get up and motion me to follow them. "No cameras in here," Dacey says as we enter their bathroom. They hold out their hand.

I take my pocketknife out, slice my finger and theirs, and press the cuts together. Ten seconds later we're both healed.

"Amazing," Tyrion whispers, waving his finger in front of his eyes.

We wipe away the blood, and I clean my knife.

"But how did you do the heart? Without scans, how do you know what you're healing?" Dacey asks.

"I hook up to the subject's nervous system. As soon as my nerves are attached to the brain stem, I have access to the entire body – I sense it as well as I sense my own. Thoughts, pain, emotions…everything."

"And you've done this how many times?" Tyrion asks.

"Just twice. Vivian and my friend."

"What happened with Vivian?"

I tell them about bringing her out of a coma, and how it took me a week to heal myself. We go back into the main room, since Dacey's afraid someone will notice if we're gone too long, and resume our seats, my back still to the camera.

"What about cancer?" Dacey whispers. "If you turn stem cells on and tell them to grow, how do you turn them off and prevent them from turning into a tumor?"

"I only produce the exact amount of Protein T I need and I only target it at the cells I want to grow, because you're right. If I left the protein floating around, it would continue to activate any nearby cells and could, theoretically, lead to cancer."

Dacey's eyes slip sideways toward Tyrion, but he doesn't turn his head.

"Are you worried about cancer?" I ask him.

He shrugs. "The others…it happened so fast. Of course, it's something I'm always alert to."

"The others?" I ask.

Dacey looks at Tyrion, whose mouth hardens into a grim line.

"What others?" I ask again.

"The others who took your proteins," Dacey says, and Tyrion growls.

"No! No, Dacey. It is not our place to tell him."

I sit back in my chair. "Dad told me four other people originally took my protein. You mean...they all developed cancer?" I swallow hard, afraid to hear their response.

Dacey nods once.

"Are they here? I can help them."

Tyrion and Dacey reach out and place a hand on top of mine. "I'm sorry, Thomas," Dacey says.

"You mean...all of them? Gone?"

They both nod. "It happened in less than twenty-four hours," Dacey says. "While they slept. They didn't feel a thing."

"But I...so my dad just injected them with Protein T, and that was it? They had no training, no warning, no inkling of what would happen?" I stand, and my voice rises as I continue. "But this is a freaking research facility! The best of the best! None of you thought about what would happen with the protein floating around? I was six years old and I could have told you! I could have stopped it! Why? Why didn't anyone ask me?"

"Thomas," Tyrion says, but I ignore him.

"This is fucking ridiculous!" I say. "I've been kept in the dark, and for what? Four Dwellers dead, because of me!"

I pace, guilt warring with anger at my father, propelling me about the room.

"Thomas, it's not your fault," Tyrion says. "You were six. No one knew what would happen. Death is a risk all of the Dwellers face on a daily basis."

I fling myself into the chair and frown. "But this was preventable, Tyrion. I could have stopped it, and I didn't."

"We had this discussion ten years ago, you know," Dacey says. "Four people volunteered to take the protein. They all died that night from massive tumors. When autopsies revealed the problem, we immediately knew what had happened. No one thought bringing you in was a good idea, Thomas. As you said, you were six. No one wanted you to have those deaths, of brave and courageous people, hanging over you. And it wasn't your fault, nor even your dad's. We were all a bit hasty in trying out something new. And it was a lesson we learned well."

I hang my head and blow out a loud breath. "Jesus, though. It's such a waste."

"No!" I jerk my head up at Dacey's sharp dismissal. "What we do here is never a waste! Those Dwellers did not die in vain, and you need to wrap your head around that right now. We learned. Even death has a purpose."

"I'm sorry," I whisper. "I didn't mean it like that."

"Have a care, Dacey," Tyrion chides softly. "Thomas is intelligent and obviously has a great deal of empathy. He's not cursing the Dwellers; he's feeling guilty."

Dacey sighs.

"I just...I've been trying to get to the Attic for years. I don't mean to imply that I'm smarter than anyone else here, but I do have things to share. I have abilities that the rest of you don't. I want to help."

Tyrion smiles. "And so here you are. We can't change the past. We can only do our best from here on out."

I nod at him. "You're right. So, Dacey, you obviously overcame the cancer issue. Why ask about it?"

Dacey lowers his head. "Tyrion, please don't be angry with me."

"For what?"

"You have cancer."

I suck in a breath. Tyrion smiles sadly.

"Did you really think you were keeping your thoughts to yourself?" Tyrion asks.

"You mean, you knew?"

Tyrion shrugs. "I may not be able to sense our body, but I can sense your thoughts and emotions. I know you've been healing me while I sleep. I figured whatever it was would come out in the tests Dr. Trent is conducting. I knew the big split was far from a done deal."

"Talk to me," I say. "What's going on?"

Dacey lifts his head, and his eyes are bloodshot and glazed. "In the beginning, after the...the first round, we were very careful. Everything was controlled. But when I began to grow Tyrion's brain in earnest, I amped up protein production, and I produced too much. Now I cannot turn the protein off. I cannot dissolve it. If I don't target the stem cells perfectly, the protein goes where it will and I cannot find the off switch."

"What cells are affected?" I ask.

"Right now, there's a tumor growing in the cerebellum. Malignant. I'm able to kill those cells, but more continue to grow as soon as I stop paying attention. There's a lot of extra Protein T floating around, and I can direct it, somewhat, but I can't get rid of it, and I'm afraid to grow more cells in the central nervous system that don't need to be there."

"You can use it," I say. "Protein T can be used to grow any cell in the body, not just the central nervous system. Direct it down to your fingertips, to the stem cells under your nails. Grow your nails longer."

"That will work?" Dacey asks.

"Try it," I say.

Dacey and Tyrion both close their eyes. I glance at my watch to keep track of the time. Tyrion's eyelids flutter, I assume, as Dacey invades his brain.

Two minutes and thirty-seven seconds later, they're still in a trance.

"Everything okay?" I ask.

Dacey speaks with his eyes still shut. "Moving past the elbow now."

The elbow? Jesus, I would have been done two minutes ago.

A few minutes later, Dacey sighs. "Growing the nails now."

I watch his hand. His index and middle fingers' nails begin to grow. I can't actually perceive the growth, but when I blink, I can tell the nails are longer. It's like trying to watch a flower bloom.

Five minutes later, Dacey's eyes open. I check the time.

"Ten minutes, twelve seconds," I say. "You got any nail clippers?"

Dacey and Tyrion look at their hand. The two nails have grown to over a foot long each, curling around in spirals. It reminds me of the picture of the man with the longest fingernails in the *Guinness Book of World Records*. His nails spiraled too, as though he had antelope horns on his fingers.

Tyrion lets out a booming laugh. "Just a bit of extra protein, eh?"

Dacey cracks a smile. "It was my first brain, Tyrion. Give me a break." Then he looks me in the eye. "Thank you."

I shrug. "You did all the work. How are you feeling?"

"Beat," he says, slumping back in his chair.

I stand. "Where's your food?"

Dacey points behind him, to a door set in the back wall I hadn't even noticed. "Through there."

I find a surprisingly well-stocked kitchen. I grab four protein bars from the pantry and four bottles of water from the fridge.

"Drink the water first," I instruct. "Dehydration is hell on the heart."

They guzzle water and finally gnaw on the bars. They both sigh in relief when the food hits their stomach.

"You seem pretty exhausted after growing fingernails," I say. "I mean, don't take this the wrong way, but I'm not sure you're in good enough shape to grow a heart."

"I didn't even pass out," Dacey says around his second protein bar. "And I think we'll be able to stay awake until bedtime. I was thinking we did pretty well."

He stares at my furrowed brow. "You mean, you can do better?"

"That's not what I meant," I say, but Tyrion sees through me.

"How long would that have taken you?" he asks. "To move the proteins and grow the nails?"

"Maybe thirty seconds total. Probably less."

They stare at me. And I can sense that they're communicating again.

"What?" I ask.

"I want you to do it," Dacey says. "Hook up to us and grow Tyrion a body."

"You promised you wouldn't say anything to anyone," I remind him.

"For the record, I'm against this," Tyrion says. "What would the effect be on your body, Thomas? What happened when you healed your friend's heart?"

"I lost two pounds, even after eating a fat-laced meal. I didn't pass out right away, I was upright about two hours, but then I slept for thirty."

"No," Tyrion says. "I forbid it. You will not do this, Thomas. If, and I mean only if, we can work it out, Dacey will do this. Not you. Two pounds for one-sixth of the heart! No!"

And the door slides open with a whoosh, and Dad steps into the room.

♥

"What's all the commotion?" he says, taking the chair beside me.

"The usual," Tyrion says smoothly. "I don't want anyone to suffer because of me."

"I understand how you feel," Dad says. "I had a thought. How about a change of scenery?"

Dacey raises an eyebrow. "You want us to move to GP?"

"I've disabled the surveillance in this room," Dad says, and Dacey bolts out of his seat.

"I won't consent, Mike! You can't do this! I won't let you kill him!"

"Dacey, sit down."

"No! You will not bloody touch him, do you understand me?"

"Dace, man, nobody's killing anyone. Quite the opposite."

"What do you mean?"

"I assume Thomas told you what he can do."

Dacey and Tyrion look at me, but I stay silent.

Dad finally looks at me. "Well?"

I shrug.

And Dad laughs. "Sit down, Dacey. I want Tyrion to live as much as you do. But we both know it's not gonna happen here."

Dacey sits back down slowly. "Why not?"

"The timetable. We know Tyrion has a malignant tumor, and you're using a hell of a lot of energy just to keep it contained. We could do a standard operation to remove it, but I suspect it won't eradicate the problem. And you're too damn slow. By Dr. Trent's calculations, it will take you ten years to create the rest of Tyrion's body safely."

"The tumor's not an issue anymore," Dacey says.

Dad raises an eyebrow at me. "You healed him?"

"Not directly," I say. "I told him what to do."

Dad smiles. "I knew you couldn't keep a secret."

I scowl.

"So yes, I propose you go back to GP. Isolation this long isn't healthy."

Dacey turns to Tyrion. "Are you up for it?"

Tyrion smiles. "I'm along for the ride."

I clear my throat and look at Dad. "Dacey has asked me to grow Tyrion a body."

Dad shoots Dacey a frown. "And what did you say?"

"I'm not opposed, but I have one major concern." They all look at me expectantly. "Physically, I believe it can be done, probably in a couple months' time. But I'm not sure it will work."

Tyrion nods in understanding. "You're worried about the soul."

I nod back, somehow unsurprised that Tyrion knew what I was thinking.

Dacey laughs. "Mike, you actually have a son who's religious?"

Dad doesn't say anything, and Dacey shuts his mouth.

"I just…I do believe we each have a soul. My best guess would be that you two share Dacey's right now. If I separate you…I just don't know."

"We've thought about this," Tyrion says. "Dacey and I believe in God, and we believe in the soul, as well. But we feel God infused me with life already, a spirit quite distinct from Dacey's. Is this fact? Your guess is as good as ours." He turns his eyes to Dad. "I do not want Thomas to do this thing. It is too dangerous. He should consult, nothing more."

Dad nods once. "We'll discuss it. Thomas isn't ready yet, even if he wants to do it. He might not be ready for a year. Dace, are you prepared to wait?"

Dacey's eyes glow. "Tyrion will not die while I have breath left in my body. We'll wait."

Chapter Fourteen

"So you caught me on tape revealing myself to Dacey and Tyrion," I say on the drive back home.

"Yep."

"And you're not angry with me?"

"Nope," Dad says. "I want Tyrion to live. I was counting on you doing the right thing."

I sit and fume, staring out the window.

"But you told me the right thing was to keep it a secret!" I explode. "You have me so confused, I'm tied up in knots! Why didn't you just tell me to tell them?"

"Because I wanted it to be your choice," he says. "I didn't want to make the choice for you."

"But you also want me to do what you say. How can I follow your orders and also have a choice?"

"Thomas, you always have a choice. That's the price of becoming a man. You have to decide what to do."

"That's a bullshit answer," I say. "I'm only sixteen, as you are so fond of reminding me. I have no say in my own life."

"I'm sorry if I gave you that impression," he says. "Maybe I assumed that because we are so much alike, you'd be a bit better at rebelling."

"So now you insult me? As though I'm not rebellious enough? What do you want from me?"

"I want you to take control," he says. "I want you to decide where you're headed. I've steered you, yes, and I will continue to give you the benefit of my expert opinion—" I snort at that, "—but I'm handing over the reins. You want to heal, we're making it happen. You want to find researchers to study with, you have my blessing. You have a steady girlfriend that you plan on marrying, and you're making a man's choices and having lots of responsible sex, again with my blessing. Though now that I think about it, maybe being away from Tessa these past two weekends has made you cranky."

I frown. "And what makes you think you know anything about my sex life?" I say.

"Please," he says. "Any man getting laid regularly isn't wound so tight."

"Oh," I scoff, "and I suppose sex is the reason you're the picture of calm right now."

Dad just smiles.

"You're seeing someone?"

He continues to smile.

"Well, are you going to tell me? Is it serious?"

He just laughs, and I sit on my hands to keep from slapping him.

♥

"It's not that girl at the grocery store, is it?"

"Thomas, give it a rest."

"But why won't you tell me? It must not be serious if you're working so hard to keep it a secret."

"We promised not to involve our kids until it's a done deal. I'm just respecting her wishes."

"Done deal? You mean I won't meet her until you're married?"

Dad laughs. "Thomas, if I'm planning to get married, or anything else earth-shattering besides regular sex, I promise to fill you in immediately."

"So it's just about sex."

"No, actually. That's just a side benefit."

I growl. "Fine. But you have to see this from my point of view. You tell me to do one thing and expect me to do the opposite. You have an important relationship you won't share with me. Four people died taking my protein and you never mentioned it, and don't think we won't talk about that later, because we will! You constantly withhold information. I can't...I don't want our relationship to be like this. I can't take it. I don't feel like I know you at all."

Dad's grip tightens on the steering wheel. "Don't say that."

"What else am I supposed to say? What else am I supposed to think?"

We sit in silence for another forty-five minutes until we pull up in our driveway. I slam my car door shut and shove my way into the house. I flop on my bed and force myself not to cry.

Dad comes in my room and sits on the edge of my bed.

"She's married, Thomas. Has been for the last five years we've been together. It's a complicated situation."

Five years. He's been seeing someone for five years, while I had no clue. And this woman's been cheating on her husband the whole time. What a loser.

"The physical part of our relationship is recent. She finally told her husband she's leaving him. We hadn't even kissed until a couple of weeks ago."

I fling my arm over my eyes. "How can you say you've had a five-year relationship if you only kissed her now?"

"I admitted my feelings back then, and she admitted she felt the same way. But she wasn't ready to end her marriage. We spend a lot of time together. We support one another. We always knew we'd be together eventually."

"How can you say you spend time together?" I ask, my words muffled by my arm. "I'd have known if you were gone a lot. Unless you're seeing her instead of going to work."

"Nope. I actually show up for work every day," he says.

"But the only person you hang out with is…"

I stop. I close my gaping mouth. I remove my arm and sit up slowly.

My dad's in love with Tessa's mom.

❤

"But Erica…you've been in love with her for five years?"

"Longer. I just didn't want to break up her marriage."

"But you did."

"That's debatable. Erica and Ron haven't been close in a long time, well before I came along. But since the three boys are out of the house, and Tessa's almost done with high school, Erica found the courage to end it."

"Are you getting married?" I ask.

"Not now. Someday, I hope."

"But Tessa and I will be brother and sister!"

Dad chuckles. "Only by marriage. It doesn't mean you can't be together."

"But I'll be kissing my sister!"

"Thomas," he sighs.

"Fine, but you can't expect me to keep this a secret from her. We don't lie to each other."

"I won't ask you to lie. I'll call Erica now and tell her you know. All I ask is that you give her time to talk to Tessa."

"Do it now," I say. "If I don't talk to Tessa tonight, I'm gonna explode."

Dad nods and leaves the room.

Just a few minutes ago, I was thinking the woman Dad's seeing is a loser for cheating on her husband. And then I find out the woman is someone I care about and respect.

I should have known, should have seen the signs. Erica runs our art gallery, The Heart. A few years ago, Dad helped her install a little bakery and coffee bar in one corner. They talk every day, about business, I assumed.

I'm at Tessa's house half the week. I haven't seen her Dad in the flesh in over a year. He's always working, always traveling. Tessa hasn't said much about it, just that she wishes he were home more.

It's a sin to cheat on your spouse. Is it a sin to develop feelings for someone else, even if you don't act on those feelings?

Is it a sin to ignore your family?

Someone knocks on our front door an hour later, and I don't have to be psychic to know it's Tessa.

But when I open the door, Erica is standing there.

"Erica," I say, surprised and uncomfortable and totally unsure of how I should act.

"Hi, Thomas," she says. Neither of us moves.

"Would you like to come in?" I ask, stepping aside.

She smiles and follows me to the kitchen.

"I'll just go get Dad," I say, but Erica stops me with a hand on my arm.

"Thomas, can we talk for a second?"

I face her.

"This...I need you to know your dad means the world to me. I tried to do the right thing with my marriage, and it just didn't happen. I want you to know...nothing about this changes my relationship with you. I mean, I won't try to take the place of your mother. I know she's irreplaceable."

I scrub a hand across my face. "Honestly, Erica, it hadn't even occurred to me. Under normal circumstances, I'd be happy for you both and that's it. But I'm worried about Tessa. You're breaking up her family."

Erica sighs. "I'm not going to make excuses, but I want to defend myself. Ron's been cheating on me for years."

I don't know what to say to that, so I stay silent.

She laughs. "Every time he went out of town. And sometimes in town. I stayed for the kids as long as I could, but Sam...he called a few weeks ago. He's having a baby."

"Sam's only nineteen," I say, confused.

She nods. "I know. My baby having a baby. And he's not even in a relationship with the girl. I thought my kids needed an intact home, but instead, I've taught them that it's okay to screw around, that women don't deserve respect. I can't...I won't teach them that anymore."

"Wow," I say, thinking about Tessa's older brother becoming a father. "I'm sorry."

"Me, too," she says, blinking back tears. "I love your dad, and Thomas, I love you, too. You're Tessa's best friend, and so respectful of her...I just hope she can see that she deserves those things, and that she demands those things."

"I meant what I said the other day," I tell her. "You're a good mom. Tessa's the best person I know, and that's because of you."

"Thanks," she says, swiping her eyes. "Think I can get a hug?"

I hug her. She hugs me back. It doesn't feel like Mom, but it feels good.

"Is Tessa coming over?" I ask when we pull apart.

She nods. "She's talking to her dad. She'll be over when she's done."

"Okay. Dad's in his room—"

Dad comes out then, into the kitchen. He automatically moves to Erica but catches himself. He stops beside her, and I notice his arms tremble, probably from the effort of not touching her.

"I thought I'd take Erica out to dinner," he says. "That okay with you?"

"Sure," I say. "Have fun."

They both smile awkwardly at me and leave.

Wow. So that's how it's gonna be. Kinda weird, but I suppose I have to get used to it.

I pour myself a stadium cup half full of orange juice, and Tessa walks in as I'm closing the fridge.

"Hey." I wrap my arms around her, and she buries her head in my chest. "You okay?"

She lifts her head, and her eyes are swollen and red. "Been better."

"You need some orange juice?"

She smiles and takes the cup from my hand. "Orange juice won't get it done."

She rummages in the cabinets until she finds a bottle of vodka. She pours a few fingers into the juice and takes a long sip.

"Ahhh. Better."

I raise an eyebrow at her. "Seriously? You're gonna get drunk?"

"Why not? Seems fitting." She takes another gulp, grimacing.

"You been holding out on me, or is this your first sip of vodka?"

"First and second and third," she says, sipping again. "You want to try it?"

I take the doctored juice and sip. It's disgusting.

"Yikes," I say. "People actually drink this voluntarily?" I sip again, just to make sure I didn't miss anything.

Tessa swipes the cup from my hand. "It gets better the more you drink. I don't think the point is the taste – the point is to get drunk."

"You want to get drunk?" I ask her.

She finishes the cup of juice and goes back to the fridge to pour more. This time, she fills the huge cup with half juice, half vodka, emptying the vodka bottle.

"I think I don't want to feel anything right now except you."

I move to her and push a stray lock of hair behind her ear. "You want to feel me, huh?"

"Yes."

We take the cup and walk hand in hand to my bedroom. I shut and lock the door.

Tessa plugs her phone into my radio and puts on some music. I sit on the bed while she moves to the rhythm, sipping her medicine.

"You want to talk about it?" I ask.

She shimmies over to me and waves the cup in my face. I take it and sip.

"Nope." She sways a bit, and I don't know if it's the alcohol or the music.

"You feeling drunk yet?"

"Mmmm." She closes her eyes, her hips moving back and forth. "A little. Like everything's swaying with me."

I take a bigger swallow of juice – Tessa's right. It's starting to taste pretty good.

I stand up and hand her the cup. I mold my body to hers, and we move to the music, our bodies pressed together, the juice passing back and forth until we finish it.

"You want more?" I ask her.

"No. My lips are numb."

I press my lips together. She's right again – I can't feel them.

I press my lips to Tessa's. She melts into me.

We dance and kiss and think of nothing at all. My hands move from her back to her stomach, and then up under her shirt, as though they have a mind of their own. Before I realize it, Tessa pulls her shirt over her head and throws it to the floor. I unhook her bra, our mouths still entwined, and she drops her arms to her sides and the bra slides to the floor.

Okay, I've touched her breasts countless times – it's like my hand is a compass needle and her breasts are due north. But I've never actually seen them, never seen any female breasts in the flesh. I stare, and Tessa stares at me staring at her.

She raises her arms above her head. "You like?"

I nod. I think.

She grabs my hands and presses them to her breasts. I squeeze lightly, testing their texture and weight.

They are amazing – there's nothing on my body that feels remotely like them. Tessa sighs, and I squeeze a little tighter, running my thumb over the nipples.

I've never done this, but I've thought about it: I drop my head and lick the swollen flesh. Tessa gasps. I take my time, savoring the soft feel of her.

As I lick, Tessa's hands wander. She tugs on the hem of my shirt, and I pull back to tug it over my head. I press my chest to hers, and Tessa's hands go for the fly of my jeans.

We're not thinking – we're feeling – so I stand up straight and smile down at her. She drops to her knees and undoes the button and zipper carefully.

I feel her nerves, or maybe they're my own. We've never taken things this far.

Tessa pushes my jeans down over my hips, and I step out of them. She stands and strips off her jeans.

We're both in our underwear.

I want to touch her, but I want to look first. Tessa seems to know this. She stands up straight in nothing but a pink thong, and she strikes a pose for me. I laugh.

She turns to give me her profile. The view is just as awe-inspiring.

And then she faces away from me. I get my first glimpse of her butt cheeks, in all their swim-toned glory.

"God, you're beautiful," I say.

She bends at the waist and gives me a sultry look over her shoulder. I shudder.

She turns back around and puts a hand on my groin. "I want to see you, too."

"You're looking at me," I say with a grin.

She grins back. "Off."

"You first."

"Same time."

Our hands go to the waistbands of our underwear at the same time. We lock gazes, and both of us get naked.

I want to look, but I sense that Tessa's bravado has given out.

I pull her into a hug, squeezing tight.

Tessa sobs into my chest.

We climb into my bed and settle under the covers wrapped around each other.

"We're drunk," I say, stating the obvious.

"I'm sorry," Tessa says through her tears.

"What are you apologizing for?"

"I don't want...I want our first time to be better than this."

"Well, I don't think it gets much better, but I wouldn't have sex with you like this. Not our first time. I hope you know that."

Tessa nods against my shoulder. "I know, and I'm sorry I pushed it."

"I'm irresistible," I say. "Understandable."

"I think I'm gonna puke."

We both rush to my bathroom. I hold Tessa's hair back while she throws up in the toilet. When she's calm, I get my robe and put it over her shoulders.

"It's okay," she says, rinsing her mouth out in the sink. "I don't need the robe. Unless you need me to cover up." She glances at my groin, where I'm pretty much standing at attention.

"It has a mind of its own," I say. "Ignore it. I'm fine."

She giggles, and we go back to bed. In five minutes, we're both snoring.

Chapter Fifteen

The saving grace for Tessa was that she threw up a lot of the alcohol in her system. She wakes up rested and energized, ready for school. I'm completely dumbfounded that we woke up together, in my bed – Dad and Erica must have checked on us at some point. Tessa goes to dress, and I groan as I head for a shower.

My head pounds, my tongue is dry, and my eyes feel like they're packed in cotton balls. Dear God, why do people get drunk?

I stand in the shower, feeling inside, trying to decide how to remedy the situation. There's still some alcohol in my system, which I can just sweat out. The real problem is dehydration, and I can't fix that without downing a gallon of water. But I shut off the nerves in my head to at least eliminate the headache.

And then it occurs to me – how would I have functioned last night, if I'd tried to use my abilities? Could I have used them?

Hmmm. That's something to think about.

I come out of the shower feeling human, and I see that Tessa is gone. Which is good, since school starts in an hour.

I go out to the kitchen, and there is Tessa. And my dad. And Erica.

"Have a seat," Dad says.

I gulp, and sit beside Tessa, who reeks of alcohol and sweat. I feel sorry for her.

"Thomas, how could you do this? What disturbs me is not that you two drank, not that you had sex, but that you did those things together, probably without thinking. Did you use a condom?"

"We didn't have sex," Tessa says before I can even process. "You might not believe that, but we didn't. And I'm the one who poured the vodka."

"Tessa!" Erica says, and it's more of a pained statement than a scolding.

"We both did it," I say. "We didn't plan it, but it happened. I'm sorry."

Erica sighs. "We just…we want you to be safe. You've been together for so many years, it's not like we don't know you have sex."

Tessa and I exchange a glance. I speak. "I guess you don't believe us, but it's the truth. We haven't had sex."

Erica and Dad exchange a look. "You haven't?" he says.

"I want to," Tessa says, "but Thomas wants to wait. He wants us to be married. Last night was the farthest I've been able to push him."

Dad looks at me like I'm an alien. Erica laughs.

I frown, trying not to be defensive. "It's a sacred thing, okay? I'm not gonna just do my future wife because I'm horny."

Dad shakes his head. Erica hides a smile behind her hand. Tessa pats my arm.

I sigh. "Well, is this conversation over?"

Erica glances at her watch. "We'll talk more after school. You two should get going. Tessa still needs a shower."

"Drive me home?" Tessa asks.

"Only if you roll down the window."

I drop Tessa off and tell her I'll be back in thirty minutes to pick her up for school. We usually walk, but we're a little crunched for time.

I head straight for the kitchen and force myself to drink that bucket of water. When my stomach's full, I push the water throughout my system, where it needs to go, and drink some more. In less than five minutes, I'm a new man with a full bladder.

I go down the hall to the bathroom, and I can hear Dad and Erica talking in his bedroom. I wonder if she spent the night, too.

"Probably," Erica says. "We've already had the confrontation, so I don't think it will be too bad. We have the money – he can go to a hotel for all I care."

"Is he angry with you for telling Tessa?"

"I gave him three weeks to talk to her. He had more than enough time for this to go down a different way."

"I'm sorry," Dad says. "I should have known Thomas would figure it out."

"You've wanted to tell him for a long time, and it's my fault you had to keep it a secret. I know how much you want to share with him. It's me who should be apologizing."

Wait. Dad actually wanted to tell me?

"You have nothing to apologize for. Thomas will understand."

"I hope so," she says. "God, Mike, how did you get so lucky?"

Dad laughs. "I did, didn't I? I wish I could say some of it was me, but it was all Trish and my mom. It's so obvious, the way he was raised. The nature part is all me. But the nurture? Trish and Mom. It seems I had no effect whatsoever."

"How can you say that? It's just been you for the last ten years."

"And look at him. Sixteen, in a committed relationship with the girl he's been planning to marry since the first grade, and he doesn't make a move on her? That's the exact opposite of his nature and the opposite of me."

"You're exactly wrong," she says, and I have to smile at Erica taking him head on. "You haven't dated in five years. Even before that, you didn't bring dates around Thomas. You respected me and our relationship, however screwed up it's been. Talk about the opposite of nature – you didn't once try to kiss me in all that time. But I know you thought about it."

"And thought about it, and dreamt about it, and fantasized about it."

Erica laughs. "See? You taught him self-control. Nobody's born with that."

"Screw self-control," Dad says, and then they go silent. Sort of.

I start to back away when Erica laughs again. "Ooooh, I have to go."

"Dinner tonight?"

"Definitely. I'll meet you here after I close up the gallery. What time will you be home?"

"I only have a half day in San Diego, then I'm going to see my mom. How about six?"

"How's your mom doing?"

"Worse. You'll see her on Monday. That's when they're painting her apartment."

"You think Thomas will do it?"

What?!

"I don't know. We'll give him the opportunity, but I honestly don't know. I can't seem to get him to break away from authority."

What the hell are they talking about???

"I don't like the way you're going about this," she says. "I know why you're doing it, but is it really necessary?"

"He has to think for himself. No God, no higher power, no father, no one telling him what's right except his own heart. He has to learn that, or his confidence will be shattered. If he ever wants to use his abilities to their fullest, he has to break out of his pattern of listening to authority."

"He's been following his heart by refusing to sleep with Tessa."

"But again, that comes from his religious beliefs. God is the authority."

"But Mike, with that logic, he can't follow any rule at all. That's ridiculous. If he's thought about a rule and decided to follow it, how can you say it's not a part of his inner belief system? I think you're being too hard on him."

"That's my job," Dad says.

"I think you just have a problem with the fact that he's bowing to religion. But look at the alternative. Would he be better off, more moral, if he rejected Christianity? He's trying to do the right things."

Silence.

And Erica continues. "I think you want him to break away from you. I think you're questioning yourself and whether you've made the right decisions with him, and if he'd just stop listening to you, you'd be off the hook."

Dad sighs loudly. "When did you become a mind reader?"

"When you healed me." Huh?!

They both laugh.

"Okay. We'll talk to the kids when we get home and then you and I can grab a bite and you can give me more of your insightful insight."

Erica laughs. "You're not worried about leaving them alone after last night?"

Dad chuckles. "I've never been less worried."

I scowl at that and slink back to the kitchen. I grab my keys and backpack, and head out to pick up Tessa.

♥

"Do you think I was born this way?"

"What way?" she asks.

"Wanting to wait to have sex until we're married."

Tessa gives me a look. "Nobody's born that way. It's your ten years of religious training with Dr. Rumson."

I frown. "I've never talked to him about sex before."

"But you're always weighing your actions against what you think God would want you to do. Would God want you to have sex outside of marriage? No."

"How do you know I do that?"

She shrugs. "I just do."

I sigh. Sometimes it sucks being so easy to read.

"It's not the potential sin that bothers me," I say.

"It's not?"

I shake my head. "And it's not God that I hear in my head when I'm trying to make a decision. It's you."

"Me?"

"You. You're the best person I know. I want to do what you think is right, and what's right for you."

Tessa laughs. "Then you have my permission to sleep with me."

I smile as we pull into the school parking lot. "But think about it. There's no upside for you. You could get pregnant. You could be branded a slut. I could take the milk and kick the cow to the curb."

"Are you calling me a cow?"

"If I were the kind of guy who'd wrestle you into the back seat and take your virginity, I might be."

Tessa sighs as I turn off the ignition. "I appreciate that you're looking out for me, Thomas, and maybe that's something I take for granted with you, but honestly, none of that applies and you know it. Okay, I could get pregnant, but we can prevent that. Hell, you can probably keep your sperm from swimming." She turns and looks me in the eye. "I love you. Completely and totally and with every breath I take. I'm ready. If you're ready, too, there's no reason to wait."

I squeeze her hand and smile. We walk into school.

I think about what she said.

For Tessa, there is no downside. Great. What about for me?

Okay, I do feel a little icky about the potential sin, but only a little. Not enough to keep me from making love to Tessa. I know we're going to be together forever.

For me, sex is the final frontier, the only physical thing I haven't experienced. I guess I've never been shot before, never jumped out of an airplane, but I've felt similar sensations. I fell thirty feet onto asphalt and felt bones break and my brain rattle in my skull. I felt my spinal cord snap. I've felt the sharp needling pain of bare nerves, growing and exposed.

I've never felt anything close to actual intercourse with a woman. And while I definitely want to feel it, I don't know how I'll react. I don't really even know what to do. It's a total unknown.

I'm used to knowing what to do, how to perform. I'm used to being the best. What if I disappoint her?

Chapter Sixteen

The Planarian Institute is 6.3 miles from my house, which would make a great walk during the summer. But since school's in session and I only have a few hours after school every day to visit (and those pesky bad guys are probably tailing me), my Explorer is finally going to put on some mileage.

Run by a husband-and-wife team of researchers, Drs. Kate and Kenneth Mullen, the institute was founded only three years ago to study brain cell regeneration. They haven't made any great discoveries yet – at least, none that are published – but I've chosen them for three reasons. One, they are close to my house. This wouldn't be a sufficient reason in and of itself, but it's convenient. Two, as husband and wife, they must talk about their research all the time. They must live and breathe it. And they have a perfect sounding board at the end of the day, someone who knows everything they know and can understand what's going on. I like that idea. I don't have that with Tessa, exactly, and that's okay, but whomever I reveal myself to is going to question my abilities. They'll want to talk about it. And I don't want them to talk about it with outsiders. In choosing a married couple, I think I have a greater chance that they'll keep the secret between themselves.

My third reason for choosing them is that they both perform two surgeries a month at Children's Hospital of Orange County for free. They heal children while still doing research – and that's exactly what I want to do, the life I want to lead. They seem to be good people.

Of course, I don't know them at all, and I have to remember that as I pull into their parking lot and turn off my ignition. I have to approach this without any preconceived idea about their character, otherwise I could be duped. And maybe dead.

I lean my forehead on the steering wheel and take a few deep breaths. I can do this.

I exit the car, lock it, and walk to the doors of the Planarian Institute.

♥

A shiver runs down my spine as the door closes behind me. It's cold enough in here that I automatically regulate my body temperature to keep my teeth from chattering.

"May I help you?"

A pretty, petite brunette in a lab coat looks up at me as I enter, a full coffee pot in one hand, mug in the other. She has an eyebrow ring, which is a little weird but kind of cool. I immediately recognize her picture from the institute's website as Dr. Kate, and I'm suddenly sweating. I didn't expect her to be the one to greet me.

"Uh, hi. I'm Thomas Van Zandt." I stick out my hand, plaster a smile on my lips, and she laughs, waving the coffee pot.

"Just a sec. Let me put this down." She pours her mug full of coffee and replaces the pot. We shake. "I'm Kate Mullen."

"It's nice to meet you, Kate, uh, Dr. Mullen."

"What can I do for you?"

I take a deep breath. "I was wondering if you could use an intern. I'm interested in regenerative research, and I'd like to offer my services."

I can see her fighting a smile as she sips her coffee. "Your services," she says. "How old are you, Thomas?"

I stand up straight. "Sixteen, ma'am. But I have a photographic memory and have been studying the nervous system my entire life. I'm up to speed on the latest research."

She cocks a hip against the coffee bar counter and considers me. "Name three marine animals that regenerate."

"The starfish, the sea cucumber, and the zebra fish," I say.

"Too easy," she says. "Who's your favorite researcher in the field and why?"

"I came here for a reason," I say, "but I know you don't want me to say you and your husband. Actually, James Thomson ranks pretty high in my book. I know he's considered the stem cell pioneer, and he seems an easy answer, but I admire his approach. He advocates more research on the body in general, rather than just a focus on stem cells, and I agree. The body as a whole has the answer. Stem cells alone won't cut it."

"Okay," she says, nodding her head. "What factors do we need to be studying to unravel the mystery of regeneration?"

"Stem cells, of course. DNA, because it dictates the stem cell's ability to grow into any cell. Protein..." I almost say Protein T, but I catch myself. "I believe a protein is necessary to activate the stem cells."

Dr. Kate squints. "Protein, singular?"

"I believe so, yes. One protein is all it would take."

She stares into her mug for a few moments. "Are you sick, Thomas?"

Wow. Off the mark and right on target. I decide, just like that, to trust her.

I take a small spiral-bound notebook and pen out of my back pocket. I flip to a clean page and write down my name and the amino acid sequence of Protein T. I rip off the page and hand it to her.

"What's this?"

"The sequence of the protein. Do you have the...is your facility capable of duplicating this?"

"Yes," she says skeptically.

I nod. "I'm kind of on a deadline here. I'll be back in three days." I turn to the door.

"Wait."

I turn back.

"You're sixteen years old, you waltz in here offering your services, then you write an amino acid sequence for a, a, a protein that's supposed to activate a stem cell...and then you leave?"

"I'm trusting you," I say softly. "I am trusting you with knowledge that people would chain me in a lab for. My girlfriend said I should try to meet you on neutral ground, get to know you, feel out what kind of people you and your husband are before I reveal myself. But honestly, that's not me. Would you feel better if I'd stalked you and struck up a conversation at the coffee house? I don't have time for that. I need help and I need it now."

"What exactly do you need help with?" she asks.

"I'm a freak, Dr. Mullen," I say. "I can produce that protein in my brain. I can regenerate any part of my body."

Dr. Kate lowers the mug from her lips. She opens her mouth, but no words come out.

"Study it," I say, pointing to the paper in her hand. "You probably won't be able to produce it in three days, but I think you'll see the possibilities by then. I'll be back."

And I leave.

Chapter Seventeen

As I pull in my driveway, Tessa rushes out the front door and yanks my car door open.

"Well?"

I stand up and close the door slowly. "It's a done deal."

Tessa raises her eyebrows but doesn't speak.

"I met Dr. Kate, I trusted her, I told her. Done deal."

"Did she believe you?"

I think about the question as we walk into the house and enter the kitchen. I pour myself some orange juice while Tessa boosts herself up on the counter, legs swinging.

"Yep."

Tessa frowns. "Yep? That's it? She believed you just like that? Did you have to demonstrate?"

I sip my juice, and I immediately feel better.

"We didn't get that far. I just gave her something to think about."

"So what did she say?"

I cock my head. "Nothing."

"Nothing?" Tessa shrieks. "Then how do you know she believed you?"

I shrug. "I just do."

Tessa sighs. "You didn't need my lessons at all, did you?"

I put my empty cup in the sink and my hands on Tessa's thighs. "Maybe I didn't exactly use them, but I definitely needed them." I kiss her, and she sighs into the kiss.

I pull back and give her one more peck on the nose. "So's my dad home yet?"

Tessa nods. "On the computer. He said he and Mom are going out to dinner."

The phone rings, and I can hear Dad answer it.

"So you want to order pizza?" I ask her.

"Sure. Bacon and extra cheese?"

I take my cell phone out of my pocket when Dad rushes in. He scoops up his keys up off the counter.

"I'm meeting Erica," he says on his way out. "Don't wait up." And he slams the door shut behind him.

"What was that about?" Tessa asks, jumping down from her perch.

"No idea."

I order pizza and Tessa lays her head in my lap on the couch while we wait for it.

I massage her scalp. "You feeling any better today?" I ask her.

"I guess," she says. "Knowing what my dad did...on one hand, it's easier to swallow the divorce, because Mom's doing the right thing and Dad's such an asshole. But on the other hand? I had no idea, Thomas. No clue. Dad's been unfaithful for years, and I never suspected. I loved him." Tessa sniffs as she starts to cry.

"You still love him, Tessa," I say. "That hasn't changed."

"That's what hurts so much," she says. "Our whole life has been a lie."

"I thought the same thing when I found out Dad has the same abilities as me. It felt like such a betrayal, him not telling me. But Dr. Rumson told me that good parents always try to spare their kids the nasty details."

Tessa snorts. "So it's a sign of good parenting, not betrayal?"

I smile. "I didn't buy it, either. I mean, I'd do the same thing with my own kids, but that doesn't make it hurt any less."

"You've never gotten over it," she says. "Ten years, and you still hold it against your dad."

"Only because he continues to lie and manipulate me. If that had been the only lie, I think I'd be over it by now."

"But he has his reasons. I believe your dad is trying to do the right thing."

"I believe the same thing about your mom."

The doorbell rings and our pizza arrives. We eat, and then Tessa goes home to finish homework. I fall asleep on the couch watching a movie and wake when I hear Dad come home a couple of hours later.

I meet him in the kitchen, where he's emptying his pockets on the counter.

"Everything okay?" I ask him. "You left in a hurry."

He scrubs a hand across his face. "Ron left."

"Good riddance," I say.

"It's worse than that. He's disappeared. He emptied the bank accounts. Even took the pieces of art they owned that were worth anything."

I gape at him. "What?"

"Their house is in foreclosure. He hasn't paid the mortgage in four months. Erica has about three weeks to pay it."

"Write them a check," I say.

He sighs. "I tried. She won't take it. She refuses to let me rescue her."

"So do it anyway."

"I can't!" he yells. "I have to respect her wishes. I can't lose her, Thomas. I love her. I have to let her do it her way."

"So marry her. You won't need two houses anyway. They can move in here." My heart thumps hard in my chest as I think about Tessa living here, with me.

"I asked her. She won't marry me until her finances are settled. She's…she's thinking of moving in with her parents."

"But they live in Arizona!"

Dad just nods.

I storm off to bed. Tessa moving to another state is unacceptable. I can't…I just can't let that happen.

Chapter Eighteen

Tessa texts me early in the morning that she's staying home from school. I understand, but I hate school without her. It's mindless and pointless and sucks.

Finally, my last class of the day, Pre-Calculus, arrives. It's probably my favorite, because the teacher's so self-absorbed he just stands and lectures. Mr. Bertram doesn't even ask questions. Which means I can zone out and think of other things.

His lecture ends twenty minutes early, and he allows us to start on our homework. I finish in about two minutes and pull the latest Jim Butcher novel out of my backpack.

"Thomas, you're supposed to use this time for your homework, not for pleasure reading," Mr. Bertram says, calling me out in front of the entire class. I fight not to scowl.

"I already finished," I say, going back to my book.

"Let me see it."

I sigh and close the book. I pull the homework out of my backpack and walk to his desk. I thrust the paper in front of his nose.

He examines it longer than I spent doing it. He finally hands it back.

"There's another issue I want to discuss," he says. He rummages through the pile of papers on his desk until he finds what he's looking for. "I'm turning this into the principal."

I take the paper from him. It's Tessa's homework from last Friday. "Why?"

"It's obviously not her work. It's yours."

"No," I say, handing it back to him. "Tessa does her own work. It's hers."

"Tessa has never done this well on a homework assignment."

"So what?" I say. "You don't believe you're the kind of teacher who can help a student improve?"

Mr. Bertram narrows his eyes at me. "You gave her the answers."

"Or maybe you don't think Tessa's smart enough. Is that it?"

"Tessa's intelligence is not at issue here. Her integrity is."

"Exactly!" I say, leaning into his personal space. "Tessa is the most upstanding person I know. Don't you dare impugn her honor in front of me."

"Then explain her answers!" Mr. Bertram hisses at me.

I stand up straight. "I don't have to. She got an A on the last test. She knows this stuff. She doesn't need to cheat."

The class has gone silent. The ever-present murmur of whispered voices is gone, and I know everyone's watching us.

"And how do you know she got an A? Maybe you helped her with that, too."

I clench my jaw. "Tessa's grades have improved because we study together. You're right – without me, she'd still be getting C's, because your teaching is so abysmal. I have never done her math homework, never helped her cheat, and I couldn't if I wanted to – Tessa is just that honest. I don't need to be here. You and I both know that. I can run circles around you. Maybe that's why you're accusing us of cheating."

Veins throb in Mr. Bertram's neck as he stares at me. "Go to the principal's office now! I will not take such disrespect in my classroom."

I laugh. "But you're allowed to disrespect me? Fuck you."

And I grab my backpack and head out the door, the whole class gaping after me.

I drive straight to Dr. Rumson's office. He's eating a salad at his desk and checking email.

I flop in a chair and sigh.

"Bad day?" he says around a piece of lettuce.

"I quit school."

He raises an eyebrow at me.

"It's bullsh...uh, bull. I don't learn anything. What's the point?"

"Exactly," he says. "You haven't needed to be in a classroom for years. So why were you?"

I shrug. "Nothing better to do."

"Then I'd say it's the right move if you have something better to do with your time."

"I go back to the Planarian Institute in two days. I'll be working there from then on."

"Oh, so they accepted you, then?"

I squirm in my chair. "It's not a done deal, but I'm pretty sure."

"And do you have a Plan B?"

My Plan B is not a second option – it's more of an option I need to make happen at the same time as Plan A.

I need to make money for Tessa and Erica. Big money. And I know I can do that if I offer to heal the sick. I haven't worked out all the details yet, but if the Planarian Institute won't work with me, I'll have plenty of time to figure it out.

"I'll just get a job," I say.

Dr. Rumson chuckles. "That's an excellent idea."

"You think so?"

"Of course," he says. "You can use the responsibility and the hard work. It'll make a man out of you."

Great. Just what I wanted to hear.

Chapter Nineteen

Tessa texts me on my way home, saying she'll be over in a couple of hours. That's good, of course, because I want to see her and talk about her dad, but it doesn't give me time or privacy to have the school talk with my dad.

But he's the one who said my life's up to me. So I text him the news:

Quit school today. Better things to do. FYI.

He doesn't reply – he's probably driving home from the Attic – and with that out of the way, I realize that the big talk with him is not the one I should be worrying about.

I need to tell Tessa I've left school. And that Mr. Bertram thinks she's cheating, but Tessa always manages to take those things in stride.

So I pace, thinking about how I'm going to tell her. I pour myself some orange juice. I pace some more, and I think about adding alcohol to my oj, but honestly, what for? I'd just feel sick, and then I'd still have to tell Tessa, and my tongue would be numb and my lips wouldn't work, and then she'd be mad at me for getting drunk without her and for not being able to understand whatever words were attempting to come out of my mouth, and then she might take advantage of me and push for sex, and then what would happen?

Maybe I should get drunk.

I sip more orange juice and debate the course of my life and the fate of my relationship with Tessa when the doorbell rings.

Show time.

I pop a mint so that I don't smell like oranges.

I open the door.

Dr. Kate and Dr. Kenneth stare at me.

"Hi," I say.

Dr. Kate gives me a smile. "Hello, Thomas. I hope we're not intruding."

I slow my heart and feel my stomach turn a cartwheel. "Not intruding," I say. "Stalking, but not intruding."

She laughs, and it seems a little nervous. Dr. Kate is nervous?

"This is my husband, Kenneth," she says.

I shake his hand. "It's a pleasure to meet you. Please, come in."

I lead them to the den, and we sit.

"I didn't stalk," Dr. Kate says suddenly. "I mean, I looked you up, but there was no stalking involved."

I smile at her. "It's okay. I'm glad you came."

Dr. Kenneth leans forward. "We have questions, of course," he says. "Lots of questions."

I settle back against the couch and rub my sweaty hands on my jeans. "Shoot."

He looks at Kate, and she nods at him. "Where did you get that protein sequence?"

"My body manufactures the protein. If I'd had the right equipment, I probably could have sequenced it myself, but it was done for me by the Attic."

They exchange a quick glance. "So the Attic knows the sequence?"

"You know about the Attic?" I ask him.

"We've heard about it, but we don't know anyone who works there, or who is connected to it."

"My dad is the director," I say. "He sequenced the protein himself. Exactly one other member of the Attic has had access to it. No one else."

"You mean, the Attic's not researching it?" Kate asks, surprised.

"No. My dad won't let them."

"Why the three-day deadline?" Kenneth asks. "You had to know we couldn't do much in three days."

"You did enough that you sought me out," I say. "That was my goal. I want to work with you."

"Why?" Kate says. "I mean, if you can do what you say you can do, and that's a big if...you could get funding on your own. I could name fifty donors that would build you your own lab. Why us?"

I blow out a breath. "I know the human body, yeah, and I know the theory behind the research, but I've never worked in a lab. I don't want to run things, I want to experiment. I want to bring what I can do to other people. I'm not in it for the money." And then I remember Tessa and Erica, and I have to backtrack. "Actually, I could use some money right now, but that has nothing to do with my long-term goals. Long-term, I want to change medicine. Short-term, I have to learn how to protect myself. My abilities have physical consequences, and I have to be able to counter them. My dad also thinks there are people or entities that already want me, and they might take extreme measures to get at the knowledge I have. I need a safe place to develop my abilities further."

"Why us?" she repeats.

"I read that you do those surgeries, to help sick kids. I like that."

Kate smiles and shakes her head. "Thomas, we appreciate that, a lot, but I'm not sure we're the best fit for you."

Kenneth frowns at her. "Why not?" I ask.

"We don't have a lot of funding yet. We're new and untried. You say you need money...our budget can't help you right now. Of course, the research will pay off in the long run, but for now...you might be better off going somewhere bigger and more established."

"Where others will dictate what I do and how I do it. Where word could get out about my abilities before I'm ready. No," I say. "I want to work with you."

Kate opens her mouth to speak again, but Kenneth squeezes her knee and she closes it.

"This discussion is a little premature," Kenneth says. "How do we know you're telling the truth?"

"You want me to demonstrate?"

"If you can," he says.

The first thought that pops into my head is Dacey. I hold out my hand in front of me. "Watch."

I activate the stem cells under my fingernails, blah, blah, blah...and my middle fingernail grows as they watch.

Kate gives a small squeak. Kenneth leans forward to get a good look.

In ten seconds, my nail has curved into a two-foot long unicorn horn.

Kenneth takes my hand in his, turning it over and around, examining the nail from every angle.

"Can you show us something with living cells?"

"Sure." I break the nail off my finger and place it on the coffee table. I stand up and fish my knife out of my pocket.

"Wait!" Kate says. "Do you have a towel? You'll get blood all over the floor."

"Don't need it," I say. "I'll clot the blood immediately. Minimal mess."

I slash my palm open and hold it in front of them. I heal it while they watch.

"Cool," Kate whispers under her breath.

"What if you cut off your finger?" Kenneth asks.

Kate slaps at his arm. "Kenneth! You want him to cut off his finger? That's torture!"

I smile and sit back down. "I've never actually done that, but I know I could. We'll try that in the lab."

"I'm not going to condone torture in my lab," she says.

"It's not torture," I say. "I just cut off the nerve signals. I don't feel a thing."

Kenneth squeezes Kate's knee again, probably his signal for her to be quiet. "So you...you said you need to learn to protect yourself. What does that involve?" he asks.

"Well, after healing, my body shuts down and forces me to sleep. I need to be able to fight that. And I burn up a huge amount of calories. One time, I lost 15% of my body weight in under an hour. On the fantastic side, if someone drugs me, can I counter the drug's effects. If someone renders me unconscious, can I bring myself out of it. If someone deprives me of sleep, can I take it. That sort of thing." I look at Kate. "I guess I do want you to torture me."

♥

We talk for another thirty minutes, discussing my abilities and the initial tests they want to perform. I tell them that I can devote myself to their lab full time for no pay, and they insist on paying me $20 an hour. It won't pay Erica's bills, but it's a start.

As they're leaving, Kate says, "You know, we get requests almost every day from people who want us to consult on certain cases. We don't have the time to answer all of them, and some of them pay pretty well. Maybe you could have a look and see if there's something you could help with. It might generate some extra money."

I agree that that sounds promising, and I shake their hands goodbye.

"See you Monday at eight," I say.

♥

"Thomas?"

I hear the front door slam shut and Tessa's unhurried steps in the kitchen. I grab my empty orange juice cup from the coffee table and meet her with a hug.

"I don't think life could get much crappier," she says into my chest.

My stomach flips. I'm about to make it a whole lot crappier.

"You guys okay?" I ask.

She shakes her head. "Everything. He took everything! How could he do that?"

I don't have an answer, so I just hold her and stroke her hair.

Tessa finally lifts her head and looks at me. "We might move," she whispers, her voice quivering.

I nod. "I heard. But Tessa, I'm gonna do everything I can to keep that from happening."

"What do you mean?"

I blow out a breath. "I got a job."

She smiles sadly. "Thomas, I appreciate that, but I don't think an after-school job is going to help."

"I know," I say. "I know you need big money, and I'm still working on that, I have a few ideas, but...I didn't get an after-school job. I...I got a full-time job."

She gasps. "You mean..."

I nod.

Tessa drops her arms from around my waist. "Full time?"

I nod again.

"You mean, no more school, no more tests, you're really gonna work at the Planarian Institute and heal people, for real?"

I sigh, bite my lip, and nod.

Tessa grins and throws her arms back around me. "Finally!"

Chapter Twenty

"Coffee?" Kate asks when I walk in the front door of the Planarian Institute the next morning. She's pouring herself a cup, and I think my first experiment should probably be finding a way to hook her up to the pot intravenously.

"Thanks," I say, "but I can pour my own."

"Ever after," she says, "but the first day, for my very first employee, I'm pouring the coffee."

I smile gratefully and take the mug she holds out to me. "So what happens first?"

She waves her hand. "Well, there's paperwork, but let's leave it 'til later. Let me show you around."

We walk through the lab. Kate points out various machines, and I'm excited to get my hands on them. She senses this, I think, because she says, "Everything's off limits. We have to train you extensively before you touch anything. It's not personal, it's just the rules."

"Got it," I say, instinctively stuffing my coffee-free hand in my pocket.

"Let me get you a notebook," she says. "You should take notes."

"I have perfect recall, Kate," I remind her. "If you tell me, I'll remember."

She surveys the room. "What was the first thing I said to you this morning?"

"'Coffee?'" I say. "I said, 'Thanks, but I can pour my own.' You said, 'Ever after, but the first day, for my very first employee, I'm pouring the coffee.'"

Kate laughs. "Okay. No notes. Got it."

She goes over protocol, cleanliness, personal protective gear, chain of custody and documentation, blah, blah, blah. It's info I need to know, but I'll spare you the details.

Kate shows me her office, where she has an extra desk set up for me. I get a new MacBook Air and iPad, on loan from Apple, Kate says, as some kind of program they have to move their products into the medical field. Sweet. She asks if she needs to show me how they work, and I just raise an eyebrow at her.

Kenneth comes out then from his office. He shakes my hand. "Thomas."

"Hello, Kenneth. Nice to see you."

He glances at Kate. "He catching on?" he asks her.

"Do you know how annoying it is to say something once and have it understood?"

Kenneth laughs. "So I got something I think we should look at it. Can we shift gears for a minute?"

"Sure," she says, glancing at me. "What's up?"

He hands her a letter, and Kate motions me over. We stand side by side, reading it.

My sixteen-year-old daughter, Olivia, was thrown from her horse on May 4th of this year. She was racing across the pasture at our home when a neighbor's dog got loose and spooked the horse. She was thrown twenty feet and landed directly on her head.

She has been in a coma since, with doctors claiming little brain function and littler chance of recovery. I am desperate, a father in daily agony. I ask for your assistance for my beautiful daughter.

Included in this package are Olivia's medical records, scans, everything her doctors have compiled these past months. Perhaps something will jump out at you that others have missed.

I'm looking for a miracle – I know that. As pastor of the Sinners Way Church, though, I also know the power of prayer and the power of faith. I have that faith that, together, we can bring Olivia back.

I'm enclosing a check. Please keep it as a donation to your facility for your time in reading this letter.

May God be with us all.

Pastor Cyrus Brooks

"Wow," I say. "Sixteen."

"It's why we do what we do," Kate says, then she fixes on Kenneth. "How much is the check for?"

"Ten large," he says, and I blink.

"He gave you $10,000 for reading the letter?"

"Let's look at the records," she says, ignoring me.

No less than twelve doctors have reviewed her case. They all come to the same conclusion:

Diffuse axonal injury – basically head trauma from extreme deceleration (her fall), where the nerves in her brain were stretched. Those nerves are no longer functioning.

Depressed skull fracture with bone fragments piercing the brain caused both swelling and bleeding in the brain.

Cerebral anoxia (lack of oxygen to the brain) for approximately ten minutes compounded the injury. Brain cells die from lack of oxygen.

Patient is being kept alive with a ventilator – her lungs don't work on their own. She is completely unresponsive.

"Well," Kenneth says, removing his glasses and rubbing his eyes, "I guess I'll take this check to the bank."

"No, you won't," Kate says, snatching it from his hands. "We can't help her. It wouldn't be right."

Kenneth sighs but doesn't argue.

"I can help her," I say.

Kenneth replaces his glasses and considers me. "At what cost to you?"

"Honestly, I don't know. I grow neurons routinely at little cost, and I've grown new brain cells in response to injury exactly twice. Once, when I brought a woman out of a coma and had to re-grow some cells, and once when I fell off a jungle gym when I was six and had a small bleed in the frontal lobe. I didn't even have to think about healing it, really. No-brainer."

"Ha, ha," Kate says with a frown.

"This would be more difficult, of course. I know that. But I also know I can do it."

"This would be an experiment," she says. "You can't experiment on a sixteen-year-old girl."

"She's basically dead," Kenneth says. "Who better to experiment on?"

Kate gapes at him. "Really?"

"Okay, no, not really," he says, "but we can work on this. Pastor Cyrus won't be pulling the plug on his daughter any time soon."

Kate turns her back on us. "If someone has a functioning brain, but suffers isolated trauma, I'm on board. That's what we're here to study. Someone like Olivia...she's gone, Kenneth. Her memory is wiped. Personality obliterated." She turns back to us. "You may be able to bring her back to life, Thomas, but she won't be Olivia. She'll be a newborn, starting from scratch. Even after therapy...she won't be the same old Olivia."

I rummage through Olivia's records and pull out a few sheets of paper.

"So, here," I say, pointing, "we have an EEG showing no rhythms in the hippocampi. The neurons there are not firing. But if you look here," and I pull out a CT scan of Olivia's brain, "you can see that the hippocampi are largely unharmed, even after the oxygen deprivation. That means her long-term memory is fairly intact. The problem is here, with the medial septal nucleus. It's damaged. And since it's responsible for neuron activity in the hippocampi, all we have to do is repair it, and I believe her long-term memory will be restored."

"What about her personality?" Kate asks.

"You're just testing me," I say with a smile. "You already know that personality can be affected by even the smallest head injury. Environment, genetics, and experience all affect personality. Neurons built over a lifetime affect personality and alter it as we go through life. Of course, she's lost a lot of those neural connections, so her personality may change significantly. But maybe not."

"Maybe not?" Kenneth says.

I take a few seconds to feel inside myself and search my brain. In the hippocampus, the long-term memory center, I find the "blueprint" of my body that I access all the time to tell me the status of things, like how many neural connections I have and where they're located. "The hippocampus records all the information on the body. I can tell how many neurons I have in the brain, for example, and where they are. If I can access that portion of Olivia's brain, if it's intact, I can re-create those exact connections for her. Her personality should be relatively unchanged."

Kate's and Kenneth's mouths drop open.

"And, there's an experiment going on in the Attic...basically, I know that memory and information can be transferred to newly grown brain cells. I'm not sure how it works, but I know it can be done. So I could potentially start Olivia off with all the basics – how to walk, talk, read, write – if those parts of her brain are damaged beyond repair. She wouldn't have to start from scratch."

Kate lets out a choked sob, and both Kenneth and I startle. We stare at her, and tears start rolling down her cheeks. Kenneth puts his arm over her shoulders.

"What's wrong?" he asks gently.

Kate sniffs, swiping the back of her hand across her nose. "This is...do you realize...so many people can be helped. So many...so many lives saved." She grabs my hand and holds it to her chest. "You're a miracle. And the fact that we get to witness it, to be a part of it..." She dislodges herself from Kenneth and throws herself at my chest, crushing me in a bear hug.

I hug her back. It means so much to me that they've invited me here, that they're listening, that they're believing me.

Kenneth just gives me a shrug and a smile behind her back.

Chapter Twenty-One

I get home a little before six o'clock, and find Dad hovering over Grandma near the stove.

"Hello, Grandma, " I say, kissing her cheek. She leans into the kiss and blows me one into the air.

"Where have you been?" she asks.

This is so familiar that tears prick my eyes. I glance at Dad, and he smiles at me.

"Work. I started a new job today."

The teakettle whistles, and Dad and Grandma reach for it at the same moment.

"I can do it, Michael," she says.

"It's hot, Mom. Let me."

They wrestle for a moment, but Dad wins. He pours the scalding water into her teacup while she glares at him.

"I'm not helpless, you know," she says.

"You're on vacation, Grandma," I tell her, and I pull out a kitchen chair and wave at her to sit. "You've taken care of us for years. Let us take care of you."

"And who are you?" she says, reluctantly sitting.

"Here's your tea, Mom," Dad says, setting the cup in front of her. She picks it up daintily with a trembling hand. "Careful now."

Grandma gives Dad the evil eye. And like a five-year-old defying her father, she takes a big gulp of tea and gasps. The teacup falls to the floor in a steaming puddle of splintery china shards.

"Grandma!" I say, squatting beside her. "Did you burn yourself?"

She nods and her face goes blank.

"Did you...how's your tongue?" I ask.

She shakes her head, as though clearing it. "My tongue? It's fine. Why wouldn't it be?"

"You burned yourself, Mom," Dad says. "Is your mouth okay?"

I watch her wiggle her tongue around in her mouth.

"I'm not burned. What nonsense is this?"

Dad and I exchange a glance over her head. Does Grandma not remember scalding herself thirty seconds ago, or did she actually heal herself?

I clean up the spill while Dad pours Grandma another cup of tea. He adds two ice cubes to cool it down before handing it to her.

"Do you have honey?" she asks.

"Mom, you don't put honey in your tea," Dad points out.

"So a girl can't change her mind?"

"Give her some honey, Dad," I say, giving the floor a final swipe.

Grandma looks down at me. "Why are you on the floor?"

"I'm just cleaning up a spill, Grandma," I say.

"You should be more careful," she says. "I could slip and fall."

"That's why I'm cleaning up," I say, getting to my feet.

She holds her cup out to me. "I'd like some honey in my tea, please."

"I don't have honey, Mom," Dad says.

"Who doesn't have honey? You have a kitchen. A kitchen without honey is like...a body without a soul."

"I'm a single guy with a son. Not a lot of honey-eating going on here," he says.

I squat down next to Grandma. "Have you known anybody without a soul, Grandma?" I ask her.

She laughs. "That would be an impossible thing. I've known people without hearts, that's for damn sure. But a soul? We don't work without a soul."

"Why not?"

She takes a small sip of tea, grimaces, and turns to me. "Let's pretend you were walking in the woods, and you find a car. Maybe it's a rusty piece of crap, maybe it's a brand new Ferrari. Doesn't matter. Do you assume the car grew out of the ground?"

"Of course not," I say. "Someone made it."

"Exactly. Now compare a car to a human body. Which is more complex?"

"The human body."

"Yes. We have a maker. Complex systems cannot spontaneously occur from rock and dust. There is more to us than that."

"But I can take that car and make it work," I say. "I can fix it. I can give it gas and a new battery and I can make it come to life," I tell her.

"And you cannot do that with a human body," she says. "Dead is dead. Feed a dead body, water it, jump-start it with electricity, it's not waking up."

"Because the cells die," I insist. "If I can re-grow the cells, or keep them from decaying, surely there's a way to bring a body back."

"If the soul has not returned to Heaven, perhaps. But at what cost? It costs us to heal. Our abilities do not work for free."

I swallow hard at her words. "You know who I am?"

"Oh, Thomas," she says, placing a hand on my cheek. "Do you know why I've lived so long? Because I stopped using my abilities. Thirty years without healing gave me enough life to come be here with you. Be choosy, Thomas. Be very choosy."

I glance at Dad. "What do you mean?"

"I'm sixty-five years old and you're what? Six? You don't look six, by the way. But six-year-olds think they have all the time in the world. You don't. Healing takes its toll."

"What is she talking about?" I ask Dad.

He sits in a chair across the table from Grandma. "Mom, you're seventy-five, and Thomas is sixteen. You've lived an amazing life."

Grandma laughs. "Seventy-five! That's ridiculous. We're lucky if we hit fifty. Harry knew that, but it turned out he was the one who went first. Ironic."

I stand up and glare at Dad. "What is she talking about?"

Grandma sips her tea again. "Do we have any honey?"

Then the front door opens, and Tessa and Erica interrupt us.

♥

The five of us have dinner, and then Dad tucks Grandma into bed. At my discreet direction to Tessa, the girls make a hasty exit afterward.

"I guess it's too much to hope for that you want to have a father-son movie night," Dad says with a small smile.

I scowl. "Have a seat. You and I need to talk."

Dad settles in his recliner and kicks his feet up. I sit on the edge of the couch.

"First. What exactly do you want me to do with Grandma?"

Dad raises an eyebrow, and his surprise seems genuine. It's not too often that I surprise him.

But he doesn't crack. He stays silent.

"I heard you tell Erica, you'd 'give me the opportunity' to do it. I assume you mean heal her. Explain yourself."

"Thomas, you heard me wrong—"

"Bullshit. Here's the deal. I'm giving you one opportunity to come clean. You tell me everything – what you want from me, what you have planned, who exactly might be following me, all of it. I may or may not agree to go along with you. That's up to me. But if you refuse to be one hundred percent honest with me here and now, I'm leaving. I'm moving out, and I will never speak to you again. I won't go back to the Attic and help Dacey and Tyrion. I won't cooperate with you at all."

Dad doesn't flinch. He doesn't move. He doesn't speak.

And then he slowly lowers the recliner to its upright position and sits forward.

"No one specific is following you, but we have gotten some letters from a father of a coma patient, and they're just short of threatening. He knows about your accident on the playground all those years ago. He knows of your relationship to Dr. Rumson and his newfound health. There's something off about the whole thing."

"Do you mean Cyrus Brooks?"

Dad startles. "He's contacted you?"

"Not directly, but I'm aware of his case. Next."

Dad scrubs a hand across his face. "You've been a controlled experiment since you were born."

This floors me, but I force myself not to react.

"Basically...we don't know of any Dwellers born outside of Dweller-family lines in the last hundred years. We all had the benefit of our parents' training. You didn't."

"Old news, Dad," I say as dismissively as I can, even though my body has started to shake. "You were a shitty parent. Tell me something I don't know."

Dad sighs. "There's something about the act of discovery. It grows neurons in ways we don't understand. We believe...you and Jack have abilities far beyond the rest of us. We believe your personal discoveries with your own bodies created these abilities."

"Jack can do what I do?"

Dad shakes his head. "No. She has unique abilities, but they're not the same as yours."

"Like what?"

Dad stays silent.

"Like what?" I repeat.

"Heal your grandmother."

"What?"

"You heard me."

I sit back and stare at my father. He's conveniently turned the conversation away from Jack to something I can't ignore. I know what he's doing, but I decide to go along and revisit the Jack issue later, because Grandma is more important.

But that doesn't mean I'm going to make it easy on him.

"What was she talking about earlier?"

Dad shrugs. "Just her religious crap. Intelligent design theory."

"I know that," I say impatiently. "Stop evading. That stuff about living longer. Do we die earlier than most people?"

Dad clenches his jaw. "Think about it. The most basic thing we do is replicate cells. We make copies. A copy is not as good as the original. Eventually, the copies break down."

"If we're healing ourselves, yeah," I say. "If I heal you, my cells aren't replicating."

"But you're straining your body. The body is a machine. Machines wear out."

I sit back on the couch. "You're the oldest person at the Attic right now, aren't you?" I ask him.

"Yes."

"So this is why you've kept my healing to a minimum."

Dad doesn't answer.

I growl. "So now you want me to heal Grandma. Why now?"

"You're ready."

"I wasn't ready last week."

"You've always been ready."

I gnash my teeth. My father is the most irritating person on the planet.

"So you're going Yoda on me," I tell him. "I've been a Jedi all along."

"You've demonstrated maturity this week I wasn't aware of," he says. "Like your decisions about Tessa."

God, he's good. So my virginity makes me a man. Yeah, right.

But what's his angle? He previously told me he thought I'd come to harm if I hooked up to Grandma, and he wasn't willing to risk my life. Now he's willing. What changed?

Actually, that was a lie he told me to keep me from doing it. He told Erica he'd give me the opportunity, that presumably he wants me to heal Grandma. Was he just trying to use reverse psychology all along? Tell me not to do something so I'd do it?

But he knows I generally follow the rules! He knows my every thought! He predicts my every action! Why tell me what to do, and then tell me the complete opposite?

He...

I close my gaping mouth, and I narrow my eyes.

I am an experiment.

I believe that's the only truthful thing he's said this entire conversation – besides the fact that we are machines that break down, which I fully believe, but which does not change my resolve. I made peace with my death a long time ago.

I am an experiment predicated on the fact that I've had no guidance, at least none that's been consistent. The only consistent thing in my life has been the inconsistency. Ultimately, it doesn't matter what Dad wants or what he thinks I should do. How I use my abilities is up to me. Fuck him and his experiment.

"I'm going to explore Grandma's body and figure out the problem," I finally say. "Maybe I'll fix it. I won't know until I get in there."

Dad nods.

"As for the rest, we'll deal with it one issue at a time. Don't think you're off the hook."

"Fair enough," he says.

I stand. "Okay then. Let's go."

Chapter Twenty-Two

In Grandma's bedroom doorway, I pause. She's breathing lightly with her mouth open, soft snores drifting through the room. I lean on the doorjamb, excited but nervous.

Dad puts his hands on my shoulders. "You okay?"

I crane my neck to look back at him. "She's going to be in pain until I can get hooked up to her brain and turn off the nerve signals. She'll wake up and be frightened, might even fight me. Do we have anything we can give her?"

Dad squeezes lightly. "I already drugged her tea."

I clench my fists and fight not to turn around and punch him. This whole thing is choreographed! He somehow knew it would come to this, that I would make this decision. How? Why am I so Goddamn easy to read?

Or maybe he would have drugged her every night of her stay, just in case.

I have no way of knowing.

So what do I want to do?

I stare at Grandma, her thin, frail little body barely making a bump under her covers. I want to heal her.

I shrug off Dad's hands and make my way to her bed. I take my knife out of my pocket, kneel beside her, and take her hand in mine.

I repeat Psalm 41:3 in my head: *The LORD sustains them on their sickbed and restores them from their bed of illness.*

Except I am not the Lord. And I know that. *God, please just guide me and watch over us,* I pray. *Give me the strength to help her.*

I take a deep breath, and it bolsters me. Maybe it's God's presence, maybe not – who's to say? – but I feel ready.

I drop Grandma's hand and slash open my palm. I grab Grandma's hand again and make an identical cut. I press our hands together.

I grow my nerves, attach them, race along the connection up to Grandma's brain. I hook up to her brain stem, block the nerve signals from her hand, and take a look around.

Her body and organs seem to be in decent shape. Her cells are slow to replicate, but I assume that's because of her age. Her brain is intact, no degeneration, but I find the problem immediately – her neurons are not firing properly, particularly in the pre-frontal lobe, which is responsible for short-term memory.

I experiment a bit. I tell the neurons to fire. Some of them do, but others won't. Then I step back and let them do their own thing. They don't.

Okay, Grandma's sleeping and drugged. No real reason for her short-term memory neurons to be firing. She needs to be awake.

I find the drug Dad supplied her with and quickly metabolize it. I gather potassium from my own cells, direct it to the cells in Grandma's brain, and order her pre-frontal lobe neurons to fire. Then I stroke Grandma's cheek with my free right hand. "Grandma?"

Her eyes flutter and settle open. She turns her head to me. "Thomas?"

I smile. "Hey. How are you feeling?"

She smiles back, then frowns, looking down her body at our hands resting on her stomach. Her eyes fly back to my face. "You're so big. So...grown up. What are you doing?"

I swallow. "Healing you."

She closes her eyes and sighs. "What have you done so far?" she asks.

"Nothing. Nothing permanent, anyway. I'm just diagnosing the problem."

"And?"

"Maybe a potassium deficiency," I say. "Your neurons aren't firing properly, and I think the potassium's responsible. Sometimes they fire, sometimes they don't."

"It's not a deficiency," she says. "My body's just not properly using the nutrients I give it anymore."

"Whatever the case, I'll figure it out," I promise her. "I'll fix it."

She smiles sadly. "I can't remember...I don't remember. How long?"

"It might take me a few sessions," I concede. "I'm not sure exactly—"

"No," she says. "Not that. How long have I been...like this?"

I glance at Dad, but he's stoic, leaning against the wall, arms crossed over his chest.

"A few years," I say.

I see Grandma's throat work as she swallows.

"Thomas, listen to me. This is...cancer I could take. Pain I can handle. This...please don't...Michael?"

Dad pushes himself off the wall and comes to stand opposite me on the other side of the bed. He takes her free hand. "Mom."

"I love you. Both of you. I would do...most anything, to stay here and be with you both. You know that, right?"

Dad nods, and in the dim light of the room, I see the sheen of a teardrop at the corner of his eye.

Grandma nods back. "I can't ask this of him, of Thomas. But I'll ask it of you, because you know how it feels to be out of control. You know, and you'd never suffer it willingly."

Dad nods again, and as the realization of what she's asking sets in, I explode. "No. No! Grandma, I can fix you. You don't have to live the way you've been living! It doesn't have to be like this!"

Grandma turns her head towards me. "And what did I tell you? That just because we can, doesn't mean we should. My body's giving out, Thomas. Like it or not. And while I respect that fact, I think I've earned the right to call it quits."

"But, no!" I scream. "That makes no sense! You respect your body? Then let it decide when it's done. You have no right to take your own life. It's God's choice!"

"And God gave me free will, Thomas," she says. "He gave me this life to do with as I see fit. He doesn't condone suffering. I believe He's with me."

"But what about us? What about me?"

Grandma squeezes my hand tight. "You don't need the burden of worrying about me and healing me. You fix this thing and something else will go wrong. Where's the end point? I've lived a good life. And you have a good life to live. I want you to live it. I want you to breathe it. I want you to save those who still have things left to accomplish."

"But I can do that if you're here. Healing you won't stop me from living."

Dad and Grandma exchange a glance.

Grandma sighs. "I love you, Thomas. And now I'm ordering you to back off. Unhook me. Now."

I shake my head. "No."

"Please," she says. "When you're out, if I still have my wits about me, I'll do it myself. Otherwise, Michael, I expect you to help me."

"Dad!" I whisper.

My father is crying, but for the tears running down his face, you wouldn't know it. He clears his throat. "You heard her, Thomas."

I choke on a sob and hold my hand to Grandma's cheek. "Please don't do this," I say. "Not now. I'm not ready...I thought I'd be healing you. Please. I'm not ready."

Grandma pulls her hand from Dad's and strokes my hair. "Your Dad didn't prepare you," she says, making it a statement. "Michael, why don't you give us a few minutes alone."

Dad nods and leaves, closing the door softly behind him.

"Don't leave me alone with him," I say.

Grandma sighs. "He loves you, Thomas."

"He said I'm an experiment. Everything he tells me to do is a test. It's a wonder I don't have any ulcers."

"He told you that?" she asks, eyebrow raised.

"You knew?"

She nods. "I knew what the Attic wanted him to do. But he said he wasn't going along with it. I believed him."

"What did the Attic want him to do?" I ask.

"Raise you until age twelve with no outside help using your abilities. At twelve, you were supposed to spend a year in residence at the Attic. Did you do that?"

"No," I say. "Dad never mentioned it. I've only been to the Attic twice now, just recently."

"So he deviated from the plan," she says. "Your Dad was always the best at taking orders. And the worst."

"So what's his plan now?" I ask her. "What's really going on?"

"I know your dad, honey. He's doing whatever's best for you. Sometimes it might feel like a test, but…think of it this way: Dad's the one in the worse position. He has to navigate the Attic while protecting you. He's probably got several ulcers by now."

"But you don't know that!" I say. "How do you know he's protecting me? He basically set me up so you could die!"

"He was making sure my wishes were carried out," she says. "Tonight was about me."

"With no thought for me," I say.

"You and I want opposite things, Thomas. He can't please the both of us in this."

"But he could have talked to me about it before. I could have been ready."

"Would you ever have been ready?" she asks gently.

I squeeze her hand. "I'm being selfish."

She squeezes back. "Never. You're demonstrating how much you love me. I...I never thought I'd have that, your love. I never thought I'd get to know you. I thought I was going to die alone in Florida."

"That's what you wanted," I say, miserable.

"It's what life handed me, and I accepted it. There's a difference between acceptance and desire."

"So you don't feel cheated?" I ask.

She laughs. "I feel like the luckiest woman in the world! But I missed out on a lot by accepting my fate. Your mom, for instance. I wish I'd been here to spend more time with her."

"Did you know her well?"

"I'd like to think so. When she and your dad got engaged, they came to visit me for two weeks. She was so smart, so in tune with your dad. She knew his flaws and worked around them, made them into assets, even. She had a knack for that. And I'd never seen him so happy. He couldn't believe a woman like that would love him."

"I doubt that," I say. "Dad thinks he's God's gift to women."

Grandma smiles. "Come now. You know him better than that. He's all talk. The truth is, your dad is the most self-aware person I've ever known. He knows his faults, all too well."

"Not when it comes to me."

"Parenthood is tough, Thomas," she says. "A parent has zero experience until he's in the trenches, bullets flying. But he loves you. He adored your mom. I trust him."

I sigh and close my eyes. "I've wanted you back for so long…I've dreamt of the day I could heal you and you could come back to us. You could stay, just for a little while."

Grandma purses her lips. "And any moment I could slip away. You and your dad would hover over me, baby me, be afraid to leave me alone. It's not fair to you."

"I don't mind—"

"But I do!" she says, voice rising. Then she sighs. "You'll have to trust your dad. I know he's trustworthy. If I thought for one minute he'd hurt you, I'd intervene." Grandma turns her head away from me and sniffles. "Other than that, we don't have a lot of time, Thomas. Is there anything else you'd like to talk to me about?"

A tear glides down my cheek and hangs on my upper lip. "Are you scared?" I whisper.

She shakes her head. "Not now. Imagine it – I'm going to see my parents again."

"You believe that?"

"I do," she says. "And your mom, my dog Rascal, my grandfather…and Harry."

"You've missed him, haven't you?"

"Desperately," she says.

"There's nothing I can say to…to change your mind?"

Grandma smiles and leans into my hand. "I love you. Always. I'll be watching over you."

We stare at each other, smiling, not because we're happy, but just…trying to convey how much we mean to each other. Tears pour from my eyes.

I have to respect her wishes.

"Dad!" I yell. I'm sure he's within earshot.

Dad comes back into the room and takes up his post opposite me.

I back out of Grandma's body. I heal us. But I don't let go of her hand.

"I love you, Michael," she says. "Take care of Thomas. He's the best of us."

Dad leans over and kisses Grandma's cheek. She throws her arm over him and they share a long hug.

"It's time," she says, turning to me.

"I'm staying," I tell her.

Dad kneels down, and we both clutch tightly to Grandma.

"Harry's here," she whispers. "I can feel him."

Grandma stops her heart.

I watch her take her last breath.

And when she's still, I lean over and rest my head on her chest and breathe her sweet vanilla scent in one last time.

Chapter Twenty-Three

As we watch the mortuary pull out of the driveway with Grandma's body, I dash the tears from my eyes and sit on the front porch steps.

"You knew this would be the outcome," I say.

Dad sighs. "Not for sure. We talked about it when she was first losing her memory. I knew she didn't want to live like this."

"Yet you did nothing."

"Would you have preferred it if I put a pillow over her face in the middle of the night?"

My whole body tenses. "You obviously thought about it."

"Of course," he says. "That's what she wanted me to do. But I was a coward."

"How can you say that?" I ask. "You couldn't kill her! That would be murder. I'm the one who was the coward. I should have healed her back when she started to slip. It's my fault."

"She didn't want it, Thomas," Dad says. He sits down beside me and I hear his knees pop. "She made me promise not to let you. If she had had her way, the cancer would have taken her."

"Again," I say, "my fault. She healed herself to come take care of me when Mom died. I kept her from the death she wanted."

"I'm the one who asked her to come out," he says, "and neither of us held a gun to her head. She wanted to be here for us. And she was. It was her final gift. She got us through the worst time in our lives."

I rub my eyes. "Did you actually want me to heal her?"

"I wanted what she wanted. I was hoping…but you know how I feel about hope. All it does is lead to disappointment. I knew her wishes. She wanted to be at home, with us."

"Did Erica know?"

"Yes."

"Then…what did you really want to happen?"

Dad leans forward and wraps his arms around his knees. "I wanted to hear her speak again. Her, the real her. I needed to know that she still wanted to let go. I would never have been able to do it otherwise. And I knew you were the only one who could bring her back for us."

"Why didn't you just say that?" I ask. "I would have brought her back to hear her wishes. Why give me false hope? Why not prepare me?"

Dad leans back on his hands and stares up at the cloudy midnight sky. "I am preparing you. Life throws us a curveball every Goddamn day. You never know what's coming next. This is me parenting, right or wrong."

I want to scream, "Goddamn right, it's wrong!" But there's a certain poetic-ness to what he said. He's preparing me…by not preparing me. The theme of my childhood.

We're sitting so close our thighs are almost touching. I feel a sudden understanding for my father. Not a liking for him – not that – but I want to touch him. To communicate this new understanding to him. Maybe even to hug him.

Before I can move, though, Dad stands.

"I'm going to bed," he says. "Long night. You coming?"

I heave myself to my feet. "Yeah. I'm coming."

Chapter Twenty-Four

If I slept, my body has no memory of it. I finally get up around 4:30, exhausted and drooping but unable to lie in bed one minute longer.

I swish some mouthwash and drive over to Tessa's house. I text her on the way, but don't expect her to get the text.

I find their house key in a little rock in the planter by the front door. I tiptoe in as quietly as possible and make my way to Tessa's room.

She's lying on her side facing me, breathing softly. I watch her for a minute, debating whether or not to wake her.

I pull my t-shirt over my head, toe off my shoes, and strip off my jeans. I climb into bed behind her, settle the covers around us, and wrap myself around her.

Tessa startles, and I squeeze tight, whispering in her ear. "It's just me."

She twists around to face me. "What's up?"

"Grandma," I manage to squeak out.

"Your grandma? Something happened?"

"She's dead."

Tessa buries her head in my neck and clings to me. "Oh, baby. I'm so sorry."

I press myself into her and sob.

Tessa holds me. She just holds me.

♥

I wake up alone to the smell of bacon.

I put my clothes on and follow my nose to the kitchen. Tessa is flipping pancakes, and a slab of crispy bacon cools on a plate next to the stove.

She goes to the fridge and pours me a giant cup full of orange juice. I take it gratefully.

"How are you feeling?"

"Shitty," I say.

"What happened?"

I tell her the story, and Tessa doesn't interrupt once.

"So then Dad, he says that this is his parenting style, letting me just deal with shit as it comes, with no warning, no help from him."

"It kind of makes sense," she says as she sets a plate of food in front of me. "I mean, in a twisted way."

I dig in. "How does it make sense?" I ask, mouth full.

"It's what you do for a toddler," she says. "As soon as they're able, you let them dress themselves. Otherwise, how will they learn?"

"I've never met a teenager who couldn't tie their own shoes," I say.

Tessa smiles. "Okay, how about chores? Mom did everything for Ian and Matty, and when they went to college, they didn't even know how to do their own laundry. Matt had to wear pink underwear and socks his entire freshman year, and that apparently went over real well with the baseball team. So when Mom found out, she started having Sam and I do our own laundry."

I glare at her. "Why are you on his side?"

"I'm not. Your grandma, and your abilities, and Mom and your Dad's relationship, none of them is equal to pink underwear. But you have to admit he has a point."

"He's sacrificing my relationship with him to make that point."

"Maybe there's a point to that, too," she says.

I snort. That's highly doubtful.

Except my dad doesn't do anything without a purpose.

I wipe my mouth. "Actually, he told me I'm an experiment."

Tessa looks at me in horror. "You're not an experiment. That's ridiculous."

"But think about it," I say. "It makes sense. I mean, I knew my dad was ordered to have a child. I was planned from the beginning. I just didn't realize the experiment continued past my birth. And my grandma confirmed it."

"That's…like a science fiction novel," she says. "I don't believe it. Your dad loves you."

"Where's the evidence for that?" I ask.

"Well, he…he provided for you," she says softly.

"The State provides for orphans."

"He made sure your grandma was around when your mom died."

"Evidence that he didn't want to take responsibility himself," I say.

Tessa sighs. "He bought the gallery for you, so you could display your sculptures."

"Grandma's idea, not his."

Tessa gets up from her stool and hugs me from the back. "I just know he loves you. In my heart. I believe that."

I just wish I believed that, too.

I go back home for a shower. Dad seems to still be asleep. I wonder if it's disrespectful to Grandma to go to work today, but the last thing I want to do is to be alone, in mourning, with Dad.

And Grandma's last wish was for me to live and heal others. I'm going to work.

Chapter Twenty-Five

I text Dr. Rumson on my drive to work, and he calls me as I pull in the parking lot of the Planarian Institute. I shut off my ignition and answer. "Hey."

"Thomas, I'm so sorry to hear about your grandma."

"Thanks," I say, leaning back in my seat. "It hasn't hit me yet, I don't think."

"Why don't you meet me at the church? We can hang out, pray, maybe write up a eulogy. I'll help you through it."

"I appreciate that," I say, "but I'm going to spend the day at work. The whole thing is complicated. Can I come by after?"

"Of course. I'll be here. Any time."

"How about 5:30? I'll come straight from work."

"Call if you need anything," he says. "I'll be standing by."

"Thanks, Dr. Rumson," I say. "See you tonight."

"Take care."

And I heave myself out of the car and into the Institute.

♥

I find Kate in our office, on the phone. I motion with my thumb over my shoulder that I'll wait outside, but Kate shakes her head and waves me to my desk.

"Yes, we looked at the files yesterday...yes, all of us...Thomas? Yes, Thomas Van Zandt recently joined our staff, but he's just an intern, Mr. Brooks...he's not quite ready to…sir, I understand your frustration, and I sympathize. I'm so sorry about your daughter, but there's nothing…" Her eyes slide to me, then back to the top of her desk. "That's not our protocol. My husband and I are well versed in cases like Olivia's, as are the other doctors who've already looked at her. If we come up with something, you'll be the first to know, but right now…no. I'm sorry. I have to go…yes. I will. Goodbye."

Kate hangs up the phone and sighs. "That is the pushiest man I've ever met."

"Do you blame him?" I ask.

She wheels her chair to face me. "Do you know Pastor Brooks?"

"No," I say, surprised. "Why?"

"He said to tell you he's very sorry for the loss of your grandmother."

I stare at her.

"Did you lose your grandmother recently?" she asks.

I swallow. "Last night."

"Oh, Thomas, I'm so sorry," she says. "What are you doing here?"

"I have some questions," I say, "and…I just didn't want to be home alone today. How did he know? I've told two people."

"Wow," she says. "This is getting a little creepy. We'll figure out how to deal with the pastor, but you…are you sure you don't want to take some time off?"

"Actually, I'm not sure," I say, "but like I said, I do have some questions, some things I want to run by the two of you."

"Let me call Kenneth in." She dials his office number and asks him to join us. "If you need to go, you just let us know."

"Thanks, Kate."

Kenneth comes in, shakes my hand, and props his butt on Kate's desk. "What's up?"

"My grandmother passed away last night. She...shit, this is long and involved, but let me see if I can simplify it. She and my dad have the same abilities I do, except they can't grow nerves in the central nervous system. That seems to be the major difference between us."

"That's a big one," Kenneth says.

"Yep. And she explained to me last night that people with our abilities die young. At seventy-five, she was the oldest Dweller ever."

"Dweller?" Kate asks.

"Attic Dweller. That's what we call ourselves. Anyway, she only lived that long because for thirty years, she stopped using her abilities completely. But she said...we're lucky if we hit fifty. My dad's almost fifty."

"So you're accelerating the aging process by healing yourself. Maybe doubly so since you're healing others," Kenneth says.

I nod. "I never really thought I'd live a long life," I say. "I mean, it's dangerous to heal. There's an immediate danger of pushing your body to its limits. But I dismissed the long-term effects. I kind of assumed I was better off long-term because I could head off disease or decay easier than most people."

"The aging process is an entirely different area of study," Kate says. "In fact, most of the thinking right now is that to stop aging, we just have to induce cells to replicate as fast as they did in our youth. I don't think anyone in the research field has posited that this may have other negative consequences."

"Is your dad in trouble?" Kenneth asks. "Do you think he's dying?"

"I have no idea," I say. "Is he getting older? Sure. Dying? He wouldn't tell me if he were. He's not that forthcoming with me. But he's been getting his affairs in order. He appointed a guardian for me if something happens to him. And last night, he—"

"Excuse me."

We all startle at the man in the doorway. None of us heard him enter.

Kenneth stands. "Can we help you?"

The man, fiftyish, graying, in a black suit and tie, holds his hand out. "I'm Cyrus Brooks. It's a pleasure to meet you in the flesh."

He and Kenneth shake. "Mr. Brooks, I'm Kenneth Mullen, and this is my wife, Kate. What can we help you with?"

Cyrus Brooks turns to me. "And this must be Thomas Van Zandt, prodigy extraordinaire."

I don't move. If he thinks he can flatter me, he's sorely mistaken. "Mr. Brooks," I say.

The three of us stare at him.

"Well, I, I couldn't give up without a fight," he says, shrugging his shoulders. "Olivia's my daughter. I had to meet with you in person and see if there's anything at all you can do to help us."

"I think I was quite clear on the phone," Kate says. "We're very sorry for your loss, but there's nothing we can do."

"I wonder if I could speak to Thomas alone for a moment. I'm sure we can help each other."

"I don't think that's a good idea," Kate says.

"Help each other with what?" I ask him.

"I'm looking at acquiring some real estate, and there's a house. The Halters own it, I believe. I'm very interested in purchasing it."

Kate and Kenneth look at me questioningly.

I stand. "Fine. Let's talk in the lobby."

Cyrus Brooks takes the only chair in the lobby while I pour myself some coffee and try to stall to think about this situation. I don't offer him any coffee, and he doesn't ask.

I decide I have to at least be confident and a little bit hostile about him gathering intelligence on me.

"You've entered stalker territory," I say to him as I start brewing a fresh pot.

"I've done my research," he says. "I will do anything to have Olivia back."

"And you're banking on the fact that I'll do anything to have my girlfriend stay in town," I say.

"You're too late. The house is lost. Erica and Tessa are moving in with me and my dad."

"Then why have Erica's parents cleared out the spare bedroom and inquired about schooling for Tessa?"

I clench my jaw and pour a cup of coffee from the half-brewed pot. "I don't know and I don't care. That's not happening."

"It is," he says decisively. "But I can prevent it. I can purchase the house outright today, for cash, and Erica's pride will be intact."

I turn around and face him. "What do you want in return?"

"Olivia, whole and unharmed."

"Impossible," I say. "Even if I can get her to wake up, she won't be unharmed."

He waves his hand. "That's debatable. Fine. You won't reveal all of what you can do, and I'm not asking you to. I want Olivia to live from this injury. If she passes away, I don't want it to be from this."

"Why?" I ask.

He sighs. "Horses were her life. I can't take knowing she died while doing what she loved. Anything else, I could understand. I just don't think the Lord would want her to die this way."

"God has nothing to do with it," I say. "He doesn't intervene, as a rule. Accidents happen."

"Not to us," he hisses. Then he laughs. "Look at me. So arrogant. So prideful. Because I have dedicated my life to Him, I believe I should be treated better. My human failings abound."

I lean back against the wall and sip my coffee. "It is human to love someone so much that we sin. One of our better failings, in my opinion."

"A sin is a sin," he says. "There's no gray area in Heaven. I want to save my daughter, and in the process, I'm making it worse." He sighs again. "But in this, we can help each other. I have the earthly means to help the Halters. If it helps Olivia in the process, why not? We both win."

I stare into my cup. "Look, I'm not even sure I can do what you're asking. I may try and fail."

Cyrus Brooks looks at me, and there's something manic in his eyes. "All I ask is that you try," he whispers. "I'll help the Halters regardless."

"This week," I say. "You'll purchase the house this week. And you'll give them thirty days to move out."

"Yes."

"And I need to get through the next couple of weeks. My grandma's funeral, stuff at home, I need two weeks. I'll visit Olivia a week from next Tuesday."

Cyrus stands and clasps my hand tight. "A week from Tuesday. First thing in the morning. At our home." He hands me a card with his address and contact information.

"Olivia's at home?" I ask.

Cyrus nods. "It's been…expensive, yes. But what's the point of having money if I don't have my daughter?"

And he leaves through the doors with a whoosh.

♥

"I do not like that man," Kate says when I come back into the office.

I sit down heavily in my chair and sigh. "He's not that bad," I say. "He's just desperate."

"Desperate people do desperate things," Kenneth says. "What did he want?"

I go over our conversation and what I agreed to do. They both frown at me.

"I should have our lawyer draw up paperwork," Kate says. "The standard patient-doctor stuff. And one of us needs to be with you at all times. Since you're our employee now, we need to be there."

"Whatever you need me to do," I say. "That's fine."

"Both of us should go the first time, and then we can split duty from there. We should also go over what you're gonna do," Kenneth says. "Maybe practice a few things."

"No," Kate says. "Thomas, you can't practice without a purpose. If you're using up your life every time you heal, you can't practice."

"This has a purpose, Kate," I say. "I'll be bringing a teenager back to life. What greater purpose is there than that?"

Kate shakes her head. "You're right. Just, make sure every move counts."

"How about this?" Kenneth says. "I want to work on a protein shake, or a pill, something with super nutrients and calories to take the strain off your body. And we can work up a plan for healing, what order you should do things in, so they go smoothly. Unless you think you need to practice?"

"Actually," I say, "that sounds great, but I do have some other things I want to work on, too."

"Right," Kate says. "The torture."

I laugh. "More like self-defense training."

Kenneth grabs a yellow pad and pen off Kate's desk. "You have specifics in mind, I'm betting," he says.

I mentally snort. Kenneth has no idea.

"First, I need to work on the sleeping issue. My body shuts down and forces me to sleep pretty much every time I heal something major. I understand why, but I need to be able to delay it, ideally for five or six hours.

"Second, I need to try to use my abilities while I'm impaired – I've never really had the opportunity before."

"Impaired how?" Kenneth asks as he scribbles.

"With alcohol, drugs…even unconscious."

Kate frowns. "Are you drunk often?"

"Only once," I admit. "But you never know. Do you guys know of any drug someone could inject me with that would produce a similar effect to alcohol?"

"That would be just about all of them, with the right dosage," Kate says. "If you're set on this one, we need your dad's consent. He should even be here during the trials."

I sigh. "That's fine. He's on board. I'll talk to him." Maybe.

"What else?" Kenneth prods.

"Unconscious," I say. "Any idea how to do that one?"

Kenneth pinches the bridge of his nose. "This one really depends on the cause, on how you are rendered unconscious. If it's a drug, you can metabolize it. If it's a blow to the head, it's going to depend on the brain damage."

"I'm thinking of something like general anesthesia, definitely a drug. If I'm conscious, yeah, I can get rid of the drug, but what if I don't do that fast enough and I pass out? I'd like to bring myself out of it, and also see if I can still use my abilities while I'm under."

"We know a few anesthesiologists," Kenneth says. "I think that's the safest option. I'll work on it. Next."

"The fun stuff," I say, grinning. "Limb regeneration first."

Kate grimaces. "Only if you promise not to stand in this office and slice your wrist off. We only do it under controlled surgical conditions."

"Of course," I say. "I think I can get to the point where I can grow a few limbs every day. If that's the case…I want to grow them for wounded vets. I'll hook them up myself."

Kate's eyes tear. "That's an amazing goal, Thomas. But one step at a time. Let's make sure you can grow them safely first."

I nod. "Then I have this idea…but I haven't really had access to the stuff I need to do it."

"Do what?" Kate asks.

"I want to build a chip to record memory. I mean, essentially we already have that chip in our brain, but I think I can transfer it to something a computer could read, so you could actually see my experiences as my brain records them."

Kenneth tosses his pen on the desk. "I know a guy in Canada who's been working on something similar, a type of video camera to record what the eye sees."

"Does he have anything yet?" I ask.

Kenneth smiles. "No. But he swears it can be done."

"The problem is that there needs to be a biological component to the chip and its interface with the brain. I've already got that part worked out. It's the mechanical components I don't have access to."

Kenneth reaches for his pen. "Do you know what you need?"

I give Kenneth a list, and he grins. "How many more of these experiments do you have brewing in your head?"

"Eighty-six," I say.

"Time to prioritize," he says. "Sleep and nutrients first. Olivia's stuff second. Drugs third. Then we do the fun stuff."

All of it's fun to me.

We spend the rest of the day theorizing about how to fight my body's urge to sleep and discussing what nutrients my body uses when I heal.

I only think about Grandma 132 times.

Chapter Twenty-Six

Dr. Rumson opens the church office door for me and pulls me into a hug. "I'm so sorry," he says.

I cling tight and nod into his shoulder. "Me, too."

"You want to talk about what happened?"

We settle on the couch and I tell him about our evening.

"So she committed suicide," I say sadly. "Do you think she'll still go to Heaven?"

"Of course," he says. "You're grandmother was a good person. The pain of living without awareness, of being dependent on people…it was too much for her. I respect that."

"You might respect that, but what about God?" I ask. "He gave her life. Shouldn't He be the one to take it away?"

"Being in pain is not a sin, Thomas," he says. "Do not worry about this. Your grandmother is in Heaven right now, right where she belongs."

I nod, and tears sting my eyes.

"You want to talk about the rest?" Dr. Rumson asks.

"Just…my dad. I think he's dying. And I don't want to care. I know that sounds horrible, but I don't think he really cares about me, so why should I care about him? But I do."

Dr. Rumson purses his lips. "Thomas, you grew up with a wonderful mother for the first six years of your life. She taught you things, gave you room to grow, supported your extraordinary abilities, hugged you every day, and told you how much she loved you. Your dad, in stark contrast, was Disneyland dad. He did fun things with you. He wasn't around to parent and didn't even bother trying when he was around. Then your mom died, and you wanted your dad to be your mom. But he wasn't. He isn't. That doesn't make him wrong."

"You think I can't appreciate him because he's nothing like my mother?"

"It's one possibility. Must people be outwardly affectionate for us to feel their love? Must they profess it ten times a day? Must they relate to us in the way we want them to? If they do those things, great. But the absence of those things doesn't mean they don't care."

"You make me sound needy and petty," I say. "Like I'm a stubborn brat who wants things his way or no way."

Dr. Rumson just looks at me sympathetically.

"You think I'm just being a brat?"

"No," he says. "I know I've simplified things a great deal. You don't trust your dad's love for you because you don't trust him, period. But I want you to really think about that for a moment, your trust in your dad. If Tessa became pregnant, would you go to him?"

I nearly choke on my tongue. "That's impossible."

"Good answer," he says with a smile. "But seriously, would you go to him for help?"

"Yes," I say reluctantly.

"If you developed a brain tumor that you couldn't heal, would you go to him?"

"Yes."

"If Tessa were in danger, would you ask him to protect her?"

"Yes."

Dr. Rumson smiles wide. "See? The most important things in your world, and you'd trust your dad with them. All is not lost."

I smile back. And then I cry, a few tears at first, and then a river pouring down my cheeks.

Dr. Rumson scoots close and throws an arm over my shoulders.

When I'm done, Dr. Rumson removes his arm. I wipe my eyes on my sleeve and lean my head back against the couch.

"Grandma was so damn funny," I say, closing my eyes. "Did I tell you about the time she told me I could make my breasts larger by shifting around the fat in my body?"

Dr. Rumson chuckles and shakes his head. "No, but I remember when she was first losing her memory, and she brought you in for one of our talks, and she and Mary Kate got to talking about a recipe, and before Mary Kate could react, your grandma started writing the recipe on her arm. And when she was done, she tried to give it to Mary Kate. Her arm, I mean."

I laugh. "She would call me out every time I farted. Even if I were alone in my room, and she was at the other end of the house, she'd say, 'I heard that!'"

He laughs. "Remember the time she swatted Mr. Newall upside the head when his son's phone rang in the middle of my sermon? She caused more of a disturbance than the phone did."

We trade stories about Grandma all evening.

I only think about Dad twice.

Chapter Twenty-Seven

At Grandma's funeral, Dr. Rumson gives a beautiful eulogy, which we wrote together, and I speak a bit about Grandma's selflessness and generous spirit. I asked Tessa ahead of time to stand at the podium with me and hold my hand for support, and she does, even though she is hiccoughing from crying and trying to stifle it so as to not interrupt me. Halfway through my speech, I pause and look at Tessa. Her entire body shakes from the effort of keeping her emotions under control, and a wave of love for her spreads from my heart to my fingertips. "Come here," I whisper, and I fold her into a tight hug.

The whole crowd sighs as we hold one another. Normally, I would find such a pause awkward, maybe uncomfortable to watch, but it feels right today. This show of emotion is for Grandma. It feels good just to feel it, to let the world know how much she meant to us.

After the service, I find I'm at peace with Grandma's death. I don't like it, and I miss her terribly, but I've thought a lot about the circumstances under which I would want to end my life. Having dementia would probably be a deal-breaker.

I understand her decision.

Tessa comes over the next morning before school, and I get my hug and a few extra kisses.

"How are you?" she asks.

"Good," I say, and I mean it. "I'm getting there."

"Good," she says. "I have awesome news. Can you hear it?"

"I could use a little awesome," I say, and Tessa squeals.

"Someone bought our house!"

Shit. I forgot all about that. It's great news, awesome news, but I didn't even think about my reaction. I mean, do I tell Tessa how it came about? I don't want Erica to know, but at the same time, I don't want to lie.

I am not my father.

"That is awesome!" I say, hugging her tight. And then I step back. "About that. I already knew."

Tessa raises her eyebrows. "Don't tell me you bought it."

I shake my head. "No, but I know who did. I agreed to try to heal his daughter."

"You're doing it for me?" she asks.

I nod. "And me. Us."

"I won't tell Mom," she says. "And before you accuse me of lying, I'm not lying. Just omitting."

"I agree," I say. "We can come clean after you graduate. She doesn't need to know right now."

Tessa pulls out a chair and sits at the kitchen table. "Will it be dangerous?"

"Not much," I hedge as I sit across from her. "Maybe a little."

She takes my hands. "Promise me you'll stay safe. No matter what. Promise you'll come back."

I squeeze tight. "I promise."

♥

After Tessa leaves for school, Dad comes out, ready to head to the Attic as I'm packing my lunch for work. He leans back on the counter and watches me.

"What's up?" I finally ask, creeped out by his silence.

"It was you, wasn't it?"

I busy myself in the cheese drawer, trying to avoid the conversation. "Maybe."

"Erica thinks it was me."

"So tell her it wasn't you," I say, slamming the fridge door shut and stuffing a yogurt in my paper lunch sack.

Dad cracks a smile. "You could have at least let her get the house on the market," he says. "She's driving herself crazy trying to figure out how Cyrus Brooks knew her house was for sale."

"There are lists out there, of houses when they go into foreclosure," I say. "Tell her his real estate agent suggested he make an offer."

"I did."

"And?" I say.

"She's not stupid," Dad says, "and neither am I."

"He just did it to get to me, Dad," I say. "So now I'll feel obligated to help him."

"Cyrus Brooks isn't stupid, either," Dad says.

"What's your point?" I say, cranky and eager to get this over with.

Dad pulls a folded sheet of paper from his back pocket and places it on the counter. "Just don't forget the big picture." He walks past me towards the front door. I scowl behind his back and grab the paper. Dad turns around. "Oh," he says. "And nice work." He has the audacity to wink at me as he heads out the door.

I crumple the paper in my fist and hold it over the sink. The big picture...

Now that he's mentioned it, there is no big picture. I wanted to save Tessa's house, or at least keep Tessa from leaving. I want to heal. Damn it, that's really all I've been thinking about.

I open my clenched fist, pull out the piece of paper, and smooth it against the edge of the counter. It's a copy of a newspaper article from September 2001.

Lora Paradis, actress and daughter of late filmmaker Arthur Paradis, died today from injuries sustained when a car hit her last week. She was 32 years old.

A spokesman for the family confirmed that she was taken off life support: "It is with great sadness that we announce that Lora Paradis passed away this morning. Lora was more than a gifted actress and the daughter of a legend; she was a truly caring mother and wife and gentle soul. She will be terribly missed."

Paradis was married in 1995 to Cyrus Brooks, a then-struggling radio personality. In 1997, the two gave up their partying ways when daughter Olivia was born, and both became Christians. The next year, Brooks founded the Sinners Ways Church in Villa Park, now one of the largest congregations in Orange County. Paradis once said, "It's our desire to help people, to show them the right path, that has led us here. Life is about more than money, more than getting high, more than finding your next fix. With the Lord's help, your life can have meaning."

Paradis recently finished filming a biopic on Meryl Streep, and her home life with Brooks seemed charmed. They were last seen together three weeks ago handing out backpacks and supplies to schoolchildren in Santa Ana.

Daughter Olivia was also injured in the accident. Mother and daughter were walking home from an afternoon of shopping when a driver ran a red light and struck them in the crosswalk.

Olivia remains in the hospital in good condition. Doctors predict she will have no lasting physical affects from the accident.

Calls to the Brooks home have been unanswered, but Paradis' cousin, Charlotte Tanner, appeared stunned when speaking with reporters.

"She was a light, such a strong light," Tanner said. "This is an absolute tragedy."

Donations can be made in Lora's honor to the Sinners Way Church.

I stare at the paper.

Wife dies tragically, unexpectedly…and Olivia was injured back then, as well.

Just don't forget the big picture…

Pastor Brooks doesn't want to lose his daughter after losing his wife.

Pastor Brooks wants to save people from themselves.

Pastor Brooks has A LOT of money, but claims money doesn't matter.

Pastor Brooks…what? What the hell is the big picture?

Damn if I can see it.

Chapter Twenty-Eight

Kenneth and one of his chemist buddies come up with a super pill that will release nutrients to my body slowly as I heal. They also doctor a giant batch of Gatorade, giving it three times the electrolytes it normally has, and they dub it *Dwellerade*. We determine that if I take one pill and drink sixteen ounces of the Dwellerade every hour, I can heal for six hours straight without any ill effects. Honestly, I could heal a lot longer (I think), but Kate won't let me.

But I'm in charge now. If I want to heal longer, I will. But I'm also not above taking good advice.

On Tuesday, Kate, Kenneth, and I head to the Brooks' home with my backpack full of pills and four bottles of Dwellerade. I don't plan on using them, but I like to be prepared.

Kate is sitting in the passenger seat. As soon as we're on the road, she whips out her notebook. "Let's go over the plan one more time," she says.

I glance at Kenneth in my rearview mirror. He rolls his eyes with a smile, and I smile back.

"Okay," I say. "First, I explore a bit. Get a feel for things, see if there's anything that might prevent me from healing her."

Kate slaps her notebook against her thigh. "I really hate that part. I know we already agreed to it, but it's too vague. Can't you be specific about the kinds of things you'll be looking for?"

"I already told you I don't think there's anything that will prevent me from healing her. I mean, I can't conceive of anything that I can't heal, given enough time."

Kate sighs. "Fine. What's the next step?"

"Back out of her body and debrief you on my findings. That's it. Then we go back to the lab and work up a more specific plan."

Kenneth catches my eye in the mirror. "What are the chances you'll actually stick to the plan?"

I fight not to smile. "I'd say 50/50."

Kate laughs, oblivious. She believes I'll stick to the plan.

But Kenneth knows me better. He gives me a solemn nod, preparing himself for anything but Kate's grand plan.

♥

The Brooks family lives in Orange Park Acres, an equestrian community. The houses are large and the lots sprawling, many of them with stables or barns or those rings they train horses in. I know very little about horses – never had the need to study them. And I've certainly never been in a private home as large as these. I'm suddenly feeling a little out of my depth.

We cruise down a winding driveway of cobblestone and park in one of the marked spaces to the right of the main house. Who has parking spaces at their house?

Pastor Brooks strides out from behind the garage, pulling off leather gloves, as we exit my car.

"Thomas!" he says, taking my hand and pumping it enthusiastically. "Thank you for coming."

"You bought the house," I say. "Just upholding my end of the bargain."

"I'm grateful," he says. "And Dr. Kate, Dr. Kenneth. Such an honor to have you all here. Please, come on inside, and you can meet Olivia's team."

Okay. She has a team?

The house is even more intimidating on the inside – stained mahogany moldings, expensive jewel-toned rugs, heavy brocade drapes. It looks more like a museum than a home. I hope he doesn't ask us to sit because I don't want to leave a butt print on the velvet couch.

"You have a beautiful home," I say.

Pastor Brooks laughs. "I know what you're thinking: this home is way too extravagant for a man of God. And it is. But it's all my late wife's money. Her father was film director Arthur Paradis. She was used to this life. And I just haven't been able to bring myself to change anything."

"I'm sorry to hear about your wife," Kate says. "Was it recent?"

He shakes his head. "Twelve years ago now. That's the other thing that makes this situation with Olivia so hard for me. She's all I have left."

We all nod sympathetically. I know what it's like to lose a mother, for a husband to lose a wife.

We follow Pastor Brooks up a split staircase to the second floor. I marvel at the cleanliness of the carpet – for horse people, their ability to keep mud off the carpet is impressive. We head left off the stairs.

"This is Olivia's wing," he says.

She has a wing?

"This is the guest bath," he says, waving a hand at the first door on the left. "Feel free to use it at need. And this is Olivia's music studio."

Pastor Brooks opens the door opposite the bathroom, and we peer politely inside.

"She's a singer. Never could keep her quiet, especially when she was little. She would sing her way through her day."

There's a booth with a microphone in the back corner, walled off in glass. There's mixing equipment, speakers, a keyboard and a guitar. Olivia sure has some expensive hobbies. Or maybe they're so loaded that every time she got a whim to try something, Pastor Brooks built her a new room for it.

"And this," he says, "is her wrapping room. She was always so generous, giving gifts to the staff or to her friends. I can't bear to go in there – it was sort of her special place – but please. Have a look."

I open the door and peer into the pitch black. I fumble for the light switch and flip it up.

It's a laundry-sized room, narrow and deep. Dowels line the back wall, each holding a roll of gift wrap. A long counter runs the length of the room, cluttered with assorted bows and baubles. Two wrapped gifts sit undisturbed, waiting to be delivered.

Who has an entire room devoted to wrapping?

Kate and Kenneth take a quick look inside. They don't comment, but I sense they're as weirded out by the room as I am. I flip off the light and close the door. "It's a unique space," I say. "I can see why Olivia liked it."

Pastor Brooks nods. "And up here, the staff have rooms right next to hers. They are on the clock, twenty-four/seven."

We pass the staff rooms and stop at the end of the hallway, at two giant mahogany double doors. I shiver for no discernible reason.

"I made sure she was decent before you arrived," he says, opening the door wide and gesturing us inside.

I take a deep breath, and we follow him into Olivia's room.

♥

We enter a sitting room with two people chatting softly in matching wing chairs. It smells like vanilla in here, and I get a sense memory of Grandma so strong I have to fight to stay on my feet.

"Welcome," a young woman in pink scrubs says, rising and taking my hand and patting it gently. "I'm Rachel, Olivia's primary nurse."

"Hello, Rachel," I say. "Thomas Van Zandt. This is Dr. Kate Mullen, and this is Dr. Kenneth Mullen." They both shake her hand.

"And this is Dr. Park," Rachel says.

I hold out my hand to Dr. Park, a sour-looking man in his mid-forties. He looks at my hand pointedly and ignores it.

"I don't believe anything Cyrus has told us about you," he says. "Let me get that out of the way right up front."

"Thomas is the real deal," Kenneth says, stepping up next to me. "I know it sounds extraordinary – we didn't believe it ourselves, at first – but I ask you to keep an open mind."

Dr. Park ignores Kenneth and focuses on me. "You won't touch Olivia unless you prove yourself."

Pastor Brooks sighs from behind me. "Now, Henry, we've had this discussion."

"She's been poked and prodded enough, Cyrus," he says. "Her condition is well-documented."

"I agree," I say. "I'm not here to conduct tests."

Dr. Park narrows his eyes. "Then why are you here?"

"To heal her."

He stares at me. And then he shakes his head. "A little laying of the hands, is it? I don't have time for this."

"Then you can leave," Pastor Brooks says. "This is happening, whether you like it or not."

And Dr. Park stands and storms out.

"So…what's the next step?" Pastor Brooks asks me.

I blink a few times, trying to regroup. It's like I've entered an alternate reality, one with hostile doctors, desperate fathers, and gorgeous nurses. I must have fallen down the rabbit hole.

"Let's take a look at her and see how she's doing," I say, improvising. Kate gives me a nod of encouragement.

Rachel smiles at me and leads the way. We round a corner and I find myself in a bedroom fit for a queen.

A queen in a coma, anyway.

Medical equipment lines the wall at the head of the bed, a hospital bed, narrow, giving her "team" easy access to the patient. Olivia herself looks young, younger than sixteen, but it's difficult to make out her facial features with the tubes hooked up to her. Her black hair is tied into a neat bun at the very top of head, allowing her to recline without lying on a lump.

I look at Pastor Brooks. He nods at me, and I approach the left side of the bed. The vanilla scent is stronger this close to her, and I wonder if the pastor is afraid of the smell of sickness.

"Hello, Olivia," I say, taking a seat in the chair beside the bed. I scoot it up close to her, so close the arm of the chair bumps the bed. Kate and Kenneth stand behind me, notebooks and pens ready to record their observations. I try to ignore them, as though I'm doing this on my own. After all, I am doing it on my own. "I'm Thomas Van Zandt. I'm going to take a look at you, see what we can do. Rachel, do you have her vitals?"

Rachel squats down next to me with a clipboard. "Everything's normal," she says, holding the records out to me. I scan them quickly, making sure Olivia's blood pressure and heart rate, especially, are where I want them to be.

"Good," I say. Rachel moves away. I shift to one hip and fish the knife out of my pocket. "May I?" I ask the pastor.

"Do what you will," he says. Then he quickly moves out of my field of vision.

I cut my palm and take Olivia's hand in my unharmed one. Her hand is swollen and plump, probably from her hydrating IV. I slice it as gently as possible and press my wounded hand to hers. I look at my watch and note the time.

I told myself I wasn't going to heal her today – we have a plan. But maybe I can do one thing, just one little thing that will start the process.

I clot her blood and cut off nerve sensation from her wound. I make my nerve connections, dragging Protein T in my wake. When I get to the top of her spinal cord and enter the base of the medulla oblongata, the center for autonomic nervous system functions, I gasp aloud – nothing happens. I don't have awareness of her, of her body. I sense nothing.

"Thomas?" Kate asks, nerves in her voice.

"Everything's fine," I assure her.

And then I relax. Of course I'm not getting anything – nothing in her brain is functioning properly. I have to blindly heal the basics before I can get the whole picture.

I glance at my watch. It's been thirteen seconds. I take quick stock of my own body, and everything's normal.

I want to heal something that will elicit an immediate change in Olivia's circumstances.

Olivia has a tracheostomy – a hole was made in her neck so she could be hooked up to a ventilator, which is breathing for her. It's a violation, this tube, this hole where no hole should be. It's like a parasitic worm planted in the tender flesh of her neck.

I want it out.

I want her to breathe on her own.

I hook in firmly to the medulla oblongata. It's called the little brain, because it controls most of the autonomic functions like breathing, heart rate, swallowing, and even vomiting. I still can't sense anything other than my immediate surroundings, so I pause.

"Rachel?"

The nurse hurries over to the opposite side of the bed and clutches the rail. "I'm here," she says.

"Usually when I do this, I have control of the patient's brain, and I can clot the blood, control pain, the whole deal, but Olivia's brain is too damaged. I don't have that control yet," I say.

"What can I do?" she asks.

"Two things," I say. "One, I'd like to sedate her. As I heal, I'm not sure at what point she'll wake, if she'll even wake, but I don't want her frightened or in pain."

"Thomas," Kate says, but Kenneth cuts her off with a "Let him work, Kate."

Rachel nods. "And two?"

"I'm going to get her breathing. I'll eventually push the trach out and heal the wound, but I don't know how fast I'll be. There may be a mess."

Rachel turns to the cabinets on the wall. She pulls out a vial and syringe, several towels, antiseptic, and gauze pads. She fills the syringe from the vial and squeezes the contents into Olivia's IV.

"Do you want me to place the towels and stand by with the rest?" she asks.

"Here," I say, patting Olivia's upper chest. "Towels here. I'll give you some warning when the trach's coming out."

Rachel arranges the towels and hovers over us.

I take a deep breath. "Pastor Brooks? Are you doing okay?" I ask.

I can't see him. I know he was last pacing behind me, but I lost track of him in my exploration of Olivia.

He clears his throat from the sitting room. "Fine," he calls, voice strained. "I'm just…around the corner."

"Okay," I say. "Just checking in. Everything's going as expected."

"Don't let me keep you," he calls back.

I turn my attention back to Olivia. "Here goes," I whisper.

♥

I examine my own body. That is Kate's Rule #1: Assess your body, ensure adequate resources are available, before proceeding with the patient. I took stock two minutes ago, but a lot can happen in two minutes.

I'm still good. I haven't done much yet but grow a few nerves. I note the time on my watch.

Kate's Rule #2: Define each move. Ensure adequate resources prior to each step. Do not heal on a whim.

Damn. Kate's probably brooding behind me, trying to figure out how to withhold coffee for a week as punishment.

I can't define each move, because I don't have a clear picture of all the damage I have to heal. But I have some information from prior scans. Particularly, the posterior part of the medulla oblongata, which contains nerves that connect to the spinal cord, appeared pinched and distorted. I need to right this part so nerve signals from the rest of her body can communicate with the brain.

I wander around. I find dead brain cells, stretched nerves, even odd blank spots, and I heal them all. I dissolve nerves that are beyond salvage and grow new ones. I find that the PICA, a main artery branch that supplies the posterior part of the medulla, is slightly blocked, so the oxygen supply to the brain is not as high as it should be. I unblock it and glance at my watch.

Three minutes, forty-five seconds.

I inwardly cringe. It's never taken me this long to heal before, but I'm used to having instant access to all the information I need. I examine my resources, find I'm slightly dehydrated, and that I need more Protein T.

I momentarily waiver. Do I stop and take some Dwellerade, or do I continue on? I'm close, so close. A few more nerve cells, then I can move on to the tracheostomy.

I hear Tessa whispering in my head. *"Promise you'll come back."*

I keep my promises.

I sit up straight and swipe my forehead with my free hand. "Rachel, could you open up my backpack and take out a bottle of Dwell...of, uh, Gatorade, please?"

The backpack is still on my back. Rachel unzips it, retrieves a bottle, and zips it back up. She twists off the cap and hands it to me over my shoulder.

"Thanks," I say, chugging half the bottle. I hand it back to her, and she places it on the nightstand next to me, then resumes her position.

"Anything else?" she asks.

I shake my head. "I've got the medulla fixed, almost. Another minute or so, then I'll push the trach out."

"She's been on it for six months," Rachel says, her brow creased. "Shouldn't we wean her off of it?"

"There's no need," I say. "I'll make sure her respiratory muscles are up to the task before I continue."

I dismiss her concern and bend forward. And then Tessa butts in again: *"A little self-doubt isn't a bad thing...you're not God, Thomas..."*

I grit my teeth. Why am I second-guessing myself now?

I sit back up. "You know, you're right, I mean, you never know...if we wanted to be prepared for the worst-case scenario, what do you need?"

Rachel looks me in the eye. "You mean if she doesn't start breathing on her own?"

I nod.

"I can keep her breathing for a bit, but we need Dr. Park. He can intubate her again if necessary."

Great. The wonderful Dr. Park. Just who I need hovering over me.

"Or we can do it," Kenneth says.

"Kenneth we're not legally supposed to—"

Kate breaks off, and I imagine Kenneth squeezing her elbow to shut her up.

"Let me get to that point, and then we can call him in," I say. "No need to waste his precious time."

Rachel cracks a small smile.

I bend back over Olivia and continue my work.

Two minutes and fifteen seconds later, I'm still working. The damage is never-ending.

I flood a few more cells with Protein T and re-grow them.

Rachel gasps.

"What?" I ask, opening my eyes and focusing on her.

"Her eyes!" she says. "Her eyes moved!"

Yippee. Eye movement. That's one for the record books.

I continue.

I make one final circuit through the medulla until I'm completely satisfied. Then I move down to Olivia's chest.

Her muscles are slightly atrophied. Nothing obvious, nothing physically deforming, but they've clearly gone flabby from disuse. I go back to Rule #2. I define my move: re-build the muscles. I assess my resources: I don't need Protein T, normally, but I still don't have control of Olivia's body, so I can't heal it using my own abilities – I need Protein T. Fine. I generate some more and hurry it along to Olivia's chest.

I'm starting to tire. Nothing unmanageable or debilitating, but I can feel it. I grab the Dwellerade bottle and finish it off.

"You okay, Thomas?" Rachel asks.

"Fine. Working on her chest."

I bulk up her muscles. Then I examine her lungs. She has a slight case of pneumonia, and I detect traces of antibiotics in her system, but they haven't had a chance to work yet. So I attack the pneumonia. I clear the lungs. And I head up to her throat.

She has significant damage to her throat from the tracheostomy – most long-term ventilator patients do, so it's not too troublesome. But I'm glad Olivia doesn't have to heal the damage on her own. It would be painful.

I smooth out the throat, heal sores and other damage, kill any bacteria I find. Then I sigh.

"Okay," I say. "She's ready. I'm pushing the trach out now."

"What about Dr. Park?" Rachel says, but I barely hear her. She's the wind rustling through the trees. She's a distant birdcall. She's the buzz of a fly beating against a window.

I contract the flesh in Olivia's neck, effectively pushing the trach out. I heal the wound as I go, and suddenly I'm out of Protein T, and instinctively I try to heal the flesh like I'd heal myself.

But it doesn't work.

The trach slips out, and a fountain of blood shoots from the wound and splatters my cheek.

"Thomas!" Rachel cries, pressing gauze to the opening in Olivia's throat. "Heal it! She'll choke on her own blood!"

I fumble around in the dark of Olivia's neck, trying to heal it. Goddamnit, why won't it work?

And then I remember: Olivia is not me. And I am not God.

♥

I finally muster the good sense to grab my Protein T and get it to the site of the injury. It takes me a good fifteen seconds, and Rachel is panicked, screaming, Kate is yelling in my ear about a plan, Kenneth is trying to shush his wife, while I try to keep my wits about me and do what I came to do.

I heal the wound.

I clear all the blood.

I destroy bacteria.

I ensure her muscles are working, the medulla firing.

I finally lean over Olivia and breathe into her mouth. She needs a kick-start.

And suddenly she's breathing on her own.

♥

I back out of her body, unhooking and repairing as I go. I heal the wounds in our hands and flop back in the chair.

"Holy Christ," I whisper, breathing heavily. I glance at Rachel, who's still wide-eyed and bent over Olivia, holding blood-soaked gauze to her neck.

I gently put my hand on Rachel's shoulder. She jumps.

"It's okay," I say, patting her softly. "She's healed. You can move away now."

Her eyes fly to my face. "You're sure?"

I nod. "Yes. She's fine. She's breathing."

Rachel turns back to Olivia. Rachel is frozen, searching for signs of life from her patient. When she's calm enough to feel Olivia's chest move, she gasps and slowly moves her blood-stained hands away.

"She's breathing," she whispers.

She runs to the trashcan, throws the gauze in, and washes her hands in the sink at the far end of the room. But her eyes are on Olivia the whole time.

She grabs more gauze and towels and begins to clean up the blood on Olivia's throat and face.

"There's no hole," she whispers to herself. "She's actually breathing!"

I watch the delicate way she cares for Olivia. Rachel takes her vitals and then pulls Olivia's eyelids up and flashes a penlight in them.

"Her pupils! They contracted!"

I nod. I'm still too breathless to speak.

"Thomas!" I look up and Rachel is kneeling beside me. "How are you feeling?"

I clear my throat. "I'm fine."

She smiles wide. "That was...I've never...I can't believe it. Let me clean you up."

Kate and Kenneth have disappeared, and I can hear them speaking with Cyrus in the sitting room. I try to rise, but Rachel pushes me gently back down. "Rest. Your face...let me clean you up."

I hold my chin out to her and she carefully cleans my face.

"This shirt may be a goner," she says. "We should get you some scrubs."

"And a brain!" Kate yells from the other room.

I laugh. "I wasn't planning on doing this or I would have been more prepared. I'm sorry."

"Sorry?" she says, standing. "What on earth are you sorry for?"

"Well," I say, following suit, "that last bit, with the trach...I got a little carried away."

Rachel smiles. "You can get carried away with me any time."

Oh boy.

As I gape at her, Kate and Kenneth come back in and Pastor Brooks pokes his head around the corner from the sitting room. "Is everything..."

"Oh, Cyrus!" Rachel says, running to him and taking his arm. "Come look. I still have to change her bedding, and her hair needs a little wash, but can you stand it, a little blood? She's breathing!"

Pastor Brooks stiffens at the mention of blood, but lets Rachel lead him to Olivia's side.

He falls to his knees beside the bed and gropes for Olivia's hand. He squeezes it tight and lays his cheek on the railing, just looking at her.

"Baby," he whispers.

I start to back away. His show of emotion seems a private thing, too raw for human consumption. My own eyes tear in response as I watch the pastor pray and listen to his daughter breathe.

And then he sits up suddenly, and with a quick swipe of his eyes, heaves himself to his feet.

"Thomas," he says.

I stop a few feet from the door.

"Thank you."

I smile. "It's a small thing, Pastor Brooks, I mean…she still has a long way to go."

"I understand," he says. "But she's still in there, isn't she? This is proof, that now she's breathing on her own."

I don't know what to say to that.

We stare at each other, and I'm the first to avert my eyes.

"I don't know. I wouldn't presume to know," I say. I steal a glance at him and he's still staring at me. "We won't know," I say, "I mean, that's not my area of expertise."

"What might your Dr. Rumson say?"

Gooseflesh covers my arms as he says my dear friend's name. I still don't like the fact that the pastor knows things about me I've never told him.

"He believes the soul stays with the body until death," I say. "And so do you, or you would have let Olivia pass months ago. I have no proof otherwise."

"But you doubt," he says. "Doubting Thomas."

"If I doubted," I say, "why would I waste my time here?"

"You doubt, and yet you hope. You are a sixteen-year-old man with the sensibilities of a child. You have more belief in yourself than you do in God."

"Pastor Brooks," Kate chides.

I feel the blood heat my cheeks. "You're wrong. I believe in myself, yes, but my abilities come from God. He made this possible."

"True," he says, "but I don't think you really believe that."

"Why do you stand there and insult me?" I say. "I come in here, work absolute fucking magic on your daughter, and you insult my belief in God? You tarnish it, you spit on it, as though it's just some trifling excuse to me?"

Pastor Brooks holds his hands up as though warding me off. "You misunderstand me," he says. "I meant no insult. I'm trying to get you to see."

"See what?"

"Whatever's in your heart."

It's on the tip of my tongue to say, "Fuck you," but I've already let my anger get the best of me.

"Let's go," I say. I turn my back on him and walk out.

Chapter Twenty-Nine

I push through the door of the Planarian Institute and go straight to my desk. I know we're about to have a come-to-Jesus talk, and it's the last thing I'm in the mood for.

Kate heads straight to the coffee bar and starts a pot brewing. Kenneth sits in the lobby chair, scribbling in his notebook.

I walk back out to them.

"Do you actually work around here?" I growl. "Or do you just drink coffee?"

She raises an eyebrow at me. "Someone's a little testy this morning."

Morning? I feel like it's dinnertime. I glance at my watch and sigh. It's only 10:15. We were honored guests at the Brooks estate for only an hour.

"Sorry," I say, scrubbing a hand through my hair. My fingers catch on something tacky, something beginning to crust, and when I look at my hand, it's covered in blood.

Kate glares at me. "In the shower. Now. We can't have blood all over the lab." I glare back. I pour myself some coffee with my non-bloody hand, and saunter off to the locker room to wash off Olivia's blood.

♥

So we sit in Kenneth's office, my hair dripping, and I make them wait for it. I busy myself with meaningless tasks – opening a Word document, sending an email to myself. I know I'm being a jerk, but I can't help it – I'm in a jerky kind of mood.

"So you healed her," Kate finally says, her lips a thin white line.

"Yes and no," I say, "but we'll get to that in a minute. The thing is, do you two believe in God?"

"Yes, absolutely," Kate says, while Kenneth says, "We do."

I let out the breath I'd been holding. Until that moment, I didn't realize how much it meant to me that they shared my beliefs.

"Great. Okay. So, God gives each of us certain abilities, and —"

"I don't believe that," Kenneth says.

Kate and I look at him. "You don't?" I ask.

"No. Sure, we get the genetic basics, but abilities are things developed, not bestowed."

"But I was born with the ability to heal my own body," I say.

"And you developed it," he says. "If you'd never chosen to exercise and practice it, you wouldn't be able to do what you do."

"I'll buy that," I say, "but the basics *were* given to me. You can't heal, no matter how much you practice."

He nods his head at me in agreement.

"So what I'm wondering is, how much is God really involved in everything we can do? I mean, I can heal. Theoretically, if the flesh is alive, I can bring anyone back to a walking, talking, thinking state. Is God involved?"

"Sometimes," Kate says. "Miracles do happen. And the flesh only stays alive because the soul is present."

"You both believe that?"

"Yes," they both say, nodding.

"Okay, so can I create life?"

"Do you mean bring someone back from the dead?" Kenneth asks.

"That's one possibility," I say. "I mean, I think I could grow a baby, either inside of me, or in someone else, or hell, even in a petri dish. But if I did, how does the soul get infused?"

Kate and Kenneth exchange a worried glance. "Thomas, is this something you're considering doing?" Kate asks.

"No," I say. "I mean, I don't know, if it ever came up…no. Really, no. But my point is, I think I could do it. Which means maybe we don't really have a soul at all."

"Because you are not God," Kenneth says.

"Exactly!" I say. "I know that! But the things I can do…I feel like I'm straddling that line, between the possible and the impossible. And if I can actually do the impossible, well, what does that mean? What are the implications?"

Kate sits back and sips her coffee. "Thomas, doctors have always felt this way, even back when they were only healers crushing herbs into tea. We're fighting death, and that's not the purview of man but of God. So when we win, what do we feel? That we've beaten him, God, in a way. We feel invincible. We grow arrogant. You're not the first to feel this way."

The air goes out of me and I sag. "You think I'm displaying arrogance." Will my folly never end?

"I just think your own abilities are causing you to question your faith," Kate says.

"You're right," I say. "I've explored every part of the human body, several bodies, and I've never felt the soul. It bothers me. I mean, if it's in there, don't you think I would have run into it by now?"

Kenneth smiles. "I've cut up many more bodies than you, and I've never seen a soul, either. Doesn't mean it's not there. Why do you believe in God at all?"

"Intelligent design," I say automatically, and Kenneth raises an eyebrow at me.

"That's all?"

I study my fingernails. "And I have had a few moments, where I was praying or asked for strength, that I felt...something."

I sneak a glance at them and they are both staring at me sympathetically.

"Fine. And if I don't believe in God, my mother's gone. Dust. Fish food. Fertilizer for all the pretty daffodils."

"Oh, Thomas," Kate says, squeezing my arm.

I hang my head and fight not to cry.

I think Kenneth senses my impending tears. He changes the subject. "So, you healed Olivia."

"A little," I say. "The medulla oblongata. Autonomic systems are functioning. She's breathing on her own, obviously."

"I'm so mad at you I want to spit," Kate says. "And I'm so in awe of you I want to hug you and never let go. I don't think I really believed it until I saw the trach come out. I mean, I did, but I didn't. It's just so incredible."

"So, you're really mad at me?" I ask.

"Yes," she says. "What if something had gone wrong? Actually, something did go wrong with the trach. What was it?"

I blow out a loud breath. "I ran out of Protein T. My first instinct was to heal her like I heal myself, but I didn't have the connection with her yet to do that. So it took me a few seconds to remember and call up more of the protein."

"You idiot," Kate says affectionately. "You forgot Rule #1. And Rule #2."

"I used them earlier," I say. "But when it came time to do the trach, I guess I got a little excited."

"Exactly why you need a plan," she says.

"Never mind the plan," Kenneth says. "You were fucking brilliant!"

"Thanks, Kenneth," I say.

"But the plan is going to keep him safe," Kate insists.

"I know," he says, "and we'll have a plan each time, but I knew the plan was a goner before we even got there."

"What?" she shrieks. "You guys planned something else without me?"

"Calm down," he says. "I'm a guy. Thomas is a guy. We're not planners. And this stuff...I think a lot of it is instinct. Thomas needs to do what he feels he should do in the moment. Shit's gonna come up that you just can't plan for."

Kate huffs a breath and sits silently, sulking.

"Start over," Kenneth says. "We need to document the entire thing. Go back to the beginning. Then we need to take your vitals and see what effect today's impromptu session had on your body."

So I begin at the beginning, both of them tapping away on their laptops as they transcribe my description of events.

Thinking about Olivia and healing her today is infinitely better than thinking about how I might not really believe in God.

Chapter Thirty

After work I drive straight to Tessa's. I promised her I'd come back.

She throws herself at me and climbs me like a koala on a tree, wrapping her legs around my waist.

"You healed her, didn't you?" she says into my neck.

I squeeze her tight. "Only a little. Nothing dangerous."

She clings for a couple of minutes then slides down my body.

"Your dad's here. He's gonna want to hear all about it."

"Later," I say, taking her hand and leading her out the front door. "Later."

♥

I drag Tessa to my lair and lock the door. I pull her shirt over her head and fumble with the zipper on her jeans.

"What are you doing?" she murmurs.

I ignore the question and get her naked and sprawled on my bed. I crawl over her body and explore every inch. Tessa sighs, she squeals, she giggles, she moans.

An hour later, I lift my head and lie down beside her. She strokes my back and faces me.

"What's gotten into you?"

"I just needed to remember," I say.

"Remember what?"

"Why I believe in God."

Tessa laughs and punches my arm. "You're such a guy."

I smile. "I'm serious. I feel like I'm being tested."

"How?"

"My faith. Olivia, this girl I healed, she's brain dead. Basically, dead. If she weren't hooked up to a ventilator, she would have passed months ago."

"How do you know that?" Tessa asks.

I give her a look.

"No, seriously, Thomas, how do you know that? Miracles happen. People come back from comas. People declared brain dead wake up. It happens."

"Just because it has happened," I say, "doesn't mean it happens regularly. She was a goner, Tessa."

"And what? You got her to wake up so you think that's proof there's no God?"

"No. I only got her breathing her own, but that really doesn't matter. I mean, I think I can do even more, like create a whole person from scratch. But if I managed to do it, what about God?"

"Why do you assume your abilities are all about you?" Tessa asks. "Maybe God is with you, helping even, while you heal."

I shake my head. "I've never felt him. Well, maybe I felt something when I was about to heal Grandma, but that could have been indigestion."

Tessa smiles. "What did you feel?"

"A strength," I whisper. "As though God Himself blew His life's breath into my lungs."

Tessa laughs. "And you want to dismiss that as indigestion?"

I laugh, too. "Maybe I'm remembering it wrong," I say.

"You don't remember anything wrong," she reminds me. "Why are you fighting this? Millions of people around the world would give their life to feel God's breath for one moment. Take His help and be grateful."

I stare at Tessa.

I remember when I was contemplating my choice of labs, and I chose Kate and Kenneth because I believed they have the perfect partner, the perfect sounding board, in each other. And my first thought was that I didn't have that with Tessa.

I'm an ass.

This beautiful person just gave me every bit of herself, body and soul, without reservation. She lets me vent, lets me question, and is the perfect counterpoint of reason to my unreasonable mind.

How could I ever have doubted it?

Tessa is my perfect match.

I just have to make sure I'm hers.

Chapter Thirty-One

I get an email from Pastor Brooks late that night, even though I've never given him my address.

Thomas,

Thank you. From the bottom of my heart, thank you.

Indulge me, please, just a moment more.

My wife Lora and I started the Sinners Way Church with no intention of leading it. Yes, we had become Christians, but I was far from a religious scholar. We hired a trained minister to oversee the budding congregation, and I figured I would be a counselor. Who better to help people lead a clean life than one who'd wallowed in the mud and found his way into the bath of God?

But the minister we hired adhered to a very loose interpretation of the Scriptures. You use drugs? God loves you anyway. You cheated on your spouse? God understands that earthly bodies may be tempted. You had an abortion at sixteen? Pray for forgiveness, and God will understand.

He gave human beings an excuse for any behavior.

I instinctively knew this to be folly.

Give human beings an excuse for their sins, and they will latch onto it like a dog to a bone.

There are no excuses.

Now that's not to say a person can't repent and make amends. But the person must be sincere, determined, and unwavering. True repentance takes time. Sometimes a lifetime.

I am still at it.

So I went to seminary school, and I studied, and I watched how the people of my congregation behaved. And when I took over the ministry at the church, and I started to preach about sin as a hole you fall into and cannot climb out of rather than sin as a human right, do you know what happened?

People ran.

As far and as fast as they could.

It took me years to refine my message, to redefine the way people think about their relationship with God.

I thought I'd learned the proper way to communicate that, but it seems I fell back on my old habits today. With you.

I do have one gift, a small thing, that has helped me tremendously with the church: I can see when a person's close to sinning. I feel it, I sense it. Then I try to avert it. I've dedicated my life to doing this.

You are a good person on the verge of greatness. But remember, too, that Hitler was great. Evil to the core, sinning with every breath he took...but great.

Thomas, when I think about what you accomplished with Olivia, my faith is bolstered. Just as it is when I see a fireman run into a burning building, or see a teacher teach a child to read, or watch Kobe Bryant defy gravity and slam dunk a shot. Human beings living and breathing and excelling and testing their limits – it's all part of God's glorious plan. We are meant to slam against the barriers and tumble them to the ground.

Where is the end point? What is truly impossible?

Only God can answer that. Because us human beings, we constantly step up to that impossible barrier and smash it down. It's what God means for us to do.

I know you need time. If and when you feel you can come back for Olivia, that you're ready to once again face the barrier, we will be here waiting. I am at your disposal.

Sincerely yours,

Cyrus

♥

Even though I can recite the email by heart, I print it out, fold it into a tightly packed two-inch square and put it under my pillow.

At three AM, I peel the covers off, hop out of bed, and open my laptop.

I open a reply message to Cyrus.

I'll be there at 10.

Then I lay my head back down and fall asleep.

Chapter Thirty-Two

I wake before the sun's up and stumble to the kitchen to make coffee. Dad's already there, waiting for the pot to brew.

"Hey," he says.

"Hey."

He scrubs a hand across his face. "Thanksgiving's coming up. Is it okay with you if Erica and her family come here?"

I raise an eyebrow at him. "You're gonna cook a turkey?"

He smiles. "No, I thought the lady of the house should do that."

"The lady of the house?"

We stare at each other, and I'm the one who cracks first. "When?"

"They have until December fifth to move, but it'll probably happen gradually. We're gonna try to move a few things every night."

My heart starts thumping like a bass drum.

"We're not sure...well, let me just lay it all out there, what we're thinking," Dad says.

"That'll be refreshing," I say.

Dad just shakes his head. "Ideally, Tessa would be out of high school, and Erica and I would be married, before taking this step. We realize that's the ideal."

"But?"

"But it's gonna take time. Erica's divorce has to be finalized, and now that Ron's flown the coop, who knows how long that will take to sort out. We don't want to wait."

"Okay," I say.

"As for you two, we want to do the right thing, but we're not sure what that is. We're afraid we're going to make your relationship with Tessa a whole lot harder."

"How's that?"

"Thomas, living with someone, it's just completely different. It's stressful. It will put a lot of pressure on you two."

"We can handle it," I say, wondering if we can.

"I hope so, I truly do, because I think you're great together. But beyond that, we're not even sure how to work out the logistics. We've decided you will have separate bedrooms, but you and I both know this isn't something we can enforce. If you sneak into Tessa's room, I'm not going in there to drag you out. I can't forbid you to have sex."

"We're not having sex," I say. *Yet.* But Dad ignores me.

"Now that you're making money, I even thought...I don't know if I should even mention this."

"Mention what?"

"Are you still planning on marrying Tessa?"

I squint my eyes at him, wondering where he's going with this. "Yes."

"And she wants to marry you, too? You've talked about it?"

I squint harder. "Yes."

"Well…maybe there's no reason you have to wait."

My jaw hits the floor.

Did Dad just suggest that Tessa and I get married?

The coffee pot beeps, and Dad stands and pours us both a cup. He hands one to me.

"Think about it," he says. And he walks back to his bedroom.

♥

Holy frickin' Mary mother of all that is freaking holy.

What the hell has gotten into my dad?

No sane parent would suggest this. No sane parent would allow it. And to actually encourage it?

"Mrs. Tessa Van Zandt," I say out loud, testing the words on my tongue.

They sound ridiculous, and they sound perfectly right.

But we're sixteen. Tessa isn't even halfway through her junior year of high school. I don't even have my diploma (which reminds me – I need to sign up for my GED before I'm labeled a high school dropout). We have no home, no tried-and-true source of steady income.

Why would my father suggest this?

I need to really think about that, because he always has an agenda.

One, it's possible he doesn't want me to sin by sleeping with Tessa before we're married.

But he thought we were already sleeping together, and he doesn't even like God, so I doubt he cares whether or not I sin.

Two, he wants a good excuse as to why he allowed his son's girlfriend to move in with us.

Maybe. But he doesn't really care what people think.

Three, maybe that was Erica's condition for moving in with us. She would be much more concerned about "how things look" and Tessa's sinning than Dad would. But I highly doubt she'd want us to get married *now*, while we're still teenagers.

I'll just ask Erica myself.

Four…what could four be?

I am an experiment. Therefore it stands to reason that this is another element of that experiment. So there's something Dad's testing, or some outcome he wants. What is the outcome of marriage?

A baby.

But no, I mean, Tessa's in high school! Dad wouldn't set her up to be a teen mom, would he? This very thing was done to him, he was forced to produce a child, and he's always told me how much of a violation it was. He wouldn't do that to someone else, let alone his son…would he?

I don't know. I don't know what goes on in his head.

But whatever it is he wants, I vow with the last beat of my heart not to give it to him.

Chapter Thirty-Three

I develop an annoying headache as I make my way to Olivia's house with Kenneth. Nothing's wrong with me, as far as I can tell, so it must be stress-induced. I dilate the veins in my forehead and will the headache away.

I get several texts as I drive, but I ignore them. I can't text back while I'm driving anyway. Kenneth asks me if I want him to check my phone, but I tell him it can wait.

As I pull into a parking space, Rachel rushes out the front door and over to my car.

"Thomas!" she yells, pulling open my door. "It's Olivia. She's in trouble."

We rush to the house. "What's going on?" I ask as I run.

"Her heart rate's been slowing over the last few hours. She," and Rachel stops talking to catch her breath as we run up the stairs. "She's gonna crash. Her blood pressure is insanely low."

We hit the landing and rush down the hall to Olivia's room.

Dr. Park is leaning over her, Cyrus pacing by the window.

"What's up?" I ask Dr. Park, taking position on the opposite side of the bed.

His face goes from frown to scowl when he sees me, but he answers. "Her blood pressure is dangerously low. And her pupils have stopped dilating. This would indicate—"

"Pressure in the brain," I say, taking my knife out of my pocket. I cut my palm open, slash open Olivia's palm, and smoosh our hands together.

"What are you doing?" Dr. Park bellows. "That's not sterile! You need—"

"Shut up for a minute," I say. I'm already making my nerve connections, producing Protein T, and racing up to Olivia's brain. "If you'd been here yesterday, you'd know how this works."

"You can't—"

"He can, Henry, and he is. Shut up and leave the man alone," Cyrus says before moving around the corner to the sitting room.

Dr. Park shoots daggers at me, but I ignore him.

I find the problem immediately.

Since I opened up the PICA, blood is moving normally into Olivia's brain from the rest of her body. But since the rest of her brain is full of damaged arteries, they can't handle the flow. Blood is backing up into her brainstem, and it's starting to undo some of the work I did yesterday.

I want to dive in and work, but I force myself to pause.

"Rachel?"

She doesn't answer.

"She's not here," Dr. Park says.

Then Rachel bursts into the room. "I've got it," she says, and I glance at her, and she's holding my backpack. I smile. "Thought you might need it."

"Thanks," I say. "A bottle of Gatorade and one pill, please."

She hands me the items, and I down the pill and swig the whole bottle of Dwellerade.

"You're taking drugs?" Dr. Park shrieks.

"It's a vitamin, Henry," I say. "Chill out."

And I set to work.

♥

We get to the Planarian Institute around four in the afternoon, and I'm beat. Physically I feel fine – the pills did their job – but mentally I feel like I've been running uphill for hours.

"Hey," Kate says to us. She gives Kenneth a peck on the cheek. "How'd it go?"

"Fantastic," Kenneth says.

"I healed all the arteries and veins in her head," I say. "The blood's a-flowin'."

"What have you been up to?" Kenneth asks.

Kate pulls out a stool and props her butt on it. "I've been brainstorming ways to keep you awake."

"Well, something's working," I say. "I've only slept three or four hours since I healed Olivia yesterday."

"That's not a good thing," Kate says. "You have to sleep, Thomas."

"Did the pills keep you up?" Kenneth asks.

"No, I just couldn't sleep. And I didn't take any pills yesterday. Only today."

"It can't be the Dwellerade," he says. "There aren't any stimulants in it."

"Maybe I'm just getting better at this," I say.

"Maybe," Kenneth says. "Or maybe you're gonna sleep another thirty hours."

"How long did you heal today?" Kate asks.

"About five hours, give or take."

"Any weight loss?"

"Nope. The pills and the Dwellerade worked. I'm the same today as I was yesterday."

Kate and Kenneth exchange a glance.

"We should have had you come in this morning and run tests. We really should have your baseline every time you heal."

"You have my records from yesterday. I know what my baseline is, and I know that it's the same as yesterday," I say.

"Humor us," she says. "We're scientists. We have to test."

I smile. "Fine. Let's run the stuff now, and I'll make sure I come in before I heal."

"Debrief first," Kate says. "I wouldn't want you to forget anything."

I laugh at that.

I go over my session with Olivia, and then we take my weight, my temperature, my blood pressure, and everything else they deem important.

My stomach growls loudly as they finish inputting data into their laptops.

"That's your signal," Kate says, patting my back. "Off to dinner with you. Be here bright and early before you go back to see Olivia. We're gonna do this all over again."

"Aye, aye, Captain," I say with a salute.

"Unless, of course, you're asleep."

I sigh. "That's a distinct possibility."

I get home to an empty house and raid the fridge. Last night's frozen lasagna doesn't stand a chance.

I text Tessa, but I know she has an English project she's doing with a couple of friends. I wish her good night and tell her I'll see her after work tomorrow.

I am sleepy, but I also feel like I have the strength to fight it. I've never felt that before. Usually when I'm tired, my body just shuts down. That's it. End of story.

But tonight, I can fight it.

I lie down on my bed and prop my hands beneath my head. I'll just lie here awake as long I can.

I study the ceiling. It's covered in plaster, over fifty years old now, cracking in several places. The largest crack makes the ceiling look like it's grinning at me.

It gives me an idea for a sculpture.

I get up and grab a chunk of clay from my studio in the garage. I bring it back to bed with me, prop my head on some pillows, and mold while I think.

I have averted the biggest disaster in my life – Tessa going. I sigh in relief just thinking about it. But the consequence of Tessa not going is that Tessa is now coming. Here. To live with us.

We'll have to share a bathroom. We have a third bathroom off the kitchen, but it doesn't have a shower or tub. So we'll both be showering in my bathroom. Sharing the same intimate space.

I'm a mess in the bathroom. Not that I keep it messy, but I'm messy in my cleanup. I don't know about you, but I cannot brush my teeth without toothpaste dribbling down my chin. When I shave in the sink, all the little hairs go everywhere and I have to rinse the entire counter to remove them. And who knows what the toilet looks like after I use it – I've never paid attention before. Gah – I need to buy some air freshener or something.

And sleeping together – I mean, actually sleeping – we've done that several times now, so I guess I don't have to worry about it. I don't snore, so that's good. I probably fart in my sleep, but everyone does, so no big deal. And Tessa could fart and stink up the entire house and I wouldn't care. She has actually, a few times that I've noticed, and we just laugh about it. Growing up with three brothers has made her immune to embarrassment where bodily functions are concerned.

And then there's the real sleeping together. Sex.

Okay, so even though I'm inexperienced, I'm not as uninformed as I may have come across. I'm a guy. I've read the respected works (and a lot of the un-respected works), I've watched…stuff. I've watched a lot of stuff, actually. It's just that it's different doing it for real, with a live person. In my head, I can be a god, and my partner can respond like I'm a god, but in reality, every woman is different. Every woman's body is different. I might be a sex god with woman A, and still flop mightily doing the same stuff with Tessa.

Ugh, why am I even worrying about this? Tessa has the same zero experience I do.

But I want to be her perfect partner.

I smoosh the clay between my palms.

To be her perfect partner, I have to be what Tessa needs. I can sit here and think all day about what I should do, but it comes down to one thing – what does Tessa need? What does Tessa want?

I think about our make-out session two days ago, and I cringe.

That was all about me.

I didn't even ask her what she wanted, if she wanted anything. I didn't ask her if she enjoyed it.

I tear the clay into two pieces and knead them, one in each fist.

Why is Tessa even with me? I'm a self-absorbed, arrogant cretin.

God, what did I do to deserve her?

I fall asleep, my fingernails dug tight into the clay, without thinking of a single answer.

Chapter Thirty-Four

At six my alarm clock goes off, and I flop my arm to the nightstand to turn it off.

Hardened clay crashes into the clock with a thud.

I sit up and rub my forearm across my eyes. I peel a few large chunks of clay from my fingers, but the rest needs to come off in the shower.

I check the date on the clock to make sure I didn't sleep the week away. I only slept ten hours. Shazam.

Knowing I got a decent – and totally normal – night's sleep gives me a boost. I get out of bed whistling.

Kenneth runs my tests himself this morning, since Kate's checking on a patient at the hospital. I think they've probably agreed that Kenneth is better in a crisis and more comfortable with my on-the-fly healing. By ten, I'm hooked up to Olivia and starting more repairs.

Kenneth sits silently in a chair beside me. Dr. Park enters and moves a chair to the opposite side of Olivia's bed and takes a seat.

"Do you mind if I watch?" he asks.

I glance at him briefly then re-focus on Olivia. "Not much to see," I say.

"Perhaps you could…talk me through what you're doing?"

I stop working and stare at him.

He gives me a small smile. "I admit," he says, "I'm curious."

"Is that your idea of an apology?" I say.

"Can you blame me? I'm a man of science."

"So am I."

Dr. Park sighs and hangs his head. "I'm sorry for the way I acted," he says. "Not for the way I felt, because I feel I had good cause, but I could have handled it differently."

"And now you see the things I can do and you want to learn more," I say. "I get it. It's a golden opportunity for you."

He nods once in acknowledgment.

"Fine, but I think you're going to be disappointed. I don't know that anything I'm doing will translate to something you can do."

"You've put me in my place," he says softly. "You can do things I never will be able to do. Got it."

And then, of course, I feel like an ass. Here am I, arrogant again.

I glance at Kenneth, who has an amused smile on his lips. "Shit," I say. "I didn't mean it like that. I only meant…forget it. I'll keep a narrative going. Stop me if you have anything to add."

Dr. Park grins. "So I may have something to add?" he says.

"Miracles happen," I say, grinning back at him, and I close my eyes and zoom deep into Olivia's brain.

♥

"I start on my own body," I say. "I have limited resources, and I have to manage them. I already took a vitamin pill, which is simplifying things, it's more of a super-nutrient, calorie-boost type thing, which keeps me fueled. Dehydration is always an issue so I keep a bottle of Gatorade nearby, but I'll drink it as I go. Right now, everything's tip-top.

"To grow or repair the nerve or brain cells, I need a protein that I manufacture. I produce it in my brain then move it into Olivia's body. Doing that now. I only produce what I need or less – extra protein floating around could activate cells we don't want activated, so I can't leave any of it unused in Olivia's body."

Dr. Park clears his throat and I pause. "How do you move the protein in the body?" he asks.

"I don't really know," I admit. "I just have perfect control of my entire body and everything in it. And once I'm hooked up to a patient's brain stem, I have control of their body as well. Finding the answer to that is key, I know. It's on my list."

Dr. Park nods.

"So I've got Olivia to a pretty good place. I've healed the medulla oblongata and associated structures, as you know, since she's now breathing and responding to basic stimuli. I've got all the veins and arteries cleared and repaired. Blood flow and oxygen levels are normal. The two big areas I have left are the cerebral cortex – the gray matter – and the reticular activating system."

"The RAS?" Dr. Park says. "I thought you healed the brain stem yesterday."

"I healed all of it except the RAS. Since the damage there is responsible for Olivia still being in a coma, we wanted to save it for last. We don't want Olivia awake and severely impaired. If she wakes, I mean, when...we want everything functioning as well as possible."

"How bad is the RAS?" he asks.

"Bad enough that healing the gray matter won't bring her out of the coma, we don't think," I say.

"We?" he asks.

"Me and both Drs. Mullen," I say. "They're the neurological experts. We've consulted extensively before I agreed to come here."

Dr. Park nods his head at Kenneth, who nods back.

"So that's what I'm tackling today – the gray matter. It's going to be tricky because these nerve connections are important to Olivia's personality and to her memory. I want Olivia to come back as close to the person she was as possible."

Dr. Park looks away, and I get a funny feeling in my stomach.

"What?" I ask him.

"Nothing," he says, forcing a smile and bringing his eyes back to me. "It's just a lot to take in, that you can do this. That's what we all want, of course. Olivia back to us, just as she was."

I go back to work and my running monologue.

I try to ignore the growing pit in my gut.

Chapter Thirty-Five

Dad and Erica are unloading boxes from her car when I pull up to the house.

"Can I help?" I ask.

Dad thrusts a box of books into my arms, and Erica swats him on the shoulder. "You could have given him the pillows."

Dad laughs. "He's got the youngest, strongest arms here. He can carry the books."

I laugh and head inside.

Tessa is in the spare bedroom, looking around with her hands on her hips.

I set the box down quietly and jump on her from behind, squeezing tight.

She squeals. "You scared me!"

I laugh and kiss her. "Eyeing your new digs?"

She giggles nervously. "Yeah."

"What's wrong?" I ask her.

"Oh, it's stupid," she says, waving a hand in the air. "I'm being silly."

"What?"

"Well, your grandma passed away in here."

I put an arm over her shoulder and nod.

"I thought…when I came in here, just now, I got the chills."

"It wouldn't surprise me if she's still here," I say.

Tessa grimaces. "Really? You believe in that?"

"I have no idea," I say. "But sometimes, I get feelings about my mom. Like, suddenly I'll think of her, when I was thinking about something else entirely. Or I'll have a dream about her that is crystal clear. Maybe it is her."

Tessa shudders. "I don't know if I can sleep in here."

"You liked my grandma, right?" I ask.

"I loved your grandma," Tessa says, and her eyes turn glassy.

"Well then, there's nothing to fear. Even if she is here, it's for a good purpose. She's looking out for us. She loved you, too."

Tessa leans into me. "You're right."

"And if you're still not comfortable," I say, "we can change rooms. I'll move in here."

She looks up at me. "You'd do that for me?"

"Whatever you need."

Tessa decides to keep the spare bedroom, with the caveat that I sleep with her for the first few nights. Fine by me.

Even though it will be a couple of weeks before she and Erica are actually sleeping here, I'm already used to the idea. And I can't imagine that once we start cuddling up at night, we're ever gonna want to stop.

It makes me think about marrying her. For real.

After Tessa and Erica go home, I call Dr. Rumson.

"How are you feeling, sir?" I ask.

"Excellent," he says. "How are you?"

"Great. Things are moving right along."

"I sense a 'but' coming," he says.

"I'm sorry," I say. "I always call you when I need something, and that's crappy of me. It really is."

"Oh, Thomas," he says. "Shut up already. Stop beating yourself up. I'm here for you."

"Just so you know I'm here for you, too," I say.

"And you have been, and I know you will continue to be. So what's up?"

I sigh. "Well, Tessa and Erica are moving in."

"Ahh," he says. "Interesting parenting choice."

"I know," I say. "So I've been thinking…maybe I should ask Tessa to marry me."

"So that you're not living in sin?"

"Yes," I say. "That's one reason."

"What are the others?"

I pause. "Well, I want to protect her virtue, yes, and I'm afraid of what living together might do to our relationship, and I've been thinking that having that commitment, pledging ourselves to each other, might make it easier."

"And have you discussed this with your father and with Erica?"

"My dad suggested it," I say.

"He what?"

"He was the one who suggested it."

Dr. Rumson falls silent.

"Are you still there?" I ask.

"Oh, yes, I'm here, I...Thomas, I think you need to give this a lot of thought."

"That's what I'm doing," I say. "That's why I'm talking to you."

"Yes, but...I think I need to give this some thought before I counsel you."

I laugh. "You mean, you don't have a ready answer for me?"

Dr. Rumson chuckles. "This was not a question I thought you'd bring up any time soon. I thought maybe you'd ask me about sex, but not marriage."

I swallow. "Okay, what would you say about sex?"

"No."

I laugh. "No. I already knew that. That's why I haven't asked."

"So sex is not on your list of reasons to marry Tessa?"

I think about that. "Not really. I'd never marry someone just to have sex."

"Good lad. Okay, then, let me think about this. Can we speak tomorrow?"

"Of course."

"Until then."

"Goodnight, sir."

♥

Of course it didn't escape my attention that Dr. Rumson needed to think about his advice as soon as he heard Dad was the one who suggested I marry Tessa now.

He's wondering about Dad's motives, just like I am.

Just don't forget the big picture.

The big picture with Dad is that his life may be close to ending.

Focus in a little bit more, to what Dad's doing now, and he's what? Moving his girlfriend in! When he may be dying! Why is he pursuing his relationship with Erica when they might not have much time together?

Does she even know?

And he's suddenly putting me on the fast track to heal. I've visited the Attic and found researchers to work with. I've been allowed to heal Olivia. All this makes sense – if he's dying, he wants to be here to guide me through these things. On the more nefarious side, he's pushing me toward something, some test, some outcome, some revelation that will help him...do what? What problem does Dad want to solve?

I squeeze my eyes shut tight and open them back up.

It's so simple, I don't know why I didn't think of it before.

But he could just ask me, be upfront with me, explain it to me, and I'd go along. He knows I'd go along.

Or maybe he doesn't.

I don't know much about it. I mean, I didn't even realize it would happen until Grandma spilled the beans. Maybe I can't do it on my own, and that's why he wants me to marry Tessa. Maybe he needs a baby to do it. Maybe…

I cross the room to my closet and pull out a duffle bag. I pack. I even throw a lump of clay in just in case I need to think, 'cause sculpting always helps me do that.

I text Kate and Cyrus to let them know I'll be gone a few days. Then I go to bed early. I have to be well rested for my drive down to the Attic and for my new project: saving Dad's life.

Chapter Thirty-Six

I wake up at 4:30 and stealthily leave the house. I have no idea about dad's schedule – maybe I'll see him at the Attic, maybe I won't. It's guaranteed that he'll find out when I show up, and there's no point in discussing anything with him. He won't give me straight answers anyway.

I pull into the facility parking lot and make my way underground. I stifle my gag reflex before I exit the elevator in anticipation of the horrid smell.

Door number twelve. I take a shallow breath, swipe my card, lean into the retinal scanner, and watch as the door whooshes open to General Population.

Only one person seems to be awake. Dr. Trent is bent over Cappy, her wrist in his hand, taking her pulse. When I enter, he lifts his head in my direction and puts up a finger, asking me to wait.

I do.

He finishes and places her hand gently on the bed. He crosses the space to me and shakes my hand.

"Thomas," he says in a whisper. "Nice to see you. I didn't realize you were coming today."

"Neither did I," I say with a smile. "It was a last-minute decision."

He clasps a hand on my shoulder. "Dacey and Tyrion will be excited to see you. They've been working on a few things."

"Oh?" I say. I didn't exactly forget about Dacey and Tyrion, but I've definitely put them on the back burner. I'm happy to hear that they're moving along without me.

"Well, I won't say more," he says. "I'm sure they'll want to surprise you. They're interacting more with all of us, but they still sleep in their isolation room – the bed's larger to accommodate them – but let me ring them. I'm sure they'll be—"

"No, no," I say quickly. "Let them sleep. I'll be around all day."

"You're sure?"

"Absolutely. I have something else, something I'd like to discuss with you. Is there somewhere we can talk?"

"Of course." He replaces the clipboard he's holding in a slot at the end of Cappy's bed. "Follow me."

♥

We end up in room fourteen (interesting that they're superstitious here – there is no room thirteen), a space with lounge chairs, over-stuffed sofas, and shag carpeting on the floor. There's even a coffee bar and donuts set out in the corner.

"Coffee?" he asks, and we both make ourselves a cup and select a donut. There are no rainbow sprinkles, so I settle for a chocolate bar.

I plop into a bulging chair and it engulfs me. I struggle to sit up without spilling my coffee while Dr. Trent laughs at me.

"I should have warned you about that chair," he says. "Let me hold that." He takes the coffee from me while I get settled, then hands it back. "How are you holding up since your grandmother's passed?"

I blink at him, trying to tune my brain to what he's said. I'm thinking about something else entirely. "Doing well," I say. "Thanks for coming to the funeral. It meant a lot to my dad."

"I wish I could have met her," he says. "Mike always spoke about how irreverent she was."

I smile. "In some ways," I say. "She was a great lady. I'm lucky to have met her."

He nods. "It's odd, isn't it? Tragedy can bring unexpected blessings. I understand you only got to meet her after your mother died."

"Yes," I say. "My grandmother rescued us. I just wish I could have returned the favor."

Dr. Trent obviously knows the story, because he nods again. "That's the tricky part about what we do as healers. We can a lead a horse to water, but we can't make him drink."

"Been in that situation before, have you?" I say.

He sighs. "Pretty much daily. I have it harder here, I think, because the Dwellers all think they know better. They self-diagnose. Sometimes, though, an outside perspective is needed. No sane doctor operates on himself."

I laugh. "Is that a warning?"

Dr. Trent smiles. "Maybe."

I sigh. "Actually, I've been thinking about that very thing. Does my dad come to you with his own medical issues?"

He takes a careful sip of his coffee, staring into the cup a bit too hard. "Perhaps not as much as I'd like."

"But you and I both know he's on the edge," I say, studying his face for a reaction. "He's close to hitting his limit."

Dr. Trent doesn't look up at me. He just continues staring into his cup. "That's the downside, for everyone here. Hell, it's the downside for human beings in general. Immortality doesn't exist."

"Have you guys worked on it?" I ask.

"Your dad did, a bit, maybe six, seven years ago. He hit it pretty hard. But one day, he just ended the experiments. Done. No explanation to the rest of us."

"What happened?"

He shakes his head, finally meeting my eyes. "I don't know."

"But every experiment is out in the open, right? You must know something about it."

"I know he was working with stem cells. I know he experimented on himself, and that he didn't involve anyone else here. That's it. You could ask him yourself."

Yeah, right.

"I'll do that," I say, thinking I won't, but not wanting Dr. Trent to know how little Dad trusts me. "What do you think…I mean, do you know…how long do you think my father has left?" I hold my breath as I wait for his answer.

He presses his lips together, thinking. "A year, two at the outside. That's my prediction based on the life expectancies of the Dwellers who've come before him. But it's really a very personal thing. It depends on how much he's healed, how hard, how fast, how much he's pushed his body past normal usage. Take Vivian, for instance. They're close to the same age, but I'd give

Vivian another five or six years. She did keep her body in stasis while in a coma, but she didn't heal much beyond that. I'd give her a much better outlook."

Vivian. I hadn't even thought of Vivian. But of course she's Dad's age.

"Has Vivian mentioned it?" I ask.

"No, but she has a much more accepting nature than your dad."

"Exactly," I say. "I can't believe Dad would give up without a fight. I'm sure he must have something in mind."

"If he does, he hasn't confided in me," Dr. Trent says. "Is that why you're here?"

I nod. "I need the records of his experiments."

Dr. Trent pierces me with a look that sees straight through to my heart. "They aren't here."

"You think he destroyed them, or didn't keep a record?"

"No," he says. "I'm certain your dad would have kept records."

"Then..." I think about the places where Dad would hide things. "I need to go back home."

Dr. Trent stops me with a hand on my arm as I start to rise. "Thomas, this isn't just about a crummy piece of paper your dad's stuffed in a drawer. These are confidential medical records. Attic experiments. Government property. Security clearance-protected. Do you understand?"

I look him the eye. "I do. And I appreciate the warning."

I stand, and Dr. Trent stares up at me. "I've seen your dad do it. Hold people who considered him a friend accountable for their actions. I'm not saying…your dad is a good man, and I know he cares about you. But watch your back."

I shiver, then hold out my hand to him. "Thanks. You, too."

♥

Dr. Trent and I exit to the white hallway.

"I know you're anxious to get home," he says, "but how about a quick visit with Dacey and Tyrion?"

"Sure," I say, thinking that Dad will think it's weird if I drove all the way down here and didn't meet with them.

We go to room number five and do our scans. The door slides open.

"Rise and shine, ladies!" Dr. Trent calls through the empty room. He gives me wink.

"Christ, Trent, can't a man take a piss in the morning without being harassed?" a voice calls from the bathroom. Dr. Trent and I both laugh.

We hear the toilet flush, and Dacey and Tyrion come out from the bathroom in their boxers, absently scratching their ass.

"You don't even wash your hands?" Dr. Trent says, still laughing.

Dacey/Tyrion give him the finger.

And I gasp. "Wow." I cross the space to them and clasp them on the forearm in a strong shake, not caring that they didn't wash their hands. "What the hell happened to you?"

Dacey smiles, and Tyrion gives me a booming laugh. "What do you think?"

I give Tyrion a good look. "Freaking amazing," I say. "My God. You're the most handsome son of a bitch I've ever seen."

Tyrion laughs again while Dacey smirks like a proud papa. "I am, aren't I?"

The transformation is stunning and seamless.

Tyrion's blob of a nose has been replaced by a thin patrician one. His eyes have been centered, and the lashes grown long and black. His head is smaller, perfectly shaped, with a thick pelt of black hair covering it. He looks vaguely like a movie star, but I can't put my finger on who.

"How long did it take you?" I ask Dacey.

"About a week. I'm getting faster as I tap stem cells from different places, rather than always using sperm cells. You helped me do that."

I grin. "Did it hurt?"

Tyrion smiles. "Like a hot poker shoved up my nose," he says. "Dacey does not have as great control of my body as his own. But it was worth it, I think."

"You've also added width to your torso, I see," I say. "What, about fourteen inches?"

"Sixteen," Dacey says. "And I've got his breast bone and rib cage built. But I slept about twenty hours afterward. And that was with three hours of sleep in between after every hour of working."

"Go dress," Dr. Trent says. "I can't stand looking at your naked chest."

They go off to dress, and I take a seat and think about Tyrion's transformation. I have to help him now – he's a full-fledged man. And then I berate myself for even thinking that. He was a man before Dacey fixed him, but he had that Frankenstein, sewn-together quality that didn't make him entirely real. I mean, he looked like an experiment. And now he doesn't.

Man, I am a horrible human being. To even think that way, that physical appearance makes someone less human, it's so abhorrent a thought, so against my basic nature, that I have a hard sitting here trapped in my own messed-up head.

"It's remarkable, isn't it?" Dr. Trent says, interrupting my thoughts.

I shake my head to clear it. "Yes."

"And it suddenly seems more real, doesn't it, more urgent that we solve their problem?"

I look at Dr. Trent in surprise. How do the Dwellers always seem to read my mind?

"Yes," I say. "But it shouldn't. Tyrion's the same man he was a few weeks ago."

"Yes and no," he says. "Don't you think as our physical appearance changes, say through simple aging or growing up, we change as a person?"

"I suppose," I say.

"Tyrion is getting his own urges now, his own dreams, things he never allowed himself to feel or think before. We're feeling that from him, a sudden burst, a yearning for a real life. It's hard not to respond to."

I want to say blaming my feelings on Tyrion's projections of his own feelings is a cop-out and giving me (and Dr. Trent himself) way too much credit, but what's the point? I nod.

They come out of the bathroom dressed in jeans and a faded navy blue t-shirt large enough to be a tent. They sit gingerly in a chair, both of them grinning.

"So what's up with you?" Dacey asks.

"I want to hear about you guys," I say. "What else have you done?"

"Like I was saying, I'm working on the bones," Dacey says. "The new bones are basically floating on one side since I don't have the shoulder and arm built, and I don't know how I'd do that anyway with him still attached. So we have to be careful when we move."

"Have you created the spine yet?"

"In progress," he says. "But it's slower going than I thought."

"I think you've done remarkably well," I say. "I was thinking organs first, but I think you're absolutely right about doing the skeleton. He has to have support."

Dr. Trent gets up and takes a bow. "Thank you. Thank you very much. That was my idea."

I smile. "So no ideas on the right arm? And you need a left arm now, Dacey."

"I'll just grow mine after we separate," he says. "As for Tyrion, I've got nothing."

"If the worst I have to deal with is no right arm, I can handle it," Tyrion says.

"Hmm," I say. "What about this? Build the arm inside your body. Dr. Trent can free it during surgery."

Dacey looks at Dr. Trent. "Would that work?"

"As long as you can keep your body from rejecting it," Dr. Trent says. "You've been lucky so far, and nothing you've created has triggered your immune system. But we have to go on the assumption that, at some point, your body will begin to reject all these new parts. I think we should leave it until the very last."

"Okay," Dacey says, nodding his head. He looks at Tyrion. "You might not be the one-armed bandit after all."

Tyrion smiles. "One thing at a time."

"Is there anything you've had trouble with? Besides falling asleep?" I ask.

Dacey presses his lips together. "Not yet. I am worried about the point when we have to grow the spinal cord and then switch Tyrion's brain over. I know this is far in the future, but I think it's the biggest hurdle."

"You shouldn't do it all alone," I say. "When you're ready for that, Tyrion should be hooked up to a cardiopulmonary bypass machine so the blood can continue to circulate. And you just go fast, but systematically fast. Take one vein, sever it, heal it, and reconnect. Maybe five seconds each. Same with the nerves and the arteries. One at a time, super fast."

Dacey's face falls. "There's no way," he says, shaking his head. "No way. It takes me seventy-three seconds to heal an artery."

"You said you've gotten faster," I point out. "Just practice."

"I have," he says through gritted teeth. "That is faster."

"Then I'll do it," I say. "When you're ready, I'll hook up and assist. In fact, maybe we could do something now."

Dacey cocks his head. "I thought you wouldn't be ready for a while."

I shrug. "I've been working on stuff. I have something that should help you, too." I pull the backpack off my shoulders and rummage through it. "Here." I hand him a bottle of Dwellerade and a bottle of pills.

Dacey takes them. "Gatorade?"

I smile. "Super charged. We're calling it Dwellerade. One bottle and one pill every hour keeps me from having to sleep. We think you can work for six hours at a time safely. I'll have some more Dwellerade sent over here."

"We?" Tyrion says.

"Just a neurosurgeon I've been working with," I say.

Dr. Trent plucks the bottles from Dacey's hand. "No offense, but I need to know what's in these before I can let Dacey have them."

"Fine by me," I say. "So are you two up for a little growth?"

Dacey grins. "What do you have in mind?"

I tap my finger on my chin. "Let's finish the spine and do the pelvis, too. I'm feeling pretty good – who knows what else we can accomplish?"

♥

We get Dacey and Tyrion lying down on their bed. Dr. Trent sets up a video camera to tape the session.

I'm not sure exactly what he thinks he'll catch on video, but I indulge him.

Dacey cuts off nerve sensation in his hand, and I slice open our palms and press them together. I run along the neural pathways up his body and stop at the heart to take a look.

It's beating at a normal pace, but something's off. The blood flow is sluggish, as though each beat isn't as powerful as it should be.

I hesitate. I don't want to alarm Dacey right now, but my initial fear about the strain on his heart is correct. Dacey's heart is working extra hard to keep Tyrion going.

I move along up to Tyrion's brain and hook up. Information about Tyrion's brain and Dacey's body floods in. Nothing else jumps out at me as abnormal.

"Okay," I say. "I'm in. Dacey, can you handle pain management while I work?"

"Just tell me where," he says.

"I think I'll be working too fast to tell you," I say. "I'm starting at the bottom of the spine where you left off. Start there, and follow me. Cut off nerve sensation as I go."

"On it," he says.

I start to work. About five minutes in, Dacey nearly comes off the bed. "Yow!" he shouts.

I chuckle. "Sorry."

Dacey and Tyrion both smile through their grimaces. "You're too damn fast," Dacey says.

"Concentrate," Tyrion says, laughing.

I go back to work.

Twenty-two minutes later, Tyrion has a spine and a pelvis. I sit back and take a pill and swig a bottle of Dwellerade.

"I'm in awe," Dacey says.

I shrug.

"I notice you're not disengaging," he says. "You want to do more?"

I glance at the camera and at Dr. Trent. "I think we need to do the heart."

Tyrion lifts his head in alarm. "Why? Something's wrong?"

"Not wrong," I say, hedging. "But Dacey's heart is working overtime. It's straining. Can you feel it?"

Dacey closes his eyes. "It's not an emergency."

"No, but it's like you're obese, four hundred pounds plus. Your heart can't keep that up forever."

"It doesn't have to," Dacey says. "There's an end point here."

"But we don't know when that will be," I say.

Dr. Trent sits on the edge of the bed. "We know the heart will be tricky under any circumstance. Are you sure you're ready for this, Thomas?"

I nod. "But I know this will be complicated. I want a specific plan worked up – what veins and arteries we'll need for now, what connections in the brain and to the brain, and we'll have to do the spinal cord, too. It's involved, I know."

"That's going to take some time," Dr. Trent says.

"A week from Saturday," I say. "Can we plan to work that weekend? We can consult by email."

Dr. Trent stands. "We'll get on it right away."

I disconnect from Tyrion and Dacey and heal us. They sit up slowly.

"Feels like I've been run over," Tyrion says.

I smile. "Catch a nap. And don't turn those nerves back on for a few days. You need to heal."

I shake their hands and head for the door.

"You're off, then?" Dr. Trent says, following me.

"Yeah. I need to deal with my dad."

He pats my back. "I'll be in touch."

Chapter Thirty-Seven

Dad's car is gone when I get home around nine. I call him and he answers on the first ring.

"Hey."

"Hey," I say. "I just got back from the Attic. Are you around today?"

"I'm just pulling in there, actually," he says. "You've been there and back?"

"Yeah, I have stuff to do today, but I wanted to see Dacey and Tyrion. Thought I'd get up early and make a quick trip."

"Were you surprised?" he says.

"I shouldn't have been," I say. "Makes sense that Dacey would work on Tyrion's appearance."

Dad chuckles. "Dacey's always been the ladies' man of the group. Ironic he created his own competition."

Only if we can separate them, I think.

"Well, okay. I'm going to work. Just wanted to know your schedule."

"I'll be here all day," he says. "Erica invited you over for dinner. She's just ordering take-out. Late, I think. Tessa has a swim meet."

I almost forgot about that.

"Yeah, I'm gonna go watch. Okay, I'll see you later."

"Later." And Dad hangs up.

Excellent.

I prowl down the hall, trying to be quiet even though I'm alone.

What if the house is bugged?

This has never occurred to me before, that I'm being watched in my own home, but it's a distinct possibility. I hover in the middle of the hallway, trying to decide what to do.

Fuck it. If Dad catches me, he catches me. Knowing him, he wants me to take this rebellious step.

I step up to his bedroom door and turn the knob.

Dad's room is OCD neat. Ridiculously neat. Disgustingly neat.

I cross over to his desk on the far wall. All that's on top is his laptop and a small notepad, with a pencil resting perfectly diagonal across it. With a nervous giggle, I knock the pencil askew just to see if he notices.

Then I reluctantly move it back. Why am I always provoking him?

I wiggle my finger across the trackpad of the laptop to wake it up. It's password-protected, of course. I don't want to mess with that except as a last resort.

The desk has five drawers – one in the middle across the top for pens and such, and two on each side. The bottom two drawers hold files.

But they're locked.

I open the other two drawers, meticulously organized with a stapler, tape dispenser, some notecards (Is he giving speeches? What the hell does he need notecards for?), a box of paperclips. I run my hand along the inside of the drawers, looking for a key. Nothing.

I get on my hands and knees and crawl under the desk. I don't have a flashlight handy, so I run my hand blindly along the edges of the desk, underneath, on the underside of the top drawer. Nothing but wood.

I reach a hand out to the front of the desk, grab the top-drawer knob, and pull the drawer out a bit. With my other hand, I feel along the back of the drawer.

And there it is, secured with a bit of tape. A key.

I peel it off and crawl back out.

I put the key in the lock of the left-hand drawer and turn. It clicks open.

I pull out the drawer and start thumbing through files.

School Reg

Vaccinations

Birth Cert

Physicals

Report Cards

This entire drawer is full of me.

I pull out the file labeled *Physicals*. Inside are Mom's notes on my height, weight, and head circumference for the first six years of my life. There's also a report from Dr. Morley, the pediatrician I went to when I was younger. I glance at the papers and replace the file. Maybe someday this stuff will interest me, but not now.

I unlock the right-hand drawer.

Insurance

Mortgage

The Heart

Car

I grab the file labeled *Insurance*. It contains annual statements on a life insurance policy on Dad, bequeathed to me, in the sum of $5,000,000.

Yowza.

The rest of the files are uninteresting, the standard day-to-day crap of life. I'm about to push the drawer closed when I notice it, a file with no label, stuck in the middle. I carefully extract it from the drawer and lay it on my lap. I open it up and read the first page.

Date: August 12, 2006

Time: 16:35

Subject assessment: Cells are exact copies. No breakdown. Systems normal. No change.

Computer-aided assessment: Slight bending to the nucleus, less than 0.001 degree (resolution = 0.001 degree, uncertainty = +/- 0.003 degree). Cells are not exact copies.

Date: August 19, 2006

Time: 16:42

Subject assessment: Cells are exact copies. No breakdown. Systems normal. No change.

Computer-aided assessment: Slight bending to the nucleus, less than 0.001 degree (resolution = 0.001 degree, uncertainty = +/- 0.003 degree). Cells are not exact copies.

Date: August 26, 2006

Time: 16:31

Subject assessment: Cells are exact copies. No breakdown. Systems normal. No change.

Computer-aided assessment: Slight bending to the nucleus, approximately 0.001 degree (resolution = 0.001 degree, uncertainty = +/- 0.003 degree). Cells are not exact copies.

Date: September 2, 2006

Time: 16:32

Subject assessment: Cells are exact copies. No breakdown. Systems normal. No change.

Computer-aided assessment: Slight bending to the nucleus, approximately 0.002 degree (resolution = 0.001 degree, uncertainty = +/- 0.003 degree). Cells are not exact copies.

The same description goes on for eleven pages, subject not detecting any change, while the computer detects increasing changes in the bend (shape?) of the nucleus. The last piece of paper is a hand-scribbled note on a sheet of neon yellow legal paper.

Date: February 9, 2007

Time: 04:03

Conclusions: We are not infallible as we once thought. Some changes in our bodies are too small to detect. I say "our," but who knows? Maybe I'm the only one with this issue??? But I have greater control and practice than most – I would venture to say my estimates are at the high end of what we can do. Except for T and J. Add this to their list.

Stem cells are the answer, but our own exhibit the nucleus bend. Starting at what age??? T's stems do not exhibit this bend as found, but after repeated use, they bend. Bend comes from repeated use AND age.

Genetic engineering is the answer, but how far to go? Results of Experiment A326311 scared the crap out of me. Too many unknowns. I know it can be done, but when my left eye turned blue...you'd think after all these years, all the experiments, the physical changes, I'd be immune to the shock. But the blue eye, it caught me unaware. The same way those tumors did. People's lives are in my hands. I cannot afford such carelessness.

Thomas, tread carefully. Your instincts are correct – I know you know what I'm talking about. But experimenting with live people...how many must die so others can live? Do we put people at risk, even if they agree to that risk? Is it really worth it? We always think we're doing the right thing if we have good intentions. But remember what they say about those.

I'm discontinuing these experiments. I'm dedicating my time and energy to medical breakthroughs that can be applied universally to heal the ill. I will not play God, and I urge you not to, either. Every life is precious, Thomas. Every life.

I stare at the paper and realize my hands are shaking violently. I replace the papers and the files, close and lock the drawers, and tape the key back in place. I'm not even too careful about it, and I can't be with my shaking hands anyway. Dad meant for me to find the papers eventually.

I lie down and stare at the ceiling cracks.

Maybe it isn't okay to experiment on people, even with risks consented to, even if the rewards are great. I can accept that.

But if I'm experimenting on myself? Do we have a moral obligation to preserve on our own life?

I don't.

Genetic engineering. On myself. That's the next step.

I laugh out loud. Maybe I'll be a monkey-man. A cheetah-man. Half man, half Wookie.

Dad's eye turned blue! I try to picture that, Dad bleary-eyed and stumbling to the toilet early one morning, and when he looks up, into the mirror, he sees...holy crap! A blue eye!

But I can't picture my father being startled – truly scared – by anything.

I try to picture myself looking in the mirror, expecting to see the same old me. I lean in close to exam a zit forming on my forehead, but wait, what's this? My eye is blue!

Maybe I need to think this through.

Chapter Thirty-Eight

I missed Tessa's swim meet last night, and I want to kick myself. I ended up falling asleep under the taunting grin of the ceiling right after I got home from work, and I'd left my phone in the kitchen, where Tessa's text reminders failed to wake me.

I'm such a jerk.

I drive to McDonald's and buy her favorite bacon, egg, and cheese biscuit and hash browns. She answers the door in her robe and takes the McDonald's bag with a grin.

"You're forgiven," she says, kissing my cheek.

"I'm sorry," I say. "I fell asleep. How'd it go?"

"Third in the relay but first in the butterfly," she says.

I hug her, smooshing the bag between us. "That's awesome. I knew you could do it."

We sit side-by-side at the kitchen island. Tessa unwraps her biscuit and carefully peels it in half. "Eat," she says.

"I ate in the car," I say. "It's for you."

She takes a big bite, chews, and swallows. "So what's going on?"

"Not too much," I say. I want to talk to her about Dad, but I don't want to upset her, and I need to find out what Erica knows about the situation. I don't want to be the one to out Dad to Erica. "If Cyrus is around, I'll probably go over and work on Olivia."

"Cyrus?" Erica says, entering the kitchen.

I freeze.

Tessa waves a hand. "Miley," she says. "Miley Cyrus. She has a dog named Olivia. Hip trouble. Thomas is going to fix it."

"You're a horrible liar," Erica says, heading for the coffee pot. "Spill it, Thomas."

Tessa looks at me. I look back. She kicks me under the counter.

"He contacted me," I say. "He has a...dog that's sick."

Erica leans forward on the island, blowing on her coffee to cool it. "You're a shitty liar, too," she says, taking a careful sip.

"Are you angry?" I ask her.

"I don't even know what you're talking about," she says. "Should I be?"

The guilt gnaws at my stomach. "I agreed to heal his daughter in exchange for buying your house."

Erica stares at me. "Is it dangerous?"

"Of course not!" Tessa exclaims a little too loudly, and Erica gives her a *Shut up!* stare.

"Is it?" Erica repeats.

"Yes," I say.

Erica's eyes grow wet while I watch. "Thank you," she says. "I...need to take a shower."

And she walks out.

"I'm sorry, Tessa," I say.

"You could have tried a bit harder with the Miley stuff," she says, staring at her biscuit. "Did you have to crumble so fast?"

"You wanted me to lie to your mother, in earnest?"

Tessa raises her nose in the air. "Never, m'lord," she says in a snotty voice. "I would not dream of asking you to debase yourself in such a manner. God forbid you put someone else's feelings above your own."

I leap to my feet. "How can you say that? I did this for you guys. I'm putting my life on the line, for you."

"Allow me to kiss your feet, m'lord," she says, slipping off the stool and going down on her knees.

"Get up, for Christ's sake," I say, pulling on her arm. "Why are you doing this?"

Tessa gets to her feet. "You hurt her. You hurt her pride. You made her feel like nothing. I mean, a house in exchange for your life? She has to live with that."

I gape at Tessa. "I did not hurt her. I would never do that. How did my telling the truth do that?"

"If you don't already know, I can't explain it to you," she says. "Go home, Thomas."

And Tessa leaves me standing in the kitchen.

♥

I stomp out to my car.

I don't get it, I absolutely freaking refuse to get it! How did I become the bad guy in this situation?

Grandma's words echo in my head: *Just because you can, Thomas, doesn't mean you should.*

I growl and thump a fist on the steering wheel.

If I can't heal when someone's sick, when can I?

If I can't tell the truth when asked a direct question, when can I?

If I can't save someone's home when they're in dire financial straits, when can I?

Screw all these people. Screw Dad, and screw Erica, and screw Tessa, and screw Cyrus for putting me in this shitty situation, and screw everyone who's ever told me I made the wrong choice. They can all fend for themselves. They can all go to hell.

I feel like I'm about to explode, like every cell in my body is bursting, ready to multiply. I feel like I'm about to fly apart.

I head for Olivia's house.

I can feel neurons growing, attaching, lengthening in my brain as I drive. Pain throbs in every part of my head, like ice picks jabbing at me. At a stoplight, I pull the visor down and flip up the mirror. Veins bulge menacingly at my temples.

I grimace. Then I scream. I grow my incisors until I look like Dracula. Freakin'A, the look matches my mood.

I dissolve the extra bits of teeth I've grown and flick the pieces out of my mouth with my tongue as I lean out the window.

I pull into the Brooks driveway and park. I sit shivering for a few minutes. I finally collect myself enough to do an assessment: blood pressure elevated, adrenaline on high, heart rate increased almost to a dangerous level. Neurons have grown, most in an effort to process emotions faster (as if I needed any help with that). And Protein T, I have like a gallon floating around.

I could get rid of the Protein T, probably should get rid of it. I really should start healing with all systems at normal, with zero extra protein.

But I'll just have to manufacture more when I get hooked up to Olivia. No sense in getting rid of it.

I exit the car and my head feels like lead, like it weighs a ton. I have to stabilize it on my neck. I really should use the protein now.

But I don't.

I lope up the steps of the house and ring the doorbell.

Chapter Thirty-Nine

Cyrus answers the door in maroon silk paisley pajamas.

"Thomas!" he says, opening the door wider to accommodate me. "Did I miss a message?"

"No, sir," I say, keeping my voice steady. "My plans changed at the last minute, and I thought I'd stop by and see if I could work today."

"Of course, of course," he says, leading me to the velvet sofas. "Just have a seat. Let me talk to Rachel and have her clean Olivia up."

I sit while he disappears up the stairs. One thing I have to give Cyrus credit for: he's always happy to see me.

I go inside my brain and once again ensure I have the proteins inactive and corralled. They are.

Then the front door opens and closes and Dr. Park walks in.

"Good morning," he says. "How are you, Thomas?"

"Fine. You?"

"Well," he says. "I'm well. Does Cyrus know you're here?"

"He went up to get Olivia ready. They weren't expecting me."

"I wondered if you would show up this weekend. Having a patient so close…it must have been difficult to stay away."

"I am anxious to see Olivia wake up," I say, neither confirming nor denying his belief.

He nods. "Will it be today, you think?"

I fight not to shrug. "All I have left is the RAS in the brain, but I want to spend some time on her muscles first. Her neck muscles haven't been used in months. Jaw, too, arms and legs. Might as well give her some strength to speed her recovery."

Dr. Park shakes his head. "Remarkable. You're making us re-think our entire protocol. Physical therapy usually comes way after all the other stuff."

"I have to admit, I'm feeling my way on this," I tell him.

"What about the stomach?" he says suddenly. "Her entire gastrointestinal system. We'll have to take the feeding tube out. Could you ready her system for solid food?"

I think about what that would entail. "I don't see why not."

I already know how the gastrointestinal system works, but Dr. Park spends fifteen minutes explaining its intricacies. He wants to contribute, and since I'm waiting anyway, I let him.

"I'll try that," I finally say. "I think the only thing we haven't taken into account is Olivia's emotional state. Dr. Kate is particularly worried about this. She thinks Olivia's going to be shocked, scared, maybe even depressed. We should be ready for the possibility that she won't take in enough calories and nutrients by eating on her own. What if she refuses food?" I don't actually know if any of this will happen, but Kate's been adamant that emotional trauma is likely.

She'd kill me if she knew I were here, doing this now, without her or Kenneth.

"Mmmm," Dr. Park says, tapping a finger against his lips. "Yes. A possibility."

"One you're set up for, I assume," I say.

"Cyrus is set up for a zombie apocalypse, nuclear fallout, and typhoid outbreak simultaneously," he says, chuckling.

"Do you, uh, need to go up?" I say, praying the answer is yes.

Dr. Park waves a hand. "If they're changing her, I'll leave them to it. We can go up together."

I nod, resigned, and continue to listen to Dr. Park remind me that I should really check Olivia's teeth for cavities before we (*We!* As if!) wake her.

♥

"Hello, Thomas," Rachel says as I enter the room ahead of Dr. Park. She gives me a blinding smile, and begrudgingly nods her head at the doctor.

"Hey," I say. "How's Olivia?"

Rachel furrows her brow. "Restless. She hasn't really settled down all night – she twitches and jumps. I haven't given her a sedative yet. I thought Dr. Park, and now you, would want to take a look."

Dr. Park steps up to the bed and grabs Olivia's wrist. He takes her pulse even though she's hooked up to a heart monitor and all of us can read her heart rate from across the room.

Olivia's legs dance beneath the sheets in small jerky movements. Her eyes roll restlessly beneath her lids.

It's hard to watch. It's as if Olivia's soul is trapped and trying to escape her body.

"This is, of course, the body's normal response to healing," Dr. Park says imperiously. "The nerve signals are firing, but they're rusty from disuse or so new they're still figuring things out. Nothing to worry about."

"Should I sedate her?" Rachel asks.

They discuss Olivia's medication, and Rachel injects some into Olivia's IV.

Cyrus squeaks from behind me, and we all turn to him. "Is it today, then?"

I put a hand on his shoulder. "Maybe. I don't know, Cyrus. I've never healed anyone in Olivia's condition before. We don't know exactly what to expect."

He nods.

"I suggest you get out of the house. No sense sitting here waiting for the moment that might not come today. Go out to the pasture for a ride."

"You want him to drive his car across the property?" Rachel asks.

"No, I was thinking of the horses. It might help you feel closer to Olivia."

Rachel opens her mouth to speak, but Cyrus cuts her off. "Yes, of course. I...I'll go down to the church. Work on my sermon. You'll call me then, if anything happens?"

"Immediately," I say.

He smiles at me and heads out.

"How long until the sedative kicks in?" I ask Dr. Park.

"It should be fairly immediate, but let's give it ten minutes or so. Let me go over her vitals with Rachel."

I nod and make my way to the window.

Olivia has a stunning view of the property from a bay window with a bench seat inset. Or she would have a stunning view, if the window allowed it.

The entire window, ten feet by six, is safety glass, criss-crossed with black wire inside. I press my eye up close to one of the diamond shapes the wire makes and study the yard, though calling it a yard is ridiculous – there's no visible endpoint to the property, no wall or fence, that I can see.

Directly below is a concrete walkway that winds around the house. Beyond is a rose garden, still in bloom even though it's November, with meandering paths of gravel and a fountain dead center. Beyond that, and to both sides, are lawn, trees, and nature.

Why would someone ruin such a beautiful view with safety glass?

"She's ready," Dr. Park says, interrupting my musings. "Nervous system is a bit jumpy, even under sedation. Will it make it difficult for you to work?"

I force myself to focus on Olivia. Just like with Tyrion, my view of her has suddenly changed. She seems more human now that she's moving. Instead of the jerky movements, though, now she's only twitching slightly.

"Should be fine," I say.

I position my chair and settle into a comfortable position.

"Wait, where's your backpack?" Rachel says.

Home, I think. *Right where I left it.*

I shake my head and take out my knife. "Fuck the backpack," I say.

♥

I do a final, methodical circuit of Olivia's entire brain. Admittedly, I've kind of been jumping around in my healing – I just followed the damage. So I lay an imaginary grid over Olivia's entire brain and systematically explore each square.

Things look great. Hell, they look better than great. I'm impressed with my work.

Until I hit the amygdala. Nerves that run there from the visual cortex are completely severed. This is odd, because the only severed nerves I've found before were where bone fragments had penetrated Olivia's brain. All the other damaged nerves were stretched, not severed.

"Dr. Park," I say, "I've found something."

He cocks his head. "In the RAS?"

"No. I'm doing a final check on the rest of the brain, and I've found severed nerves leading to the amygdala. The injury seems out of place."

"Can you heal them?" he asks.

"Yes," I say. "I just...there's no other nerve damage of the kind nearby. What would cause that, do you think? If it were an old injury, Olivia would have had emotional difficulties, since the amygdala processes emotions. I mean, this is something that would have been noticeable, and there's nothing in her medical history to suggest such a thing."

He waves his hand. "I don't think the why is important," he says. "Her brain damage was so extensive...who knows what caused it? I don't think you can rule out her accident. Maybe you cut them accidentally."

I grit my teeth. "I did not cut them."

"Then heal them and move on."

The nerves are damaged, so I should heal them. But something feels off about it. Instinctively, I know they weren't cut during Olivia's fall.

I made a promise to myself that I would bring Olivia back as close as I could to the person she was before the accident. Healing these nerves will certainly change her. And if I'm wrong, I can always go back in and fix them later.

I leave them alone and continue working.

Two hours later, I unhook myself and sit back in the chair. I swipe my forearm across my sweat-beaded brow.

"Give me a sec," I say to no one in particular, and I make my way to the bathroom down the hall.

Olivia's body is totally ready. I've bulked up muscles, fired every neuron in her body to make sure it's functioning, healed her stomach lining and intestines in preparation for solid food. Physically, she should feel like she's barely spent a day in bed.

I turn on the faucet and splash some water on my face.

I'm fine. Physically, I'm fine, except for a little dehydrated. I cup my hands under the running water, and swallow four big mouthfuls.

Mentally, my emotions are still running high. I'm mad at the world, and I recognize that. But healing Olivia has given me a purpose, and it's helped. A bit.

I still have plenty of Protein T from my initial burst this morning. Holy hell, I let things get out of control. I didn't even know I was capable of that kind of loss of control.

Scary, if I think about it too hard.

The smart thing to do would be to end the session for today. I healed a lot with little consequence. I should quit while I'm ahead.

Promise you'll come back.

I should go.

Go home, Thomas.

I should stay.

Olivia is almost there.

I turn off the faucet and head back to her room.

"So this is it?" Rachel asks as I walk back into the room.

I sit in my chair and lean forward, elbows on my knees. "Maybe. We won't know until it happens."

"I know it'll happen," she whispers. "I know it."

Wish I had her confidence.

"Have you had much experience with coma patients?" I ask Dr. Park.

He takes the chair across the bed from me and nods. "They're my specialty. I've worked in private facilities with coma patients for my entire career."

"Then you can tell us what to expect," I say.

He sighs through pursed lips. "Normally, the process follows similar patterns. When everything in the brain is ready, the patient begins to gain awareness, slowly. Response to stimuli increases. Normal sleep patterns resume. A patient will begin to communicate, usually without speech. We start therapy, encourage them to respond to us, to indicate preferences and awareness. It's different for every patient, but it usually takes a while. Days. Sometimes weeks."

"But you don't think that will be the case here," I say.

"I've never had a patient wake up from being in a coma this long. And Olivia will be waking up without physical deterioration. She won't have the physical barriers to overcome that all coma patients have. You've said that her long-term memory is intact. You've indicated that even speech and balance centers are intact. Maybe Olivia will wake up and speak to us. Maybe it will take a while. I just don't know."

"What's you best guess?" I ask him.

"Well, you've seen how the nervous system is not functioning perfectly – it takes time. I would guess it will be the same with all her systems. She'll gain awareness slowly, over a period of days. Things will take time to run smoothly."

I glance at Olivia. She's perfectly still, breathing evenly.

"I fixed the nervous system issues," I say.

They both look at Olivia.

"I thought the sedative had kicked in," Rachel says.

"Nope, you didn't give her enough to stop the twitching. That was me."

"Then maybe she will wake up talking and walking," she says.

I rub my eyes. "I guess it's useless to speculate. Let's just prepare for the worst. There's always the possibility that I missed something, that I hooked something up wrong. She might not wake at all."

Dr. Park speaks. "Do you think you've missed something?"

I shrug. "Not really. But I'm not God."

And I take out my knife, slash us both open, and tunnel through Olivia's body to the RAS.

Chapter Forty

I sense the moment when Olivia gains awareness.

I've had access to her entire body for two days, so I now have a perfect snapshot of her brain, all her systems, and I can heal most cells without using Protein T. The healing came much faster once I had this access.

But it also caused some distractions. Her pain receptors were suddenly firing and the signals registering in the brain. It's hard to work on someone, knowing that each move you make is painful.

But it was also pain that Olivia wasn't aware of. I could ignore it, sort of, knowing that Olivia was oblivious.

Now she isn't.

"She's coming to," I say, and Dr. Park initiates the blood pressure cuff on Olivia's arm to take a reading.

"Blood pressure up," he says. "Heart rate increasing."

The first thing I do is temporarily numb her pain receptors. Then I tune in to Olivia's thoughts.

I can't move, I can't see, I must be dead.

"You're not dead, Olivia," I say out loud. "You're alive. Come back to us."

Who's there? Who's...I'm not dead? I have to be dead. I fell.

"I'm a doctor, Olivia," I say. "We're healing you. You're gonna be okay."

Olivia's eyes roll in her head, but the lids don't open.

"You can open your eyes. It's okay. Everything's fixed. Open your eyes for us."

But I...I can't. I don't want to. I don't want to be here.

"You're at home," I say gently. "Nothing scary is here. Just a couple of doctors and a nurse to take care of you. You're healthy now. Open your eyes."

Olivia thrashes from side to side, fighting it.

I don't want...no! I don't want to be here!

"Shhh, now," I say, patting her hand in mine. "Relax. You're going to be okay."

I begin to unhook from her brain.

What are you doing?

"We've got you hooked up, so we could heal you. I'm just unhooking you. You won't feel a thing."

You're leaving?

"No, no," I say. "I'm right here. You're all better now. You can open your eyes."

Olivia scrunches her eyes tight, refusing to open them. *Don't make me, please don't make me. I don't want to be here.*

I glance at Rachel and Dr. Park. They are riveted to my half of our conversation, and they're both frowning.

Something here is off. I re-grow my neural connections, so I can think to her, rather than speaking aloud.

Why don't you want to be here? I ask her.

I just want to die. I want to be with my mother.

Chills run down my arms. *But you're healed now. You won't be disabled or anything. You're perfectly healthy.*

Olivia screams in her head. *I don't want to be healthy! I don't want to live! I jumped for a reason!*

I'm so startled at the venom, the absolute certainty, in her voice that I pull back from her suddenly, almost breaking the connection in our hands. Olivia screams again in her head, this time in pain, as the nerves pull taut. I recover and quickly numb the pain.

What do you mean, you don't want to live? I ask her.

I jumped, she thinks. *I smashed my window and I jumped! How did I live through that?*

I don't have an answer, since apparently everything I've been told about Olivia's injuries was a lie.

My mother. Where is she?

I swallow hard. *In Heaven, Olivia. I assume she's in Heaven.*

But she's been with me forever. She's been holding my hand. Where is she?

Olivia, your mother wouldn't want you to die, I think carefully. *She loves you and would want you to live. Live for her.*

You don't know her! she screams. *You don't know anything about her! She wants me to be happy. I can't be happy...I just want to die.*

I close my eyes and take a few measured breaths. *You have to open your eyes. If you wake up, we'll sort this out together. I won't make you do anything you don't want to do.*

You'll let me die, then?

I choke on the marble in my throat. *I can't let you die. I'm a doctor. I heal people.*

Then I hate you! I hate you! Leave me alone!

Olivia, you have to wake up. Open your eyes and yell at me. Tell me how horrible I am.

No, she whispers. *No. It's a trick.*

I sit back, careful of our hands, and consider the situation.

I was tricked myself into thinking Olivia was in an accident. She wasn't. She tried to commit suicide.

How does that change things for me?

It doesn't, not really. What's done is done.

I'm leaving now, I tell her. *I'm sorry you hurt so much. I never wanted to hurt you.*

Olivia doesn't respond. She just waits, engulfed in sadness.

I won't be able to communicate with you anymore unless you speak out loud to me. Do you understand?

Olivia doesn't think anything, but I get the impression that she hears me.

My name is Thomas, Thomas Van Zandt. If you ask for me, I'll come see you. I'm sorry, Olivia. If I'd known you didn't want to wake up...I don't know. Maybe I would have done things differently.

You didn't know?

No. I thought I was healing a sick teenager who has her whole life ahead of her. I thought I was doing the right thing. Goodbye.

I don't wait for her response. I unhook from her brain and back out her body. I heal our hands and cradle my clenched fists to my chest.

"She's awake?" Dr. Park asks.

I nod. I slowly climb to my feet. "You knew."

"Knew what?"

"You knew. How she hurt herself."

Dr. Park's Adam's apple jumps as he swallows. "It changes nothing."

"It changes everything," I say softly.

"You mean you wouldn't have healed her?"

"I don't know," I say. "I would have given it a helluva lot more thought. I could have erased that part of her memory."

"You balk at healing someone who was suicidal, then think nothing of altering her memory?"

"I don't know!" I scream. "All I know is that Olivia's back, because of me, and she doesn't want to be! She's exactly in the same mental state she was in when she attempted to end her life! How does that help anything?"

"She has a second chance now," he says. "A chance at life."

"Do you even know why she did it?" I ask him.

He shakes his head.

"Neither do I. What if it's horrible? What if she's being abused? She's still here, in the lion's den!"

"Thomas, calm down," Rachel says. "I don't believe for one minute that Cyrus would hurt Olivia. We've been living here, night and day, for months. We'd know if something like that were going on."

"Would you?" I say. "You better be sure, because you guys are the only ones keeping her safe. And I'm holding you to that. Anything happens to Olivia, and I'll make sure you're held accountable."

I walk quickly to the door but stop with my hand on the jamb.

"And you can be the ones to tell Cyrus she's awake and aware and in perfect agony. I don't trust myself to speak to him ever again."

And with that, I fling myself out of Olivia's life.

Chapter Forty-One

I screech out of the parking spot and haul ass down the picturesque cobblestone drive.

Why? Why did this have to happen? My greatest achievement, and it turned out I was duped and used and turned into the perfect weapon to fight the pastor's daughter's hell-bent soul.

He lied to me. Lied! I hate liars!

But Dad warned me. He warned me something like this was going on. He told me to look at the Big Picture.

Well, screw that. I'm a kid. I don't have access to an army of private investigators like Cyrus has, or to classified information like my dad has. I'm one person. How am I supposed to know what the real story is?

An image of Grandma floats in my head. What would have happened if I'd healed her, against her wishes? What would she have done if she didn't have this otherworldly gift to so easily and cleanly end her own life?

I would have endured, she whispers in my head. *But I would have hated you a little bit.*

I jerk to a stop just in time, almost blowing through a stop sign.

Did Grandma just speak to me? *Did you just speak to me?*

I don't get an answer. Maybe it was Grandma, or maybe it was just my version of her and what I think she'd say if she were here.

Olivia has a second chance at life, true. But she doesn't want it, didn't ask for it. She's sixteen years old, same as me. Aren't we old enough to decide the course of our own lives? Shouldn't she have had a choice?

I don't support suicide, but I did make peace with Grandma's decision. How do I reconcile that? If I agree that suicide is acceptable in one case, how do I say it's unacceptable in another? How do you measure pain and suffering? I can't tell someone their pain is worth less than, is not as bad as, someone else's.

If I had a daughter...I have no idea how parents feel. Tessa, then. If Tessa tried to commit suicide, would I heal her, knowing she wanted to die?

Hell, yes! is my first instinct.

But let me really think about that. If Tessa were in so much pain that she wanted to end her life, the reality is...I'd help her. I wouldn't want to, I'd do everything in my power to convince her otherwise, but ultimately, I'd help her.

I wonder if that makes me evil. Murder is evil. But it's not really murder, it's...

And now I'm just rationalizing.

Doctors take an oath to do no harm. I'm not a doctor, exactly, but what I do amounts to the same thing. I have no wish to hurt anyone. I only want to help.

Can assisted suicide be considered a help?

I feel itchy and unsettled even thinking it. My skin crawls. Perhaps the devil is whispering in my ear at this very moment.

"Hey, God!" I shout out loud in the confines of my car. "Are you there? Have you been paying attention? What am I doing? Am I on some sick crusade to make myself a hero, to validate all the effort I've put into my abilities, everyone else be damned? Or am I doing the right thing? Tell me, please. I want to do Your will. Tell me I'm on the right path."

A car honks at me from behind, indicating the light has changed. I step on the gas and hurtle forward.

"Tell me!" I scream.

Only silence.

I pull into our driveway, nearly clipping the mailbox, and slam on the breaks. I grab my keys and thrust my way into the house.

I feel dirty.

I take off my clothes and step into the shower, turning the water on as hot as I can make it. My skin turns red, the water stings sharply, but I ignore the pain.

Maybe I am evil. Maybe I need the scalding water to burn the devil right out of me.

When I get out of the shower, my fingers and toes are prunes. I half-heartedly towel myself dry and crawl into bed.

I feel wrung out.

I sleep.

♥

Thomas?

I'm dreaming I'm in a hallway with thousands of doors, stretching miles, so many miles I cannot see the end. Tessa is calling to me.

Thomas?

I run down the hallway to meet her. I hear her but can't see her, there's no end, no Tessa in sight, so I run, and I pass doors, so many doors, but I know they're not the right ones. They're a distraction. Tessa is at the end of the hallway, I have to get to the end, I just have to run...

"Thomas?"

I turn over and prop myself on one elbow. I'm tangled in the sheets, as though I've been thrashing about in my sleep.

"Tessa?"

"It's me," she says from my bedroom doorway. "Can we talk?"

"Yeah, okay, of course," I say, fumbling around. I'm trying to get the sheet unwound from my body, but it's caught on something, my leg, maybe.

"Can I turn on the light?" she asks.

"What time is it?"

"Eight thirty."

I finally sit up. "Yeah, go ahead."

I can hear Tessa's hand running along the wall as she searches for the light. She flicks up the switch, and I'm momentarily blinded.

Tessa screams.

♥

"What?" I ask her, trying to shield my eyes against the light.

Tessa just keeps screaming, and I can hear footsteps running down the hall.

"Tessa! What is it?" Dad pokes his head in the room and throws an arm around Tessa's shoulders. "Tessa!"

She's sobbing now. She plants her head in dad's chest and points at me.

"What?" I ask again.

Dad's eyes widen as he looks at me. He hustles Tessa out of the room.

"Erica, take Tessa. Thomas, he...he's got a costume on and it scared her. Thomas is upset...let me talk to him. Keep her away for a bit."

Dad comes back into the room and closes the door.

"You didn't do this on purpose, did you?" he says.

"Do what?" I ask him. "What are you talking about?"

He points to the bathroom. "Have a look."

I throw my legs off the bed and stand. But it feels like I'm wearing high heels (not that I know what that feels like) – I lose my balance, my feet slip out from under me, and I fall on my butt.

"What the..."

Dad walks over to me, chuckling. He bends over, hands on his knees, and laughs his ass off.

I sit up and look at my feet, but I have no feet. Instead, I have cloven hooves.

And I'm sitting on something lumpy. I twist my body sideways to look at my butt, and growing out of my tailbone is a three-foot long tail, lumpy with ridges of cartilage and pointed at the end.

I'm so startled, I twist the other way, trying to get away from the tail. But it follows me. I try to get to my feet (hooves) again, and have to clutch my headboard to stay upright.

"What's happening?" I say, voice shaky.

"A little too much emotion, I'd say," Dad says, finally standing tall. "Feeling devilish, my son?"

I growl at him, and Dad laughs again. "Nice fangs."

I reach up and carefully feel my teeth. They're sharp.

"And how'd you…" Dad reaches out and touches the top of my head. "Good lord, it's bone."

"What's bone?" I feel my head, which now has two rigid horns sprouting from the top.

"Bone's tricky," he says. "I may have to saw them off."

"Like hell," I say.

I let go of the headboard and gingerly make my way to the bathroom, clomping all the way. I stare into the mirror.

"How did this happen?" I say, swallowing hard.

"This has never happened to you before?" Dad asks, leaning in the doorway.

"Of course not!" I say. "I think I'd know it if I'd turned into Satan before."

"No, I know you haven't turned into this, but you've never changed your body in your sleep before?"

"No," I say. "Well, earlier when I was mad I grew fangs, but I was awake and really, really pissed off."

"Did you go to bed mad?" he asks.

"A bit," I concede.

"No harm done," Dad says. "It's like a wet dream. I can't believe you haven't experienced it before."

"I've never felt out of control before."

Dad raises an eyebrow. "What made you feel out of control?"

I put both hands on the counter and lean in close to the mirror. Dried blood is clotted around the base of both horns in my hair. I curl my top lip and get a good look at my teeth. Every one has elongated and ends in a lethal point.

I close my eyes and change the shape of my teeth. I put my mouth under the faucet and catch a mouthful of water. I swish it around my mouth and spit into the sink. This time when I smile, my teeth are back to normal.

"Impressive," Dad says.

Then I dissolve the bone cells in my skull that are connected to the horns. I gently pry the horns off and throw them in the trash. Then I seal my skull back up, add hair follicles, and grow my missing hair.

Dad's mouth drops open. "I've never seen anyone do that," he says, admiration in his voice.

"Stick with me, kid," I say. "I'll show you a thing or two."

He shakes his head. "So you were saying you felt out of control?"

I sigh and turn around to face him. I try to prop my butt on the counter, but the tail's in the way. "Just a minute."

I clip-clop back to the bedroom and grab my dirty jeans from the floor. I finally find my knife in the front pocket and take it back to the bathroom with me.

"Here," I say, turning around. "Hold my tail out taut for me."

Dad takes the tail and stretches it out. "Bet you never thought you'd hear yourself say that."

I ignore him. I cut off the nerve endings to the tail. Then I saw it off with the knife, clotting the blood as I go and healing the wound.

Dad holds the tail up. "What the hell do we do with this?"

"Chop it up and burn it," I say. "Or bury it. Who cares?"

"Tessa and Erica are here."

I grab the tail and throw it into the shower. "We'll deal with it after they leave. Let's go."

"Wait," he says, a smile creeping back onto his face. "Your feet."

"Shit," I say, looking down at my hooves.

I sit on the closed toilet and grow new feet from the ankle down. I disconnect the offending tissue and the hooves fall to the floor. I deposit them in the trash with the horns.

"Am I done?"

"No," Dad says.

I pat my face and neck, looking for something I've missed. "What?"

"Tell me what made you do this."

I stare at my toes. I wiggle them just because I can.

"It was all too much. I felt...first I felt guilty after I fell asleep and missed Tessa's swim meet. Then Erica cornered me about Cyrus, and I told her the truth, and Tessa made me feel like an ass, even though I thought I'd done the right thing. Then...there are the issues with you, you know what they are, and they make me feel like I'm living with a stranger. And then I heal Olivia, for real, all the way, I was so...so elated to get to her to that place, to see all that effort pay off, I mean, she's alive! But she didn't want it, Dad. You were right. I should never have healed her."

Dad sits down on the bathroom floor beside me. "What do you mean, she didn't want it?"

"She didn't fall off a horse. She tried to commit suicide."

"Was it a side effect of that car accident?"

I cock my head. "What do you mean?"

"The article I gave you. I thought she might have lingering injuries from that accident, or emotional problems from witnessing her mother's death. Did you not do additional research?"

"The article said Olivia was fine. It never occurred to me to do research. What made you think otherwise?"

"Cyrus," he says. "He told me Olivia had no other medical issues prior to falling off her horse."

"You talked to him?" I ask.

"Of course. He's been trying to get in touch with you for months. He sounded sincere in our phone conversations, but then I found that article. Any normal parent would mention it. Sure, you might forget about the time your kid falls off a swing, but you'd never forget the accident that killed your wife."

I swallow. "I did find something odd in Olivia's brain."

"What?"

"Nerves from her visual cortex to her amygdala had been severed. I knew it was an old injury."

"That might result in Capgras Delusion," Dad says.

"I've read about that," I tell him. "It's when someone believes the people close to him, like a wife or a mother or father, are impostors. They say that, yes, this person looks exactly like my mother, and she knows all the things my mother knows, but she's not my mother."

"Exactly," Dad says. "The neuroscientist V.S. Ramachandran posits the delusion is created because these patients have lost the emotional connection that usually comes with recognizing a face. I would imagine such a delusion could drive a person to suicide. They feel like they're living with strangers."

I draw in a sharp breath. "But I didn't heal those nerves," I say. "I left them alone, thinking Olivia would want to return to her former self. I didn't realize."

"We're just speculating," he says. "We don't know if that's the reason she tried to kill herself."

"And that's the other thing," I say. "She still wants to die. I brought her back against her wishes."

"You still did the right thing, Thomas," he says softly.

"Did I? I don't know anymore. I don't know if anything I've ever done has been the right thing."

"The right thing isn't always easy," he says. "And sometimes the right thing for one person may be the exact wrong thing for someone else. Trust me, you've always been on the side of right."

I shake my head. "Sadly, I can't trust a single word that comes out of your mouth."

Dad hangs his head. "So that's how it is, huh?"

"That's how it is."

"Is that how it's always gonna be?"

"That's up to you," I say.

"You know," he says, "when I was your age, my biggest dilemma was how to get Becky Parsons into bed with me." I glance at Dad, but he's staring at his hands. "It never occurred to me that my abilities could help others. Never even crossed my mind. Then I knew I wanted to get the hell out of Dodge, so I joined the Navy, went to the Attic, was ordered to become a father, ordered to do experiment after experiment, and for a long time, I thought, I'm just a pawn. A plaything. Someone's whipping boy. I never had a say in my own life. I sucked it up and followed orders and never did one Goddamn thing for myself. Always for the military. Always for my country. Always for someone else."

"You want sympathy?" I ask.

"You were the only thing I did my way. I raised you the way I thought best. I molded you into the man you are."

I bristle at that but stay silent.

"You're the best person I know," he says. "You care about others and about doing the right thing. As a father, I...I couldn't be more proud of you. I'd trust you with my life."

I blink hard to keep the tears from falling. "That's exactly what you're doing, isn't it?"

"No," he says. "Not mine. I always knew I'd have about fifty years, give or take, and that would be that."

"But you have Erica now. Surely things have changed."

"Not that," he says. "Erica knows about our lifespan, and we've agreed to squeeze every single drop of happiness we can out of the time I have left. I'm not looking for miracles for me."

"Then who?" I say.

"Thomas, I don't know if you're ready—"

"Who!"

Dad blows out a loud breath. "Tessa."

Chapter Forty-Two

"How dare you?" I say. "How dare you try to manipulate me by using Tessa!"

"I wish this were a game, Thomas, but it's not," Dad says.

"What are you talking about? There's nothing wrong with Tessa."

"Erica's mom gave birth to two babies with Down Syndrome. Did you know that?"

I nod. "Tessa told me."

"One died shortly after birth, and Erica's sister, Lydia, died when she was three. They knew there was a genetic component to Down's and to some of the other disorders the babies had, so Erica did a full battery of genetic tests on each of her kids while they were in utero. All the boys were fine."

"There's nothing wrong with Tessa," I say again, more forcefully.

"She has a mutation on chromosome 4."

"Huntington's Disease?" I say. "That's impossible. She'd have to inherit it from a parent. Erica doesn't even have any symptoms." I sound stubborn to my own ears, but I'm not conceding that Tessa's sick.

"She did," Dad says softly. "Symptoms started eight or nine years ago. Another reason why Erica was reluctant to leave her marriage."

"So you healed her?"

Dad shakes his head. "I can't do what you can do. I've just been managing the symptoms. At some point, though, the disease will take over. Or I won't be here to manage it anymore."

I care about Erica, but I can't get past the fact that he thinks Tessa is sick. "Tessa's completely symptom free," I say, making it a prayer.

"Typical onset is around age 30, 35. She won't develop the disease for a while. But this is real, Thomas. She has the mutation. Huntington's is inevitable."

I get to my feet and pace the small bathroom. Tessa can't be sick. I would know it. I would know.

"Does Tessa know?" I ask.

"No."

I growl. "Jesus, doesn't anyone around here tell the truth? This is Tessa's life, and nobody thought to mention this to her?"

"They were planning to come clean after Tessa graduates high school. They were trying to give her a happy childhood."

I hang my head. Looking down the length of my body, I suddenly realize I'm naked.

I push past Dad and walk back into my room. I grab a fresh pair of boxers and some sweatpants and pull them on. Dad appears as I'm thrusting my arms into a t-shirt.

"So are you leaving it up to me?" I ask. "Am I supposed to be the one who tells her?"

"Erica would like to wait until after graduation."

"Too fucking bad," I say. "You blew it. No way I'm keeping this from her."

"You have no right to go over Erica's head on this," he says.

"I will do exactly as I see fit," I say. "Every fucking second is going to count. I have to start working on this now."

"Thomas, sit down for just a minute. Let's talk this through."

"Why?" I scream. "She's a ticking time bomb. The disease could kick in at any moment!"

"Thomas, think about this. Think! You have no idea what her reaction will be. You haven't thought about how to break it to her. Unlike you, Tessa has probably never heard of Huntington's. At least give it some thought. For her."

I suddenly realize that I'm crying, and I wipe the tears from my chin. "You two are such pussies," I say. "You're the adults. You should be handling this like adults, like parents, and instead you're pawning it off on me. You knew I wouldn't keep this from her. You knew I'd have to act on it."

Dad holds out his hands, pleading with me. "Thomas, I don't know how long I'll be around," he says. "If I had time left, I'd do it myself, without involving you. I went against Erica's wishes and told you, because I know you're the only one who can save her. I know that no matter what you're doing, you won't do it without Tessa. You'd hate me even more if I kept this secret any longer."

"And you suggested we get married!" I say. "Talk about the ultimate dodge in responsibility."

"You should be the one to make medical decisions for her, if it comes to that."

"That's years away, Dad. That's what you said. What's the rush?"

"You never know," he whispers. "If I'd married Vivian...maybe things would have gone down differently."

I sigh. "How long have you known about Tessa?"

"Since the day I first told you I was taking you to the Attic."

♥

Tessa has calmed down by the time I go out to see her in the kitchen. She's drinking hot chocolate and chatting with Erica.

"I'm sorry I scared you," I whisper behind her.

She turns in her chair to look at me. "I overreacted," she says. "You looked...I thought you'd turned into a monster."

"The inside coming to the outside, huh?"

Tessa sighs and stands. "You're not a monster, Thomas."

I turn to Erica. "I'm so sorry. I never meant...I was only trying to help."

Erica gets up and puts her arms around me. "I know," she whispers. "You're the most amazing young man, and you have nothing to apologize for."

"You're sure?" I say, pulling back from her.

"Sure," she says.

I turn back to Tessa. "I'm sorry."

Tessa lays her head on my chest. "Me, too."

I wrap my arms around her and hold on.

Chapter Forty-Three

"Come on," Tessa says, taking my hand. "Let's go for a walk."

We wave goodbye to Dad and Erica and walk hand in hand around the neighborhood.

"That wasn't a costume, was it?" Tessa says.

"No," I say.

"Why did you grow horns?"

I sigh. "I didn't mean to. It happened in my sleep. I was feeling…like a bad person."

Tessa squeezes my hand. "And I made you feel that way."

"Some," I say, "but nothing I didn't deserve. Olivia woke up today."

"And that made you feel like a bad person? That's amazing, Thomas."

"But she didn't want to wake up. I found out she tried to kill herself."

"Wow," Tessa whispers.

I nod. "And before the last few weeks, I would have said I did the right thing anyway. That suicide is a sin. But there's Grandma. And then Olivia…God, Tessa, she was in so much pain. I don't blame her for wanting to end it."

Tessa doesn't say anything to that.

We walk along the dark sidewalk in silence for several minutes. Then Tessa says, "Sophie broke up with Todd yesterday."

"There's a shocker," I say. Sophie Barone hasn't been able to keep a boyfriend longer than a week since I first kissed her ten years ago.

Tessa smiles. "Karina told Abbey who told me that Sophie said she measures every kiss against the one you gave her in the first grade, and none of them can compete."

I laugh. "Sophie dumped me. Has she forgotten?"

"It's just an excuse," she says. "Sophie's just like her mom, always looking for the next best thing."

"Kinda sad," I say. "Todd's a good guy. I feel sorry for people who don't value what they have."

Tessa stops walking and pulls on my hand. She looks me in the eye. "Thomas...I love you. You know that, right?"

I raise an eyebrow at her. "Of course."

"I want to say something, but I don't want to hurt your feelings."

A strange bolt of energy zaps every nerve ending in my body and I suddenly feel light-headed. I swallow hard. "Okay."

"Do you think...you're a very serious person, and I love that about you. I mean, I value it, the way you question things and we talk about issues and stuff. That's a good thing."

"But?"

Tessa smiles. "But sometimes, it might be nice if we had a little fun. So much shit has gone on lately and...I'd just like to take a break from it every once in a while, you know?"

"We have fun," I say.

Tessa sighs. "We enjoy our time together, I mean, I love being with you, but we don't have a lot of fun."

"Fun," I say.

"Fun."

"You mean like this?" And I scoop Tessa off her feet and throw her over my shoulder. She squeals.

I run with her down the street while she pummels my back.

"Put me down!" she shrieks, laughing.

"Not until we have a little fun!"

I drop to my knees on my neighbor's grass and roll Tessa off my shoulder and onto her back. She throws herself at me and wrestles me to the ground. I could pin her in two seconds flat, but I let her win, and she straddles me.

"I'm gonna make you pay for that," she says. She digs her fingers under my ribs and tries to tickle me.

"You know I'm not ticklish," I tell her.

Her fingers stop, and she wiggles her bottom against my groin. "Have you ever felt a tickle?"

"Nope."

"Could you let yourself feel it?"

I think about that. "I don't see how."

Tessa glares at me. "We're having fun, remember? Stop controlling everything. Let go. A little tickle won't kill you."

"It's not like that," I say. "My nerves just don't respond that way."

"Make them," she says. "If anyone can do it, you can."

Ah, a challenge.

"Actually," she says, "this raises a question: do you control what your nerves feel all the time?"

I prop myself up on my elbows. "That's…a very interesting question."

"Well? Do you?"

"I…I don't know."

Tessa leans forward and strokes a finger down the length of my throat. "What did that feel like?"

"Like you touched my throat," I say.

Tessa rolls her eyes. "Do it to me."

I run the pad of my index finger from the bottom of her lower lip, down her chin, and under to her throat. Tessa shivers.

"What did you feel?"

"Electricity," she whispers.

I lie back down flat and close my eyes. I imagine myself opening an imaginary clenched fist, letting go of my control. "Do it again."

She does. It feels like the brush of butterfly wings until she reaches my clavicle bone, where her touch almost makes me jump out of my skin. My whole body shudders and I feel it – electricity! – shoot straight to my, ahem, groin.

Tessa grins. "You did it."

"No," I say, shaking my head and pulling her down to my lips. "You did it."

We share a kiss and walk back home. All is dark.

Tessa and I cuddle up in bed, and we spend two hours exploring my nerve endings.

Chapter Forty-Four

I wake to an empty house and a fresh pot of coffee. I have to grudgingly give Dad credit for that.

I sip my coffee while I read the news on my laptop. A new email message pops up. Grrr – it's from that liar, Cyrus.

Thomas, please hear me out.

Olivia is inconsolable, uncontrollable, and self-destructive. I will probably have to admit her to a mental institution if we cannot fix her.

Here is the truth: she has Capgras Delusion. She thinks I am a pod person, a murderer who has killed her father and taken his place.

The reason I didn't reveal this to you is that this has caused us trouble to no end. I'd hoped you would heal her and the delusion would be over. But I see now that I may have doomed both Olivia and myself to hell on earth.

Imagine it – your daughter thinks you are a skilled actor, nothing more. Worse, you did something heinous to her real father in order to take his place. I have been called a murderer, a liar, a thief, an alien. Olivia has called the police, social services, even posted on Internet sites about her "fake" father. I have done damage control as best I could, but these accusations are a matter of record. The police have been investigating me on and off for years.

And then, as I try to hold my own life together, my daughter grows depressed. Despondent. She's genuinely afraid of me. She feels she's alone in the house with a stranger. She tries to commit suicide to get away from me, and to, finally, be with her parents in Heaven.

I thought you would fix her. Of course, I am forever in your debt that Olivia is alive. That in itself is enough for me. Truly.

But I would be a horrible parent if I didn't try everything in my power to get Olivia the help she requires. She's in agony, Thomas. She's so afraid, and there's nothing I can do. She won't take comfort from the enemy.

What do you require? An apology?

You'll never know how sorry I am for not being upfront with you.

Money?

Name your price.

Counsel? Spiritual guidance? My fucking life? Take it. It's yours. Everything.

Just, please.

Cyrus

♥

I drive over to Olivia's house and knock on the door. It's only 7AM, but Cyrus opens the door quickly. He looks like he hasn't slept.

"So," I say.

Cyrus just stares at me. And then a choked gargle erupts from his throat, and he bursts into tears. Before I can react, he flings himself at me and hugs tight.

"Thank you," he whispers. "Thank you."

I pat his back awkwardly. "I won't leave her like this," I whisper back.

♥

Dr. Park is scribbling notes in the sitting room when Cyrus and I enter. He jumps to his feet and shakes my hand. "Thank God you're here."

"How's she doing?" I ask.

Dr. Park sighs. "We've got her sedated. But if she doesn't eat soon, we'll have to put the feeding tube back in."

I nod. "Cyrus, I need you to stay out of sight until I'm finished. Not a word, understand?"

He nods back. "I'll wait right here."

I look at Dr. Park. "Let's go."

The first thing I do once I'm hooked up is metabolize the sedative. Olivia slowly comes around, and I'm grateful she's strapped to the bed. I don't want her pulling her hand out of mine.

"Olivia?"

She opens her eyes and meets mine. "Who?"

"I'm Thomas Van Zandt, the doctor who healed you. Do you remember me?"

She nods slowly. "What…what are you doing?"

"I'm just checking a few things to make sure I healed you properly. Is that okay with you?"

"I can't stop you," she says. "Is he here?"

"He who?"

"That man," she says. "The one pretending to be my father."

"I have some news about that," I say. "That man is gone. The police took him away."

Olivia tries to sit up but can't move much against her restraints. She lifts her head. "They did?"

"Yes. And they found your real dad."

"He's alive?" she whispers.

I nod. "They need you to make the final verdict about his identity, but they believe so, yes. Since your injuries were so terrible, they want me to do one more check on your brain to make sure you're okay, and then we'll bring him in."

Olivia lays her head back down and squeezes her eyes shut against the sudden tears. "Will it hurt?"

"If you hold still, not a bit. Just keep your eyes closed, and we'll be done in a couple of minutes, okay?"

Her breath hitches. "Okay."

I quickly focus on the amygdala and the nerves that run there from the visual cortex. I heal those nerves. In less than thirty seconds, I'm backing out and healing our hands.

I pat Olivia on the arm. "All done."

She opens her eyes. "I can see my dad now?"

I stand. "Cyrus, you can come in now."

Cyrus rounds the corner slowly and comes to stand next to the bed. "Hey, baby."

Olivia blinks a few times. "Daddy?"

He grips the side rail tight. "It's me. It's really me."

Olivia tries to raise her arm to him, but she can't. She looks at me, pleading.

I undo the Velcro straps at her wrists and ankles. Dr. Park takes care of the one across her chest. She sits up and places her hand on top of her father's.

"Daddy," she whispers.

Cyrus folds her into his arms.

I smile. Then I back away and head on down the stairs.

♥

Whistling, I head for home.

I could call Kate and Kenneth, probably should, but I'll see them in the morning. I want to talk to Dr. Rumson, but he's conducting services. I want to tell Dad that I righted the wrong. But there's only one person who should hear my news first.

It's barely eight o'clock, and Tessa likes to sleep in. I'll generously give her until nine.

I pull into the driveway behind Erica's car, where Tessa is pulling a box from the backseat.

I slam my door shut. "You're up early."

She gives me a sideways kiss – the box between us is awkward. "Thought I'd help Mom."

I squint towards the house. "Can she do without you for a few hours?"

Tessa smiles. "Maybe. If it's important."

I take the box from her and we head for the house. "Oh, it's important. We need to have a little f-u-n."

"F-u-n?" she whispers. "That's a dirty word."

I laugh. "Promise?"

♥

I take Tessa to Knott's Berry Farm. We ride the roller coasters (I have to suppress the urge to vomit), we eat funnel cake, and we get soaked on the log ride.

We even pose for a caricature. The artist draws our likenesses surprising well, with huge heads and little teeny bodies holding hands.

"I love it," she says when the artist hands her the drawing. "Could I try?"

"You're an artist?" he asks.

Tessa blushes and nods.

He laughs and hands her his black marker.

Tessa sits on his stool, sticks her tongue out of the corner of her lips, and does an awesome caricature of the artist.

She won't let him peek until she's done. He grins when he sees it.

"You want a job here?"

Tessa's cheeks burn red again. "Thanks for the compliment," she says. "But I already have a job."

♥

On the ride home, I squeeze Tessa's knee.

"What did you mean, you already have a job?"

Tessa smiles. "I was thinking you'll probably need help, like with handling the press, marketing, I don't know. Paperwork. Errands. Someone to run your life while you're saving people."

I smile back. "So you're a PR expert, are you?"

She shrugs. "I could be. I'm serious. You'll need someone you trust to do all that stuff. You're going to be a brand. Someone should manage that. I'll major in business."

I'd never thought of that – the Thomas Van Zandt brand. Kind of ridiculous, but hey – maybe she's right.

"And I want to be a part of it, a part of you," she says.

"You're hired."

Chapter Forty-Five

Tessa and I get home in the early afternoon and fall asleep for a nap tangled together. Dad and Erica don't say a word.

I wake up around five and spend half an hour just looking at Tessa, watching her sleep, studying the slope of her pert nose, the curve of her lips, the length of her lashes. It's impossible to believe that in ten or twenty years she'll start being affected by a deadly disease. That she'll have trouble walking, talking, and swallowing. That she'll die young, in terrible pain.

I reach out to touch her shoulder, to gently wake her, but I pause with my hand in mid-air. What advantage is there to telling Tessa now? She'll find out soon enough. Let her have a few more days of peace.

I get up and shove my feet in my Converse. I need to go to church.

♥

It's the 7 PM evening service, and the pews are only half-full. I sit in the last row and settle in.

When Dr. Rumson enters, he spots me right away and gives me a smile. I give him a half-hearted one back.

I want to talk to him so badly! I want to get out of this church and into the comfort and safety of his office and spill my secrets and share my problems and have him tell me what I should do.

But that is a child's wish.

I listen to the sermon with half an ear, and sing with half a voice, and pray with the whole of my being.

I have to be what Tessa needs.

Directly after the service, I do what I've never done in the decade I've attended St. Paul's Church: I leave.

I drive to Oak Glen Park, grab a notebook and pen out of my backpack, plop down under a lamp on the dewy grass, and systematically write down each and every thing I have to do to be what Tessa needs.

It's a long list.

But it's what I was born to do.

Chapter Forty-Six

Every experiment I've ever wanted to try is off the table. Saving Tessa is my only goal.

Kate and Kenneth are working on using Protein T to activate stem cells in a laboratory environment so the protein can be used universally in the medical field. This is our back-up plan to healing Tessa, in case full-blown genetic engineering doesn't work.

I'm working on the genetic engineering.

My first experiment will be on Tyrion. He's not coded as a Dweller – so I'm going to make him coded. If he can assist in his own growth and healing, he has a much better shot at staying alive.

That's the theory, at least.

I still haven't told Tessa about her impending disease, and it's gnawing at me. We don't lie to each other, we don't withhold information. This has been the longest eight weeks of my life.

Thank God she hasn't asked me if she's healthy. I couldn't lie to a direct question. But as long as it doesn't come up, I'm able to keep my mouth shut.

I've rationalized it like this: Tessa's ignorance is for her own good. Until I have a workable plan to heal her, I'm keeping quiet. She'd just be worried and stressed otherwise.

Right?

I feel like such an asshole.

I just pray that when the time's right to tell her, Tessa understands.

♥

We've got Tyrion and Dacey prepped and ready for some gene replacement. Dad's with me, assisting Dr. Trent and a couple of nurses who are monitoring the procedure.

I've spent the last two months helping Dacey grow Tyrion's body. He's got everything now except for a right arm and legs. The process was remarkably smooth, especially once Tyrion's new heart was pumping. The strain on Dacey's heart has eased.

When I explained my genetic engineering experiments and proposed trying them on Tyrion, he jumped at the chance. I suspect that he doesn't really care about being an official Dweller – he just wants to help me out. That's the kind of guy Tyrion is.

So this procedure is weighing on me. I can't screw it up. Tyrion's life is in my hands.

There are several ways to get new DNA into existing cells. The tried-and-true method involves viruses – put the new DNA into a virus, and the virus can penetrate cells. But sometimes those viruses can do funky things, so I decided on a different method.

I'm going to inject naked DNA directly into the cells.

Researchers have had a tough time doing this – you have to make the cell membrane porous to get the DNA in. But since I have control of my cells (and those of anyone I'm hooked up to), I can inject the DNA easily.

We're going to do several rounds. Today, I'm focusing on the brain. If I can successfully integrate the new DNA (Dacey's) into Tyrion's brain cells, the rest of the body should be easy.

Dr. Trent sedates Tyrion by giving him some local injections – anything else would affect Dacey, too, and we want him awake and participating. Tyrion's eyes roll slowly into his head and his eyelids close.

"Injecting now," Dr. Trent says, and he inserts a syringe directly into Tyrion's eyeball and depresses the plunger.

I cringe. Thank goodness I'm not getting that injection.

"Is the DNA on your radar?" Dr. Trent asks me.

"Got it," I say, and I begin to corral the DNA and disperse it throughout Tyrion's brain.

At minute seven, I feel my body tiring. I drink some Dwellerade and pop a pill.

At minute eleven, I sense a change in Tyrion's body.

"Immune system kicking in," I say, and Dacey immediately stiffens.

"I don't feel it," he says.

"T cells are heading my way," I say. "Damn it, I didn't think it would happen this fast."

"I'm on it," Dacey says, "but I still don't see them."

"Blood flow is increasing – do you feel that?" I ask.

"Yes. White blood cell count is up, but it might be the fact that you're here, Thomas."

"Except that Tyrion's body has never reacted to mine before," I say.

"How bad is it?" Dad asks.

"His immune system is ramping up," I say. "I don't know how bad it will get, but the reactions are there."

"Let's stop now," Dr. Trent says. "We're prepared for an autoimmune response – it's a miracle it hasn't happened earlier – but there's no need to push our luck. Let's deal with it before we proceed."

"I agree," Dad says. "Thomas?"

"Yeah," I nod. "Let me get rid of the rest of the DNA, and I'll unhook."

I start to dissolve the DNA I haven't moved into a cell. Tyrion's heart rate increases as I work, and T cells begin to enter the brain.

"T cells have arrived," I say. "You want me to destroy them?"

"Yes," Dr. Trent says. "Any in the immediate area. Dacey, shut down Tyrion's immune system. You'll be on a virus duty tonight."

"Shutting down now," Dacey says.

I finish up and back out of Tyrion's body. I heal our wounds and sit back in my chair.

"Damn it," I say again.

Dad puts his hand on my shoulder. "We knew this was a distinct possibility."

"Still," I say. "It stinks." Dad's hand squeezes tight.

"Let's let Tyrion rest," Dr. Trent says. "No more work today. We'll monitor the situation and I'll keep you updated, Thomas. Why don't you guys catch some Zs."

I want to stay with Dacey and Tyrion, but I don't feel well. It's probably just nerves and stress over Tyrion's condition, but a nap sounds great.

"We'll check back this afternoon," Dad says, pulling me to my feet. "Call us if anything changes."

♥

I'm blissfully sleeping in isolation room three when Dad shakes me awake.

"Thomas!"

"What?" I roll over and squint my eyes at him.

"Dacey needs you."

I push off the bed and grab my jeans. I shove my legs in and bend down to put on my shoes. "How bad?" I ask.

"Bad."

♥

Dacey's heart stopped while he was keeping Tyrion's immune system from attacking the brain.

They managed to restart his heart, but he hasn't woken up. Which means Tyrion's body is free to destroy itself.

I hook up and assess. "Tyrion's immune system is still shut down," I say. "But it looks like Dacey's has kicked in to replace it."

"The focus is on the new DNA in the brain?" Dr. Trent asks.

I shake my head. "Looks like it's going after the rest of Tyrion's body. It must recognize those brain cells as part of itself. Tyrion's other organs are taking a beating. What should I do?"

"Attack back," Dr. Trent says.

"There's no end point with that approach," Dad says. "Unless we take out Dacey's immune system, we're not going to be able to stop it."

I look at Dad. He looks at me.

I gulp. "It's time for the split?"

Dad nods. "Time for the split."

Chapter Forty-Seven

I try to sleep while Tyrion and Dacey are in surgery, but I can't. Well, I suppose I could force myself to sleep, but I'm too afraid of missing something. I comfort myself by sitting in their room and playing chess by myself.

Dad comes in around the three-hour mark.

"How's it going?" I ask.

"Well," he says, taking a seat. "They're fine."

I nod. I move my black queen to take the white bishop.

"Still worried about Tyrion's soul?"

I jump and accidently knock over half the pieces on the board. I sigh. "Aren't you?"

"No," he says. "Why worry about something we can't change?"

"Lots of doctors have said that over the years," I say. "Maybe someday it will be something we can change."

Dad glances at me sideways, but doesn't speak.

"Do you believe in the soul?" I ask him.

"Yes."

I raise my eyebrows. "But do you think Tyrion has one?"

He shrugs.

Then the door slides open and Vivian pokes her head in. "Hey. There you two are."

Dad jumps to his feet. "Is something wrong with Dacey?"

"No, no," Vivian says as she walks into the room. The door slides closed. She puts a hand on Dad's arm. "Mike, don't be mad."

I can't see Dad's expression – his back is to me – but I can see him stiffen. "You didn't."

Vivian smiles sadly. "I think it's fitting. And important, Mike. This is important."

Dad wrenches his arm away and turns his back on her. "No! I won't see her."

Vivian wraps her arms around Dad's waist from behind. "She's right outside, and I'm bringing her in."

"No," he whispers.

Vivian pushes on his shoulder and spins him around. "Don't belittle this. Don't turn this into something bad. I'm doing it for the man I love, and for us. For all of us. It was Dacey's last wish."

Dad grabs her arms hard. "The man you love is sending you to your death?"

"He doesn't know," she says. "He just wants Tyrion to live."

"This isn't about Tyrion's life!" he screams. "This will not save him! This is about your life!"

"Yes," Vivian says. "My life. My most important contribution."

Dad hangs his head. His shoulders begin to shake. Sobs escape his throat. Vivian wraps herself around him and holds him.

"What's going on?" I ask.

Vivian peeks around Dad's shoulder. "Are you ready to meet Jack?"

I shoot to my feet. "Jack's the one outside the door?"

Vivian nods her head.

"What, is she going to kill you?"

Vivian presses her lips together. "Jack can see a bit of the future – when a person's going to die. She says it's written on our very souls."

I gulp. Wow. The soul IS real, and Jack can see it? And she knows when other people are going to die? What a horrible thing to live with.

"So you want her to see if Dacey and Tyrion are going to live?" I guess. "And she's seen your death?"

Dad's body still trembles, but at least his sobs have quieted.

"She saw two things about my death. One, I would die the day after she met her father. And two, my death would give another life."

"That's why Dad's refused to meet her."

Vivian nods.

"How do you give someone life?"

"I don't know, exactly," she says. "But I feel, in my heart, that it has to do with Dacey."

Dad untangles Vivian's arms and marches straight into the bathroom, slamming the door.

"You're really doing this?" I ask her.

"Yes."

"You're ready?"

Vivian sighs and pulls out a chair to sit. "I don't know that anyone's ever completely ready."

"What will Dacey say?"

She smiles. "The good part about this is that I won't be around to hear whatever it is."

My eyes tear at that.

Vivian laughs. "No tears! God, I've cried enough. My death has a purpose. How many people can say that?"

I walk around the table, bend down, and give Vivian a crushing hug. "You can," I whisper.

"You think I'm making the right choice," she whispers back.

I pull away and look into her eyes. "For love. For all of us to know if someone like Tyrion really has a soul. Yeah. You're doing the greatest thing ever."

"Thank you."

The bathroom door opens and Dad comes out. His face is blotchy and his eyes swollen.

"You're sure?" he says. He looks like he's stifling a scream.

"I'm sure, Mikey."

Tears leak from Dad's eyes again, and he nods. "Okay, then. Bring her in."

♥

I've had a thousand different versions of this moment in my head.

I meet Jack, and she ruffles my hair and says, "Hey, squirt."

We run into each other on the bus (I've never ridden a city bus in my life), our eyes meet, and we just know we're related. She squeaks and throws her arms around me.

Dad introduces us and she shakes my hand and won't meet my eyes because she doesn't like anyone to see her cry (wait, that's me).

Vivian goes outside to get Jack. I turn to Dad. "You ready?"

Dad takes a deep breath. "I'm sorry, Thomas."

"For what?"

"Keeping you from your sister."

"Don't apologize," I say. "I didn't understand. I should be the one apologizing to you."

"I wanted you to find your own way with God. It wasn't all about Vivian. I wanted you to find your faith on your own."

"I actually appreciate that," I say.

Dad looks at his feet. "Thanks."

"And you sacrificed your relationship with Jack for me and Viv. You're sort of amazing."

"Don't," Dad whispers. "Don't go there. I've hurt as much as I've helped."

It's a difficult time for Dad to take comfort. I get that.

Words are inadequate. So I walk over to Dad and lock him in a hug.

He buries his head in my shoulder and hugs me back.

♥

The door slides open.

I don't even know if Vivian is still here, if she's in the room or standing on my shoulders. All I see is Jack.

Is it unoriginal, even arrogant, to say, "She looks like me?"

She does. And she doesn't.

We have the same black hair, but hers is shorter and spiked. She has Dad's dark, fathomless eyes, and we share his Roman nose, his chin cleft, a dimple at the left corner of our lips.

I notice the dimple because she's smiling, nervously, I think.

She stops two feet in front of us, and I blink hard.

My family. I have more family. And she's standing right in front of me. I clear my throat, and her eyes move from Dad to me.

"Jack," I say, and I want to say my name, welcome her here, to our lives, but no more words come. The nerves in her eyes drain away, and she is the one now blinking hard.

"Thomas?"

I nod, I think, and suddenly we're hugging, and my eyes feel like they've been stung by bees.

"My turn," Dad eventually whispers, after how long, I don't know, and Jack pulls back from me.

They embrace.

"You've read my letters?" he whispers.

She nods into his chest. "About a million times."

Dad straightens and raises her chin with his finger. "You're beautiful," he says. "I'm so proud of you."

Tears stream down Jack's face, and she brushes them away. "I didn't want to come," she says. "I thought you'd hate me for that."

Dad smiles. "I didn't want you to come, and I was sure you hated me for that."

"I don't hate you," she says.

Dad closes his eyes. He opens them when Vivian takes his hand.

"So here she is," Vivian says. "Our daughter."

Anger flashes in Dad's eyes, but he squashes it down. "Jack, can you read her?"

Jack looks at Vivian and frowns. "It's the same. Tomorrow, but early. Probably not long after midnight."

"Can you tell how?"

Jack looks away and sniffles. "Brain aneurysm."

Dad's lips harden to a grim line, and Vivian slaps his chest. "No more. That's it. I want to get out of here."

"Where do you want to go?" Dad asks her.

"The beach."

Chapter Forty-Eight

The four of us return to the Attic after dinner. Vivian goes to spend time at Dacey's bedside in recovery, and Dad says he needs some time to himself.

Jack and I head to the lounge.

"So how come you're not married?" I ask her.

"How do you know I'm not married?"

"No ring," I say.

Jack grimaces. "Tough to commit to someone when you know how they're going to die."

"But everyone's going to die," I say. "That shouldn't stop you from living."

Jack unlaces her combat boots and pulls them off. She props her neon pink-socked feet on the coffee table. "Have you ever been in love, Thomas?"

"I have a girlfriend."

Jack smiles. "Do you love her?"

"More than anything in the world."

"Then you can imagine it. What if you knew she were going to get cancer in ten years and die?"

This conversation is eerily coincidental. I shudder. Then I explain Tessa's situation to Jack.

"I think maybe we were meant to be together," I say. "Maybe it's God's plan that I'm able to heal her."

"Maybe Tessa just lucked out," she says.

"Do you really believe that? I mean, you can see souls. You know God's up there, doing his thing. Coincidence can't just be coincidence."

Jack doesn't say anything.

"Well?" I say. "I want to hear what you think."

Jack puts her feet on the floor and leans forward. "I think I don't know, but I do know I don't have a purpose in this life. I can see things, and so many times I've tried to help people, to avert disaster, and I've never done any good. Not once. Those people always die."

"Maybe your purpose isn't to keep them alive," I say. "Maybe it's to improve the life they have left."

Jack cocks her head like I've said something interesting.

"Look what you did with Vivian," I say. "She got to say goodbye. She spent her last day exactly the way she wanted to spend it. She's going to save a life, somehow. Because of you. All that, because of you."

Jack puts her head down on her knees, and her shoulders shake with her sobs.

It's around one AM. I'm sitting with Tyrion, watching him rest. I said my goodbyes to Vivian, and then I was banished from her room. Dad thought I might get heroic and try to save her.

He's right. I've thought about it all day. Why the hell *not* save her?

Except her death is supposed to save someone else.

There's sudden commotion in the hallway, and I open the door and peer out. Dr. Trent zooms by, then a nurse.

"What's up?" I ask her, racing two steps behind.

"Dacey's coded again."

My God...Dacey. That's who Vivian is supposed to save.

I rush back the other way to isolation room one, where Vivian is holed up. I do my scans and open the door.

Vivian, Dad, and Jack are playing cards, laughing.

"Hey, Thomas," Vivian says. "Want to buy in?"

"It's Dacey," I say, breathless.

Vivian throws her cards on the table and stands. "What's Dacey?"

"He coded, just now. I think he's the one you're supposed to save."

Vivian freezes. Dad picks up a phone on the wall and dials. After barking some questions, he hangs up.

"Well?" Vivian asks.

"His heart's done," Dad says. "They can keep him alive for a bit."

"How long?"

Dad shrugs, palms up.

Vivian throws herself at Jack and kisses her forehead. "Don't forget," Vivian says to her. "Don't ever forget."

Jack kisses her back and nods.

Vivian moves to Dad. "First love," she says, and Dad smiles. "Best friend. Catch me?"

"Always."

Dad opens his arms and Vivian falls into them.

Her eyes flutter. Her body twitches obscenely. Her legs give out, and Dad catches her. He puts one arm underneath her knees and picks her up.

"Door," Dad says, and I open it.

Dad strides down the hall to surgery.

Do you have a website? Visit me at www.andrearing.net. If you comment on my blog or send me an email, I will answer.

Have you written any other books? *Nervous System* is the first book in *The System Series*, and it introduces Thomas and his amazing abilities. *A Yellow Wood* is about Leni, a 17-year-old girl haunted by her past and learning how to trust herself. *Into the Trees* follows Leni's teenage daughters on their journey to discover if anyone can love the real them. Drs. Kate and Kenneth Mullen's love story is part of this book.

Is Tessa going to die? Mike? Erica? What about Sam's baby? Will Jack ever find love? Does Tyrion have a soul? Lots of loose ends, I know. Book 3, *Operating System*, comes out this fall, and it will answer some/most/all of these questions.

Do you have any writing advice you can share? The best advice I can give you is to trust yourself. You've been reading for many years, so you already know, instinctively, about story structure, about plot, when dialogue sounds wooden. Write a story you'd love to read, characters you really care about, and your work will find an audience. Visit my website for more details. I love helping teens, especially, write (I've been a writing and lit tutor since college).

Note to my readers: Thank you for following the journey of Thomas and Tessa. I'd love to hear from you! Send me an email. Write a review on Amazon. Comment on my blog. You're the reason I write, and I'll never forget that.

Book 3 in Andrea Ring's *The System Series,*

Operating System

Coming Fall 2014

A tidbit from Andrea Ring's

A Yellow Wood

Now in paperback and e-book for Kindle

I sit sipping my vanilla latte and doodling in my notebook. A heart, a star, a sun. I'm not all that imaginative when I'm nervous.

I'm worried about the impression I'm about to make. I've never spoken with a grad student before, let alone a male one studying philosophy. I'm not worldly or sophisticated. I don't particularly care what Clark thinks of me personally, I mean, for myself, but I know our meeting will be reported back to Dr. Jones. And I want to come off well for her.

I wish I knew what this Clark guy looks like. When I asked Dr. Jones, she sorta frowned and waved an imperious hand, saying, "Like a philosophy student."

I have no idea what that means. I imagine it's quite collegiate. Clark probably wears wire-rimmed glasses and corduroy blazers with leather patches at the elbows. I'm looking for a geeky professor type. But I see no one like that.

Paper rustles to my left, and I turn to see a scary goth guy folding up the front page of the *Wall Street Journal*. He has a foot-tall, green-tinged mohawk and more piercings than a pin cushion. Huh. Our eyes meet. I want to look away, but his eyes are perfectly rimmed with black liner, and I'm fascinated that there's no sign of smudging.

Scary Spice grins, and my eyes grow wide.

He laughs.

"You're Leni, right?" he asks, setting the paper aside and turning his chair toward me. He holds out his hand. "I'm Clark."

I shake his hand before I can conjure up a response. But my training runs deep.

"It's nice to meet you, Clark," I say.

We're still holding hands. And Clark is still smiling. And I cannot think of a single thing to say.

His green eyes twinkle. He squeezes my hand gently and pulls back.

"I think we were both expecting someone a little different," he says.

"We were?" I say automatically, and we both laugh.

"Linda said you were, and I quote, 'a studious, bright young woman eager for knowledge and nothing more.'" Clark leans back in his chair and lifts one ankle to his knee. The buckles up the length of his combat boot jingle.

"Linda?" I ask. "You mean Dr. Jones?"

"That is her name, last time I checked."

"Oh, well, yes, I could certainly use your help," I fumble.

Clark smiles. "I thought you'd be a total nerd."

I want to frown, but I keep my face thoughtful. "Is that because you study philosophy and you're a nerd?"

Clark tips his head to me. "Point taken. We are both more than we appear to be."

"Are we? We don't know anything about each other."

"Let's remedy that," he says. He sips his coffee, watching me. "You shop at the mall on the weekends. True or false?"

"False. I don't shop unless I need something. You listen to the Smiths. True or False?"

"False, although I do like Depeche Mode. You have a mirror in your purse. True or false?"

"False. I don't even carry makeup. You're an anarchist. True or false?"

"False. I'm a Libertarian. You collect purses. True or false?"

"False. I own exactly one purse, and the question offends me. You have a Prince Albert. True or false?"

Clark raises a pierced eyebrow at me. "A sweet, innocent little nerd like you knows what a Prince Albert is?"

I grin. "True or false?"

Clark grins back, and that smile I thought so sinister five minutes ago now seems sexy.

"My aunt will kill me if I answer that," he says.

"She's your aunt? She didn't tell me that."

"She hates to admit we're related," he says.

"Really?" I say, thinking that the Dr. Jones I've come to know doesn't seem that close-minded.

"No. Not really."

About the Author

Andrea Ring was born and raised in Orange County, California. At age eight, she wrote an essay proclaiming she wanted to be an "auther" when she grew up. It only took her thirty years to realize her dream.

She enjoys beating her four children at Boggle, reading science fiction and fantasy, and eating bacon. She hates to exercise, but loves taking walks with her family through Old Towne Orange. She's lucky to be married to the love of her life.

Her favorite ride at Disneyland is Indiana Jones.

Her favorite movies are *The Princess Bride* and *Better Off Dead*.

Her favorite authors are Jim Butcher and Susan Elizabeth Phillips.

She thinks every book should contain a love story.

Did we mention her love of bacon?